MEASURE OF
DEVOTION

CAETHES FARON

ISBN-13: 978-0615669106
ISBN-10: 0615669107

Measure of Devotion

CHAPTER ONE

Kale stole a glance from beneath his eyelashes and grimaced. Jason Wadsworth was staring at him, his face red and jaw clenched.

Kale knew his life depended on the mood of the man in front of him. Being a slave was a game of survival. Up until this point, Kale had played the game well. Hunching his shoulders and lowering his head further, he adopted as submissive a pose as possible. He didn't know why his new owner was mad, but he damned sure wasn't going to make it worse.

"Go ahead and take a look at him, son." Robert gestured toward Kale, as if Jason might not be sure who "him" was.

The last thing Kale wanted was more attention. When Jason walked around him, Kale darted his eyes up again only to find the entire room staring at him. It felt like the whole county had shown up for Jason's going away party, and Kale was the highlight, a rite of passage. Apparently, you weren't a man until you owned another.

"Father, I thought Demetri—"

"Yes, I know you wanted Demetri, son, but I thought Kale here was a better choice. He's been serving as Carter Cartwright's valet and companion. You know the Cartwrights."

Jason looked toward Carter and James Cartwright, giving

1

a slight nod that did little to hide the distaste on his face. Kale followed his gaze and wondered briefly which would be worse: belonging to someone who clearly despised you and wanted someone else or being returned to your previous owner as rejected goods.

"Fine, Father, I suppose you're right. Thank you for the gift." Jason reached for the rope binding Kale's wrists.

When Robert handed Jason the rope, Kale sank to his knees. He tried to make the move look graceful, but grace wasn't something he did well. When his knees hit the floor, he murmured, "Master."

After a brief silence, Kale raised his eyes and was relieved to see the servile display had worked. The gleam in the other boy's eye said he felt a thrill at his newfound ownership, that he thought himself officially a man now. If only that thrill could last.

"Demetri, take him to my room. Once he's tied to the bed, you may leave."

Again, the rope changed hands. As soon as Kale stood, Jason turned away, and the party resumed. The murmur of voices and clink of glasses were a welcome change from the focused silence of a few moments before. Once out of the room, Kale raised his head and straightened his shoulders.

How he would be of any use to a young man in the city was beyond him. He had never been outside of Malar County. Tonight was one of the most formal affairs he had ever attended. Social functions in this part of Arine consisted of barbecues, picnics, and the occasional ball if the free folk were feeling particularly fancy. Hell, the people here could barely read enough to reply to a party invitation. Why would a university student want Kale? If he were Jason, he wouldn't want him, either.

The walk was spent in a frosty silence. Demetri tugged the rope unnecessarily and walked quicker than required, causing Kale to stumble in the gas fixtures' dim light. It must be annoying losing out on the chance to go to Perdana. As far as Kale was concerned, Demetri was welcome to it. He would much rather have stayed in the familiar territory of the county.

Once in Jason's room, Demetri lit the gas lamp, tied Kale to the bedpost, and left. Kale eyed the knot and rolled his eyes. Why did free people insist on behaving as if slaves were stupid? Did Jason really think that knotted rope would hold him should he decide to attack or escape?

Kale looked around his new master's room to try to get a feel for him. He was somewhat familiar with the senior Wadsworth, Robert being a common hunting companion of his former master's father, but he had never seen Jason. From the contents of the room, it appeared that the resemblance between father and son ended at their shared brown hair. A telescope stood near the window, and charts of the skies decorated the walls. Dozens of books were crammed into bookcases and stacked on tables and a writing desk. In the corner, several trunks were packed and ready for the next day's journey to the capital.

An unfamiliar feeling of apprehension assaulted Kale at the sight of the trunks. This was only the second time in his life he had been sold, and getting used to a new master's preferences and moods would be hard enough without the added pressure of a new environment. The Wadsworth home was like every other home in the county. Though larger with richer furnishings, it was essentially a ranch. The in-house politics and the day-to-day activities would be much the same as at the Cartwright's. In the city, though, he wouldn't have any familiarity with which to ground himself.

Kale must have nodded off because he awoke with a start at the sound of a man stumbling heavily up the stairs. Moving to his knees from the more relaxed sitting position he had adopted during his wait, he prepared to greet his new master. With any luck, he could show Jason just how submissive he was and that he would be no trouble.

The door slammed open, and Jason stood, or rather

swayed, in the doorway. For a few moments, he stared at Kale as if he had forgotten about him. Then he grunted, took a few unsteady steps, and crashed onto his bed. Barely a minute passed before he started to snore.

Kale knelt beside the bed, stunned. This wasn't good at all. A moment later, he heard the loudest, rattling snore of his life and turned toward the bed. His master reminded him of a schoolboy who had gotten into his father's liquor closet. Normally, Kale would have busied himself with removing his master's boots and making him more comfortable, but with his hands tied, he was left with nothing to do but study his master for the first time. Jason didn't look like he had ever spent a day outside in his life. Not only was his skin pale, it appeared as smooth as silk. He had high cheekbones, a well-shaped nose, and long fingers rested on a slim jaw. The delicate features of youth waiting on manhood.

Once it was clear Jason wouldn't be waking up anytime soon, Kale decided to situate himself for sleep. With his hands tied to the bedpost, comfort was impossible. It was unsettling that his master had forgotten about him so soon. Would Jason remember to let him eat? Buy him clothes? Let him use the bathroom?

Dammit, now he had to pee. Groaning, he shifted once more and tried to think of anything but the pressure in his bladder.

◆ ◆ ◆

The next morning, Kale wondered how anyone could snore so much without waking himself. Heavy sleep must be the luxury of one who has never had to wake early a day in his life.

Jason would need to be up soon if they were going to leave on time. That presented something of a challenge. Would it be presumptuous to wake him without orders? Kale shuddered; of course it would. Not to mention that Jason was sure to have a hangover, and given his state last night, Kale doubted he knew how to take care of one. Kale could do plenty to help, but there was the small problem of his hands still being tied to the bed. The binding itself was not an issue —Kale could free himself in less than thirty seconds—the issue was whether or not his master would beat him for doing so.

Under ordinary circumstances, Kale would never dream of untying himself. Honestly, being tied was easy. Being tied meant you couldn't make a mistake. You resigned yourself to take whatever came. But it was clear last night that Jason had completely forgotten about Kale's existence. Tying Kale to the bed and leaving him there meant he was entirely useless. No master wanted a useless slave.

It didn't help that he still needed to pee. It was just Kale's luck to be sold to a man who forgot that slaves were actually people with all the same necessary functions as other people. Kale was sure his master would be furious if he awoke to a slave who had soiled himself. Some masters might leave a slave in that condition as a punishment, but Jason clearly acted out of ignorance and not malice.

That decided it. There was no way in hell Kale was just going to sit and piss himself because he had been sold to an idiot.

Using a combination of teeth and hands, Kale rapidly freed himself. Quietly, he crept to a door in the corner that he had eyed the previous night. If the Wadsworths were wealthy enough to install gas lighting, they almost certainly had indoor plumbing as well. Sure enough, the door opened on a nice bathroom. Normally, Kale wouldn't be so bold as to use his master's bathroom, but no other provision had been made, and he wasn't quite ready to go traipsing around the house looking for the slaves' facilities.

After relieving himself, Kale returned to his master's bedside. Looking down at Jason, Kale contemplated what he should do next. The thought of somehow tying himself back up was not appealing. Would Jason remember leaving him there? If so, being caught anywhere else would surely be bad. However, given last night's drunkenness, and the fact that neither the drool presently dripping down his face, nor the abominable snoring had woken him, it was doubtful Jason would be coherent enough to remember much of anything.

Walking to the bedroom door, he put his ear to it, listening for the sounds of a household waking. Sure enough, he could hear the stairs creak under slaves' feet and the hall drapes being flung open. Kale glanced back at his master and weighed his options. If Jason overslept and they didn't leave on time, Kale would probably be blamed. However, if he woke Jason, there was no telling what firestorm would ensue. What Kale really wanted was to wake his new master with breakfast and coffee. Hopefully, that would keep the after-effects of last night's celebration to a minimum. It might even get them on the road on time, and how could a man be upset at waking to a piping hot breakfast?

Venturing out of Jason's room, Kale made it to the kitchen unnoticed as the rest of the household slaves went about their morning work. The quiet of the house gave way to the clanking of pots and pans and the bustle of slaves preparing breakfast for free men and slaves alike. The smell of buttery biscuits set his stomach growling, and Kale was relieved to see that the head of the kitchen was a stout woman with a kind face. Even if he was only going to be here for one day, this woman could either make his first morning with his master a success or a failure, which would affect the rest of the day.

Kale approached the cook, adopting a submissive pose with his head slightly lowered, and looked up at her through his lashes. "Excuse me, ma'am, I was wondering if you might help me get my master's breakfast. I'm new here."

Cook looked him up and down, as if judging whether or not he was worthy of her time. "Ah yes, you're young Master

Jason's new slave. Didn't get to meet you last night."

"No, ma'am, he sent me straight up to his room. I'd still be there, except he came to bed as drunk as can be and I was hoping to get him some bacon and coffee to ward off a hangover."

"What's your name, boy?"

"Kale, ma'am."

"And I'm Darlene. Did you eat anything last night?"

"No, ma'am."

"You hungry now?"

"I wouldn't turn away food, but I don't want to be gone when my master wakes up."

Darlene waved her spatula in the air. "Nah, that boy hasn't woken up before ten o'clock a day in his life. You'll sit here and eat some breakfast. Trust me. You'll need it with that one. Then I'll send you up with a tray."

"Yes, ma'am." Kale went over to the large pot of oatmeal and ladled out a bowlful. Walking over to the table, he was waylaid by the cook, who put a few strips of bacon on top of his bowl. Kale lifted his eyebrows and looked at her.

"That's 'cause I won't get a chance to spoil you, and you look like the type I'd spoil."

Kale smiled at the twinkle in her eye and nodded his thanks. He downed the meal quickly, not willing to bet his hide on the fact that his master would stay asleep. When he was done, the cook handed him a tray. "I've put some strong coffee on there and a glass of water. Try to get him to drink the water first. There's a whole container of cream and several cubes of sugar. That boy drinks his coffee like a child, but this way he'll at least have to drink some of it black to make room. Just leave the tray on his desk when he's done, and I'll send someone up to fetch it. You'll have your hands full enough trying to get him out the door."

"Thank you, ma'am. I'm sorry I won't be around for all that spoiling you promised."

"It's probably for the best, though. You'd break my poor

7

heart with those dimples."

Kale just grinned and ducked his head, shuffling out the door to the sound of her laughter. Once out of the kitchen, he straightened his head and walked swiftly back to Jason's room. It was a pity he wouldn't be staying here longer; he and Darlene would have gotten along well.

Back in Jason's room, Kale arranged the breakfast tray on the bedside table and stood back. Here was the hard part: waiting for Jason to wake up. He hoped the smell of food would be enough to rouse him, but the only movement Kale saw was the vibration of nose and mouth as Jason released yet another snore. Dear gods, hopefully the snoring was just a side effect of coming to bed drunk. Kale didn't think he could manage listening to this every day. After the third snore, this one accompanied by a not inconsiderable amount of drool, Kale sighed. Clearly, he was going to have to take action. He stepped forward and leaned down, "Master? Master, it's time to be getting up."

Silence. And then a snore as he rolled over.

Kale clenched his fist at his side. Did he dare? Why couldn't his first morning with a new master be the least bit easy? Slowly, he lifted his hand, flexing and clenching it several times before laying it on Jason's shoulder. The sleeping man didn't stir. Kale gave one little shake and then another. Still nothing. Taking a deep breath, he shook Jason again and said, louder than before, "Master, it's time to be getting up."

Jason stirred, and at the first hint of movement, Kale snatched his hand away and took a step back. Jason wiped away the drool on his chin before stretching in what looked like preparation to roll over and fall back asleep.

"Excuse me, master, but your breakfast is here."

Jason's eyes fluttered open, and he screwed up his face in confusion when his eyes focused on Kale. "Who are you?"

Kale clenched his jaw and then forced it to relax. "Kale, sir, your new slave."

"Oh, yes, of course. Stop standing around then, and get things ready to go. We need to be leaving soon." Jason swung his legs off the bed and reached for the glass of water, downing it in three large gulps.

Kale glanced around. What on earth was he supposed to do? He was ready, all of Jason's trunks were packed, and the only thing left was to get Jason himself ready and downstairs. Hoping that dressing Jason wouldn't be too difficult, Kale walked to a large wardrobe and opened it. Luckily, some thoughtful person had neatly presented Jason's traveling clothes. Kale laid them on the opposite side of the bed from Jason and waited for him to finish breakfast.

"I'm not an animal; I bathe before I dress. Get a bath ready." Evidently, they weren't so late as to worry Jason about holding everyone up while he took a leisurely bath.

"Of course, sir."

"And you can drop the attitude."

Kale stopped on his way to the bathroom. This boy was under some serious delusions if he thought that Kale had given him attitude. Still, better to avoid trouble than to invite it. "Yes, sir. Sorry, sir."

A very tense hour and a half later, Jason was ready to go. Apparently, it was important to look one's best for an all-day carriage ride with no one but a slave for company. Kale wondered if he should feel flattered. Somehow, he couldn't summon the emotion.

◆ ◆ ◆

"Kneel on the floor, slave."

Kale shot an incredulous look at Jason. He couldn't be serious? An entire day's journey on his knees on the hard floor of a carriage?

"You heard me."

Jason tried to stare Kale down, but all Kale saw was a

child playing at being a man. It was so tempting to return the stare, to intimidate Jason the way he would a fellow slave who had gotten to thinking he was better than the others. This pale, soft boy before him would never be able to make his way in a man's world.

Closing his eyes, Kale shook the thought away and bowed his head. Of course he couldn't do what he wanted. He needed to get used to the fact that his new master wasn't the kind of man his former one was. It just felt more humiliating having to submit to a man he didn't respect. Taking orders from a mere boy who couldn't even hold his liquor was demeaning. Knowing that this was a battle in which he couldn't even engage, much less win, Kale knelt on the floor. Even with his head bowed, his eyes still drifted up to see Jason's smile of satisfaction.

Once they were under way, Jason cuffed Kale on the back of the head. "Don't ever stare at me again. You keep your eyes lowered around me and other free men, you understand?"

"Yes, sir."

The beginning of the trip passed in silence with Jason gazing out the window, brows furrowed in thought. Kale, meanwhile, used all his willpower to simply stay still. The atmosphere in the carriage was oppressive, and he knew that fidgeting would bring unwanted attention. Still, how was a man supposed to kneel for this long on a hard surface? The Cartwrights had never been big on ceremony. They demanded respect and hard work from their slaves, but they didn't put much stock in purely formal actions. They'd lay into you with the strap for no other reason than the fact that they were angry, but they never required this kind of behavior. Kale found himself wishing he were back with them. At least he'd understood that world.

After an hour, Kale couldn't stand it anymore and began to shift his weight back and forth between his legs. This didn't alleviate the pain of kneeling, it just turned it into a different pain, but any change was welcome. Kale was staring at the floor trying to will away the ache, so he didn't see Jason's hand strike his head for the second time that day.

"Can't you keep still? Dear saints, Demetri was never this fidgety."

Well, Demetri Wonder-Knees was welcome to take his spot on this journey. "Sorry, sir."

"Just look at you. I could have been entering Perdana with a real gentleman's slave, tall, blond hair, blue eyes; the kind of slave people pay good money for." What was his fascination with this slave? "You, though, you look like father went shopping in the bargain barrel. Demetri could have helped me climb the social ladder. Did you know that he once served a count? A count, for saints' sake!"

Jason paused, as if expecting an answer. What was Kale supposed to say? "No, sir, I didn't know."

"No, you didn't. I don't suppose you know much of anything. Do you even have experience as a valet?"

"Yes, sir. I valeted for my previous master."

"Ah, yes. Carter Cartwright. So I suppose I can expect to look like a backward country nitwit. Do you miss Carter?"

"Miss him, sir? No, sir. Why should I? He used to be my master, and now you are."

"I can see loyalty is important to you."

Kale bristled. Loyalty? Loyalty to what, the purse-strings that purchased you? "I tried to serve him well, sir, as I will you."

"We'll see about that. It's going to take a lot more than just trying to please me. I expect you to be an asset to me. If you're not, I'll get rid of you. I've no use for a slave who eats my food and wears my clothes without contributing."

A short while later, Kale began to hear the blasted snoring that had pushed its way into his dreams the previous night. Looking up, he saw that Jason had fallen asleep with his head perched against the side of the carriage. Seizing the opportunity, Kale cracked his neck and worked the muscles of his shoulders and back, getting out the kinks. Once he was as relaxed as he could be in his present position, he studied Jason. Guessing he was going to be out for a while, Kale took a chance and got up to sit on the bench opposite Jason and then stretched his legs. Realizing all he had to do was listen out for Jason's snoring to keep himself from getting caught, he looked out the window. He had never been out of the countryside before, and here he was on his way to the capital. As rolling green hills morphed into mountain ranges, his eyes savored the sight of a world he'd never thought to see.

CHAPTER TWO

Jason looked out the window of the carriage, awestruck. Having slept on and off through most of the journey, he perked up as soon as Perdana came into view. He had only ever been to the capital once before when he was a small child, back when his mother was still alive. That visit with her had stayed with him all these years. After she died, he'd clung to the memory of it, holding out hope that if he just bided his time, he would be able to return to this glittering city where he and his mother had always belonged.

Everything in the capital seemed better. The streets were paved instead of carved out of dirt. Buildings were more than just utilitarian, they were works of art. His mother had taken him to the theater, and all the beautiful people amazed Jason. People here wore nice clothes, spoke with sophisticated accents, and were interested in things more highbrow than calving.

He was finally returning, and this time it wasn't for a visit, but to live. Instead of seeing the passing city with the eyes of an excited boy, he looked at it as a man appraising his new home. It was night, and gas lamps lit the city. Even at this hour, activity buzzed down every street. Excitement fluttered in his stomach.

Life in the city was going to be different from life on the ranch. There would be new opportunities. People would

13

understand him. He wouldn't be the misfit he so often felt with his father. If only his father had granted him Demetri. Jason wanted more than anything to be accepted into this new world, and Demetri would have been a help, having already served in high society.

Along the journey, Jason took plenty of time to study his new slave. Nothing about Kale was like Demetri. Instead of a tall, slender frame, Kale was barely taller than Jason and had a stocky build. Where Demetri was blond and fair skinned, Kale's hair was a messy mix between blond and brown, and his honey-toned skin was too tanned to pass for someone who spent most of his time indoors. Instead of the blue eyes prized in personal slaves, Kale had pale green. In short, he came across as what he was: a backwoods slave. There was nothing worse. The last thing Jason wanted was for people to see through him, and Kale seemed a dead giveaway that Jason didn't belong.

It wasn't long before they pulled up to a white stone townhouse with blue shutters and a black front door in a posh neighborhood of identical three-story townhouses. Jason stepped out and stretched his legs, gazing up at the place that he would now call home. Walking up the front steps, he didn't have a chance to use the big brass knocker. The front door swung open to reveal a short, middle-aged woman with wild black hair in a sloppy bun and blue eyes framed with crow's feet. Despite her stained apron and disheveled appearance, she had an air of confidence and control about her, more like the lady of the house than a servant.

"You must be Mr. Jason Wadsworth. I'm Ms. Collins, the cook and housekeeper."

Jason tipped his head in acknowledgement. "Yes, Ms. Collins, I am. It's a pleasure to meet you."

For a moment she seemed to appraise him, as if determining whether he was worthy of entering her domain. Either he passed or she remembered that he was paying for the privilege, but she eventually turned aside and gestured at the house. "Please, come in."

Stepping inside, he was struck by how cramped the place felt. It was elegantly decorated and looked like the respectable boarding house it was, but Jason was used to the sprawling cattle lodge he had been raised in.

"The parlor is off to the side here." Ms. Collins indicated a room on her right. "This is where you may entertain female guests. To maintain our reputation, we don't allow girls on the other floors. Over here is the dining room. You can either take your meals here or in your room. If you'll follow me upstairs, I'll show you to your suite."

Jason marveled as he followed Ms. Collins. This place was immaculately clean. At home, dust dragged in by his father and the ranch hands covered everything. Once they reached the second floor, Ms. Collins pulled out a key and opened one of the two doors on the floor. "This is your room, Mr. Wadsworth." It was strange being called mister; that had always been his father. "The other gentleman on this floor is Mr. Carl Bonham. Upstairs are Mr. Phineas Thalomew and Mr. Timothy Hatchett. Here is your key. I'll send your slave up with your things."

Jason had completely forgotten about Kale. "Where is his room?"

"The slaves sleep in the basement near the kitchen. Of course, you are allowed to keep your slave in your rooms if you wish. Now, unless you have any questions, I'll leave you to settle in."

After she left, Jason stood in his room relishing the novel feeling. In his hand, he held the key to his own place, separate from his father, in a city as different from his hometown as night from day. It felt good.

A knock at the door interrupted his thoughts. He didn't look up as he said, "Come in," but when the door opened, he turned to see who it was. Kale stood there with a large trunk on his shoulder.

"Where would you like this, master?"

Jason looked around his room for the first time. The bedroom was quite large and had an en suite bathroom. Off to the left was a sitting area with a brown leather sofa, coffee table, and an overstuffed chair with its own side table. A table and chairs appropriate for eating, or perhaps entertaining, sat in the corner. To the right of the door was a desk, and beyond that, a large cherry wood bed with a plush hunter green comforter. Beside the bed, a wrought iron balcony overlooked the back garden.

"Anywhere is fine. I want you to get all of my bags up here and then start unpacking. At seven, you'll go and get my dinner from the kitchen and serve it to me here."

"Yes, sir."

Kale put the trunk in the sitting area and left to get the rest of the luggage. Jason plopped down in the overstuffed chair, surveying his room. It was stylish and comfortable, and more importantly, it was all his. Tipping his head back, he smiled. His life had finally begun.

CHAPTER THREE

When Kale woke up in the morning, only one other slave was stirring. After unpacking Jason's things last night, he had been pointed to his bed by another slave, whose name he didn't know, and promptly fell asleep. As much as he would have liked to stay in bed longer, the tension of sleeping in an unfamiliar place made it impossible. It would be a while before he felt safe enough to sleep peacefully.

"You an early riser, too?" Kale looked at the towheaded man addressing him and wondered what kind of crazy slave he was. Why on earth would anyone choose to wake up earlier than absolutely necessary?

"Nah, not usually. Not if I don't have to be. What time is it?"

"It's five-thirty. Simon and Jacob will both sleep for another couple of hours. They're in the room across the hall. I'm the only one who gets up early. Gives me time to gather my thoughts."

"And you are?"

"Oh, I'm Charlie." He walked forward with his hand outstretched and a grin that made it nearly impossible to not like him, despite the annoyingly early hours he kept.

"I'm Kale." Kale shook Charlie's hand, liking the firm grip that met his own.

"You want to join me outside?"

No, what Kale really wanted to do was curl up and go back to sleep, but he knew he needed to get his bearings, and this seemed as good a time as any. At least he could get a feel for the place before he had to go take care of Jason. "Sure, that sounds good."

Once outside, Kale was taken aback. Before him was a fenced in yard with a few shrubs and flower bushes. A gardening shed took up about as much space as the garden it was meant to serve. There was barely enough room for the wrought iron bench. His whole life had been spent in the country where neighbors couldn't even see each other for all the acreage they had. He looked around at the small garden and realized this little bit of earth was all that separated them from the surrounding city. Kale felt almost claustrophobic as he saw the other townhouses that enclosed them.

"So, what's your master like?" While it seemed that Charlie asked out of idle curiosity, Kale could tell he wanted to know how the balance in the house would be affected by the new arrivals.

"Couldn't really say. I was just given to him night before last as a present from his old man. So far, he's acted like a little boy trying to prove he's a man. Keeps exerting his dominance, as if I don't know I'm a slave."

"That's rough. I'll try to steer clear of him."

"I wish I could. Is there much work we're expected to do besides taking care of our masters? Are there other slaves who take care of the house?"

"We all help out with the house. Marge does the cooking and what cleaning she can. Your first responsibility is to your master, of course, but you're expected to do what Marge says as well. She's a free woman and lives in her own apartment."

"When do I get to meet her?"

"You already did. She goes by Ms. Collins to the tenants here, but she's Marge to us. You'll like her; she's a softie, likes to act like she's our mother more than our superior. Be respectful to the free men and you'll be fine. Simon and Jacob are good guys, we all get along well." *And it's going to stay that way.* Kale could practically hear the words in the silence. It was easy to believe they all got along given Charlie's easy smile, and Kale was not one to rock the boat. He was confident in his ability to fit in with the other slaves. The problem was going to be working out his relationship with his own master.

After a few more moments of watching the rays of sun begin to peek over the fence and between nearby buildings, the two men went back inside. Kale figured it would be in his best interest to be ready and waiting in his master's room. He had no idea what time Jason would get up, but after the tense carriage ride, he didn't want to be late.

When Kale reached Jason's room, he held his breath and carefully opened the door. As soon as it was open, the sound of snoring wafted out, and he released the breath he had been holding. Apparently, the snoring was not just due to alcohol. What a pity. Once the door was silently closed behind him, he found a comfortable spot on the floor and lay down, trusting that he would hear his master wake and be able to move before Jason gained enough consciousness to notice.

Kale's assumption proved correct. There was plenty of time between the cessation of the snoring and Jason being alert enough to be aware of his surroundings for Kale to stand up.

"Don't just stand there, go fetch me some breakfast. Holy heaven, are you completely worthless?" Jason got up from the bed and walked to the en suite bathroom, rubbing sleep from his eyes. Kale thought it would be wise to refrain from mentioning the fact that if he had been given an approximate time at which Jason would like breakfast, he would have had it waiting for him. Instead, he just gritted his teeth and left.

When Kale returned with the breakfast tray, Jason was at the table in the sitting area in his bathrobe. He glared as Kale set down the tray. "I'll expect to have my coffee waiting for me when I wake up from now on."

"Yes, sir. And what time will you be rising each day?"

"Well, I don't know what time I'll get up every day. But you'll know my schedule and you can figure it out from the first appointment of the day."

Oh yes, this was going to be fun. Nothing like playing mind reader with the man who held your life in his hands.

"I'll also expect you to have the paper waiting for me in the morning. I like to read during breakfast."

"Yes, sir. Would you like me to get you one now?"

"No, it looks like this morning I'm going to have to teach you how to serve me properly. Demetri would have already figured this all out, but my father seems to think my time is worthless enough to spend on teaching slaves their own business."

Kale clenched his fists and then flexed his hands, willing the anger to drain through them. If he heard one more thing about this damned Demetri, he was ready to walk back to Malar County and bring the man here himself. "I'm sorry I'm not better prepared to serve you, sir. I promise you, though, I'm a quick study. Once you show me what you like, you won't have to do it again."

"I find that hard to believe. Lesson one: you are to speak as little as possible and only when spoken to. Only relay relevant information. I'm not interested in conversing with you. Lesson two: you're to be formal at all times. I know you're used to serving in a home that is more like a barn than a house, but I won't have you being familiar or informal here. That means when you're not doing something, you should be standing as out of the way as possible with your hands behind your back. Lesson three: you're to keep your language clean. No swearing, and speak clearly. Are all of these rules clear to you?"

"Yes, sir."

"Good. Now I'll show you how you're to help me get ready."

The rest of the morning was much the same. With each additional rule and sharp remark, Kale further resigned himself to a miserable life with this boy. Kale did nothing to cause offense, yet Jason continued to act as if he was offended by Kale's very existence.

"I'm here to not only further my education, but to further myself in the world. Perdana is the home of the elite, and I plan to be part of the elite scene. That means I'll be busy most of the time I'm not in class, going to parties and different social functions. For the most part, you'll stay here. You're not nearly nice enough to be seen with. However, I imagine there will be some events where your attendance will be required. I certainly won't be showing up to an event as the only man without a slave. So for those times, you are to be on your best behavior. If you embarrass me, you will pay for it. I'm finally away from Malar County, among my type of people, and I won't have you reminding everyone where I come from. It's bad enough Father felt the need to remind me by giving you to me. Do you understand all of this?"

"Yes, sir." Gods willing, Jason would be spending a lot of time at these events that wouldn't require his presence. It was quickly becoming apparent that Kale's best chance at a good life with this man was to not be near him.

"When I'm not here, you're to be cleaning and keeping my room in order. I want everything ready for me each day when I come home, and you're to be here waiting for me. Other than that, I don't particularly care how you spend your time. Just remember that your actions reflect upon me, and if you do anything to tarnish my reputation, there will be hell to pay."

Kale had a hard time repressing a smile as he looked at Jason. This boy was shorter than him by about an inch and was easily fifty pounds lighter. In a different world, this child wouldn't be able to do a thing to him. The thought of Jason causing hell for anyone was laughable.

"Do you have something to say, slave?" Jason must have

caught the little twitch of Kale's lips.

"No, sir."

"You sure?" Jason took a step closer. "It looked as if you had something to say to me. Did something I say strike you as funny?"

"No, sir." Why couldn't he just let it go? He was being respectful.

"You seem to doubt my authority. You obviously don't respect me, or you wouldn't be lying to me. Perhaps it's time to teach you a lesson. Go fetch my riding crop."

Kale's eyes had been on the floor, but now they snapped to Jason's face. Was he serious? For a moment, Kale's natural urges pushed to the forefront of his mind, and he found himself clenching his fists and shifting his weight to the balls of his feet, preparing for a fight. Who did this scrawny kid think he was?

His master. His owner. The hard reality set in: Kale was this boy's property now. Kale hated Jason at that moment. If Kale's people hadn't been conquered generations ago, he would never have had to submit to this child. But the reality was that Arine's wealth had been acquired through battle and built by the slaves who were the spoils of war.

Before, he had been owned by men who were respected and feared. Their very presence commanded obedience. With this boy, though, it was easy to forget his place. Knowing there was no other choice, he went and got Jason's riding crop. When he handed it to Jason, Kale didn't bother trying to mask the defiance in his eyes.

Jason took the crop and twirled it in his hand. As his eyes studied Kale, they held a mischievous glint that made Kale uncomfortable. Whatever Jason had in store for him would not be pleasant. Jason's lips twisted into a sneer. "Face the wall and place both your hands against it." Kale walked toward the wall Jason indicated, and just as he was about to get into position, Jason spoke again. "Oh, and drop your pants."

Kale's head whipped around and his biceps twitched. Jason returned his look with a hint of amusement. He had Kale and he knew it. What else could Kale do but obey? He turned back to the wall and undid his belt. As he slid his pants down and leaned against the wall, he cursed himself for the red flush that settled on his skin. If there was anything worse than letting this boy get to him, it was letting the boy know it.

Kale didn't know how many times Jason hit him with the crop, and he didn't care. It stung, but the pain wasn't too bad. He'd had worse. It was the humiliation that was eating him. Surely Jason knew that he would never be able to physically measure up to Kale, but he could certainly humiliate him.

When Jason finished, Kale moved his hands to pull his pants back up and was met with another blow to his backside. "I didn't give you permission to move." Kale put his hands back on the wall and hung his head. Jason wasn't going to make anything easy for him. "Let's see if the lesson was learned. Who is the master here?"

"You are, sir."

"And who is the slave?"

"I am, sir."

"Is there anything funny about that?"

"No, sir."

"Do you believe me when I say I can make your life hell?"

"Yes, sir." Kale's mouth tasted bitter.

"Good. You may now pull up your pants. I hope this won't be necessary in the future, but make no mistake, I will not hesitate to punish you if I find you lacking." Kale turned back to face Jason when his clothes were straight, and Jason looked him up and down. "Too bad for you it looks like I'll be finding you lacking quite a bit."

◆ ◆ ◆

That night, all Kale wanted to do was fall into bed and hope to wake up back at the Cartwright's. No such luck. When he got down to the basement, Charlie was sitting at a table with two men Kale assumed were Simon and Jacob, looking as if they were waiting for him.

"Hey there, Kale!" Charlie bounded up and patted him on the back. "Just the man we were waiting for. Thought we'd have a little fun tonight to welcome you to the building."

Now that Kale was further into the room, he saw that a deck of cards sat on the table next to bottles of beer.

"You guys get beer here?" Kale looked at Charlie with his eyebrows raised. Maybe this wasn't such a bad place after all.

"Yeah, not all the time or anything. One of the perks of being a high class valet. You'll find that we gamble quite a bit. Sometimes with stolen stuff, sometimes with what's rightfully ours. Just don't ask too many questions and don't let it interfere with your work." Charlie gave Kale a wink and led him to the table. As he approached, one of the men stood and stretched out his hand.

"My name's Simon, and this here's Jacob." Simon gestured to the other man who just nodded before going back to shuffling the cards. "Charlie told us he met you this morning. Jacob and I tend to sleep later."

"So I heard." Kale took the only empty seat at the table.

"Are we going to just sit here and talk, or are we going to play some poker?" Jacob began to tap the deck of cards.

"That depends. You know how to play poker, Kale?" Charlie asked.

"Yeah, I know how to play. Might be a little rusty, but I can hold my own. I don't have anything to gamble with." Honestly, Kale was a damn good poker player, and he was looking forward to being in a house where gambling was a regular occurrence.

"Marge made you some honey biscuits. Was going to give them to you herself, but she said she hardly saw you today and that every time she did, you looked like you were in too

24

much of a hurry. You can play with them if you want. Drink your beer, though. We won't take that from you." Charlie gave him another one of his winks while Jacob grumbled and dealt the cards. "Is there something in particular you'd like if we can get our hands on it?"

Kale was a little taken aback by the question. "Actually, I wouldn't mind some drawing materials. Charcoal, pencils, paper, that sort of thing."

"You draw?" Charlie looked genuinely interested.

"What else would he want drawing materials for, dimwit?" Simon picked up his cards.

Charlie laughed at the jibe, not seeming disturbed at all by the ribbing.

"When I can. I don't get much opportunity, but it's relaxing." Kale leaned back in his chair and glanced at his cards.

"So, how was your first real day with your new master? Did I tell you all that today was Kale's first day with his master?"

"Yeah, Charlie, you told us." Simon spoke with the long suffering tone an older brother might use with a younger sibling. Kale liked him already.

"How'd it go?" Charlie turned back to Kale.

"He's something else. Thinks somehow I'll forget I'm a slave unless he constantly humiliates me. I'll handle him well enough, though. Hopefully he'll get active in the social scene and leave me be. He certainly seems keen enough on it."

"Well, you'll see, there's plenty of socializing to do here," Simon said. "These folks make a regular sport out of it. Why do you think Jacob and I get to sleep in so late? Our masters are always out getting drunk, and then running around just in time to get to class the next day. Ain't that right, Jacob?"

The only response Jacob offered was a grunt. Some might take him to be rude, but Kale thought he might be the kind of man who just didn't see the point in talking much.

"The best thing your master can do is make an

25

appearance at these social events, but not get too involved," Charlie said. "Get close, but not close enough that any of the mud lands on him, and mud's always getting flung in one direction or another. That's how my master is. He comes from an old family and is well liked in the social scene, but he also takes his schooling seriously. He aims to graduate without anyone having a reason to hate him." Charlie looked immensely proud of his master. Simon, however, rolled his eyes.

"That's also why he's boring as all fuck." Simon turned to Kale. "Hey, speaking of fucking, do you, Kale?"

"In general, or with other men?"

"You see any women around here?" Simon spread his hands and looked mockingly around the room.

Kale laughed. "Yeah, I fuck."

"Good, it'll be nice to have more than these two sorry asses to choose from."

"Your ass wasn't complaining last night when I chose you." Jacob didn't even lift his eyes from his cards, but there was a little twinkle in them. Exactly as Kale thought, Jacob only chose to speak when he felt he had something to add.

Simon punched Jacob good-naturedly in the arm. "You little prick."

"Not as small as some," Jacob said. Now Kale was really laughing.

Simon turned red and slumped in his chair. "I thought you wanted to play poker."

"I do. Now shut up and let's get to it."

CHAPTER FOUR

Walking around campus the next day, Jason could barely contain himself. Classes would start tomorrow, but today was new student orientation. He had hoped to attend with at least one of his housemates, but none of them were going. From what he could gather, Carl was in his second year, and both Phineas and Timothy had already attended for one term and didn't think it worth getting out of bed for. Jason woke up earlier than he ever had in his life, the anticipation making it impossible to stay in bed. He met up with his assigned tour guide, an upperclassman named Joshua, and a group of nineteen other freshmen for a tour of the university.

It couldn't have been a more beautiful day. Spring was getting underway, and the sun shone down on the little tour party with gentle warmth. The grounds were immaculate, and everywhere Jason looked, there were not only majestic buildings, but flowers in bloom and towering trees thick with leaves. It was easy to forget that he was in the biggest city in the country.

"And to your left is Rosemont Hall."

Jason whipped his head around when Joshua pointed out the ivy covered brick building.

"For those of you who don't know, Rosemont Hall is home to the Thistle Society," Joshua continued. At the mention of the Thistle Society, a ripple of excitement went

27

through the group, and even those that had been indifferent for the rest of the morning perked up. "It is both the oldest and most exclusive brotherhood in the country, the apex of society. Members include prime ministers, titans of industry, and lowly freshman orientation tour guides."

Jason looked at Joshua with new respect. To be this close to the Thistle Society was a thrill, but to be standing with an actual member was surreal. Jason had dreamed of becoming a member ever since Demetri first told him about it. As a young man, Jason had been intrigued by the tales his father's new slave told of his former master, an influential count who was a member of the society. Becoming a member was more than a hope and a dream; it was a goal. It was the only way to know that he had truly left Malar County for good and was accepted into high society.

The group continued on their way. As Jason rounded the corner of a building, he gasped at the sight before him. The campus radiated out from a central circle, and in the center stood the largest library in Arine, a cathedral to higher learning. Of all the buildings in Perdana, it was the most impressive. It was both daunting in its expanse, and welcoming in its offer of knowledge.

Stepping inside, Jason was awed. The entryway led to a towering rotunda. Joshua explained the layout and the contents of each branching wing. In front of them was a large study hall, outfitted with both wooden desks and comfortable sofas and chairs for reading. Since classes weren't yet in session, few people were present, but it was surprising to see a woman sitting at one of the desks hunched over an archaic tome.

"And as you can see, the library is open to the public, and that includes women. A few years ago there was a large protest to allow women to attend the university. While nothing came of it, allowing them to use the library was our concession. Don't worry though, only students may check out materials." Joshua continued leading them around.

Jason didn't care who else they let use the library as long as he was allowed. After a lifetime of having to make do with whatever books he could mail order or scavenge in the one-room library that served several counties back home, this was a paradise. He would have been happy to spend the rest of the day wandering its halls, but the group was moving on to another building.

The rest of the tour passed without him seeing much of interest until he found himself in the middle of an amphitheater. The university was connected to the city's public park, and all the tour groups were meeting there for a welcome address from the university president. The president's remarks were dry and generally boring, but Jason felt inspired. This was his chance to make something of himself, and he wasn't going to let it get away.

CHAPTER FIVE

"Charlie, you've got to help me get my master invited to something, anything. He's driving me crazy." Kale sat with Charlie in the kitchen, helping Marge peel and chop vegetables for dinner while both their masters were on campus. School had been in session for a few weeks, and in that time Jason had divided his time between classes, the library, and home.

"Things really that bad?"

"You have no idea. Whenever he's home, all he does is moan and nitpick. I need to get him out of this house."

"It's not healthy how much time that boy spends indoors. He needs some sun on his skin." Marge collected their finished carrots and potatoes to add to a large pot on the stove.

"Exactly, Marge. Thank you. The kid needs some fresh air."

Marge gave Kale a skeptical eye. "Aye, and I suppose it's just his health you'd be concerned about, yes?"

"You know how it is, Marge. What's the harm in making my life a little easier, especially if it's better for my master?"

Marge grinned. "Nothing, dear, as long as you don't go getting yourself in trouble. There's blessed little rest in this life; I won't begrudge you what you can get." Marge went back to tending her soup.

"What's he on your case for?" Charlie reached for another potato.

"He has yet to be invited anywhere. I know he thinks it's because he's from an outlying county, but the boy is as socially awkward as they come. You've seen him around the others in the house. Every night, he has me ironing perfectly starched clothes all over again, or some other nonsense. Nothing's good enough for him, and I can't take any more of his ridiculous punishments. You have to help me out here." It was difficult to keep the pleading note out of his voice.

Charlie chuckled, but Kale wasn't amused. Jason humiliated him daily, but he wasn't about to get into the details with Charlie.

"And how do you think I can help?"

"I want you to tell me everything you can about the social scene. What events can Jason attend where he won't need a slave?"

Charlie quirked his eyebrow over the potato he was peeling. "Quite the list of requirements you've got there. Nice to see how much you care for your master's social fortunes."

"Oh, come off it. We both know he's better off not being seen in public with me anyway. Now just tell me what I need to know."

For the next thirty minutes, Charlie taught Kale the basics of Perdana society. Which events required slaves, and which did not. It boiled down to the rich liking to show off by having a valet shadow them. However, most of the school events hosted by the university or city were laid back enough that no one would be carting a slave along. There might be exceptions. After all, some students saw fit to have a slave accompany them to classes, but there were plenty of casual functions that could keep Jason busy and leave Kale, mercifully, at home.

"I'll keep an ear out and let you know what's going on. In fact, there's an open house tomorrow night at the opera. Just a casual get together before the spring season starts. You know, to try and drum up community interest. There won't be any slaves present."

"Does he need an invitation or anything?"

"No, my master's family is on the board of trustees, and he'll be going. I'll suggest he invite Mr. Wadsworth to share a cab."

Gratitude poured through Kale. "Thank you, Charlie. I owe you one."

"Don't worry about it. If I'd known things were this bad, I would have done it before now."

A few hours later, Jason came home from the library. When Kale entered his master's room, he was unsurprised by Jason's irritable mood. He had come to expect it.

"There you are. Is it too much to ask that you be waiting for me when I return? Are there pressing engagements you must attend to while I'm away?"

Walking forward to help Jason take off his suit coat, Kale bit down on the response he wanted to make, reminding himself that he had good news. "I beg your pardon, sir. I was actually talking to Charlie." Jason's vacant look showed that he had no idea who Charlie was. "Mr. Bonham's slave, sir. He told me that there is an open house tomorrow at the opera, and Mr. Bonham would like you to attend." It was a small lie, but worth the risk.

"Really?" Kale had succeeded in piquing Jason's interest. There was a glimmer of happiness in his expression, as if he didn't dare hope it might be true.

"Yes, sir. He'll be catching a cab at five-thirty and invites you to join him. May I tell him you'll attend?"

"Absolutely." The happiness that had been peeking through now came bursting to the forefront. It was the first time Kale had seen a smile like that from Jason. "Will you talk to this Charlie and pick out an appropriate outfit for me?"

"Of course, master." Was that uncertainty Kale heard in his voice?

Jason began to pace. "I've been to the opera house once

before, you know, with my mother when I was a child. I haven't gotten around to seeing it again." Jason stopped moving and looked at Kale. "You're sure that Mr. Bonham wants me to come? I've barely said two words to him."

This was quite the departure from Jason's usual attitude, and it was the first time he had ever said anything approaching personal to Kale. For a moment, Kale felt bad about his little lie, but looking into Jason's hopeful face, he couldn't reveal the truth. "Why else would Charlie tell me to pass along the invite, master?"

"Of course, of course."

"Would you like your dinner now, sir?"

"Yes, that would be good." Jason sat on the overstuffed chair, his knee bouncing as he stared at nothing in particular, lost in his thoughts.

Kale bowed and left. Once he was outside Jason's rooms, he leaned against the wall and chuckled to himself. That had been too easy. And the look on Jason's face? You'd never believe that was the same kid who humiliated his slave for sheer sport. If this was how he was going to be every time he got invited out, Kale would have to start working a little harder at making it happen.

◆ ◆ ◆

The next night, Kale tried to ease out of Charlie's bed as quietly as possible. Charlie had fallen asleep right after they finished having sex, and Kale didn't want to wake him. The last few days, Jason had kept him so busy that he hadn't had time for much else. It felt like it had been forever since he'd gotten laid. Fortunately, Charlie was more than accommodating and was willing to let Kale top. While all the slaves slept with each other, Simon and Jacob commonly paired off—Kale had a suspicion they harbored feelings for each other—and that left Charlie with Kale, which suited him just fine. Charlie was a fun fuck, responsive and eager, and afterward he was content to roll over and sleep or get up and go about his business. It appeared the only sure way to halt Charlie's incessant talking was to fuck him.

Jason being gone all night made this the most carefree day since Kale had become Jason's slave. Even Marge was happy for him, and had fixed some special scones to go with dinner. Simon and Jacob were both out with their masters, so Kale and Charlie had the house to themselves. Before climbing into bed, they had played cards and relaxed in the garden, but now it was time for Kale to get up to Jason's room to await his arrival.

Jason entered not long after, humming.

"How was your evening, master?"

"It was wonderful. Mr. Bonham introduced me to everyone. There was actually a duke there. A duke! He's one of the trustees. I've never seen so many diamonds as I did on his wife. I thought the poor lady was going to tip right over at one point…" On and on Jason prattled as Kale helped him undress. Everything from the people he met to the way the opera house looked was described in perfect—and time consuming—detail. Kale listened as attentively as he could, not wanting to disturb Jason's good mood. It was actually kind of funny to watch Jason relate the evening. Everything was larger than life, and he spoke with such animation. It was like he was a completely different man.

When Kale finally got Jason squared away and was free to leave, he was surprised to find Charlie awake and waiting for him.

"My gods, what on earth took so long?"

"Well, did you know that the drapes at the opera house are the most stunning shade of violet—not a royal purple or baby purple, but violet—that you've ever seen? Or that Mr. Woodhausen, yes of those Woodhausens, is the most interesting storyteller? I swear I was this close to walking out."

"Really? Then why are you smiling?"

Kale checked himself and noticed for the first time that he was, indeed, smiling. "It was just fun seeing him all flustered, that's all."

"You think it will last?"

Kale smoothed out his smile as he climbed into his bed. "I hope so. I guess we'll see soon enough. All I know is that you've got to start telling me about every social event."

"After the night we had tonight, you can bet on it."

The next day, Jason was still in a good mood. Instead of calling Kale out on a dozen different things that were not up to his level of perfection, he merely grunted and left it at that. It wasn't exactly friendly, but it was more than Kale had hoped for.

Life settled into a comfortable pattern. Charlie kept Kale informed of what was going on around town, and Kale managed to send Jason to several events a week. Between his now busy social calendar and school, Jason was hardly ever home. After a few hours of work each day, Kale was left with time to draw, gamble, and fool around with the other slaves.

Of course, things were too good to last. Jason began to change. It was gradual and subtle, but Kale noticed. Jason began to come home looking bored or preoccupied. At first, Kale figured it was normal, that Jason was just settling in and acclimating to his new life. Then Jason began to come home agitated, and Kale started to suspect that something more was going on. He had the disturbing feeling that his comfortable situation was about to get turned on its head. There was a storm brewing, and Kale just hoped he could escape the worst of it.

CHAPTER SIX

That storm broke on one of the last days of spring. Jason came home from a festival in the park, muttering to himself with a heat Kale had never seen. Tonight is the night that things are going to change, Kale thought, watching Jason fidget.

Jason glanced at Kale, and then proceeded to ignore him. He paced around the room and appeared to grow more agitated as time passed. There was no way for Kale to escape the room, and it didn't appear as if Jason was going to say anything to him. The only thing Kale could think to do was speak. Jason would be short with him for it, he knew, but better to do it now and get it over with than let the pressure build and deal with worse later in the night.

"Is there something wrong, master?" Kale knew that being referred to as master stroked Jason's ego and could typically be counted on to put him in a better mood.

"What do you think, Kale? Does it look like everything is all right?"

"No, sir. Is there anything I can do?"

"Not unless you can get me an invitation to the Thistle Society."

"I'm sorry, sir?" Kale furrowed his brow in confusion.

"You wouldn't understand."

As if Kale's brain somehow didn't work as well as Jason's.

All right, so maybe it didn't when it came to intellectual matters, but that was still no reason to treat him like an idiot. He certainly knew how to play Jason well enough. "No, sir, maybe not. But it might help to talk about it."

Jason sighed and looked at Kale, as if considering the idea. "I'm at the bottom of the social ladder, Kale. The Thistle Society had their biggest party of the season tonight, and I didn't even know about it. I came here to be around the best, not just trade one mediocre social life for another."

"So why don't you start going to the parties where you want to be seen?"

"You really are stupid." Jason looked at him with disgust. "Even if I could get invited, it's not like I have an appropriate slave to take with me." Jason gripped the back of a chair until his knuckles turned white. "Get out. I don't want to see you right now."

This wouldn't do. Kale needed his old, happy master back —and quickly. Kale hurried from the room and made his way downstairs. Everyone was busy, so he waited for Charlie in their room, calming himself by sketching with some charcoal and paper he won at last night's poker game.

"Your master out?"

Kale saw Charlie entering the room. So absorbed was Kale in his drawing, that he didn't hear Charlie coming. "No, he's here, just doesn't want me around. Can't say I really want to be around him either."

"What's the trouble?" Charlie took a seat on his bed, facing Kale.

"You heard of the Thistle Society?"

Charlie scoffed. "Of course, who hasn't?" Kale glared at him. "Oh, right. Well, there's no reason anyone should know about them, really. It's just a bunch of rich boys playing at being their daddies. Think they own the world. Why?"

"Apparently my master's heart is set on becoming a member. He's tired of his social scene and wants to move up."

38

"You're talking about the highest rung of Perdana society. They're not an easy nut to crack, and if you ask me, they're not worth it."

"Yeah, well, he's miserable."

"What do you care?"

Kale narrowed his eyes. "Because he's going to make my life hell. You know that. Stop trying to turn this in to something it isn't."

"Sorry, didn't realize you were so touchy. You should know, though, that the circles he'd have to run in to meet up with members of the Thistle Society are going to require your presence at some point. They're all about showing off, and personal slaves are a big part of it."

"Well, I don't really have much of a choice. I can stand a few uncomfortable nights if it means relative peace the rest of the time."

"I might be able to swing you an invite to one of the more exclusive events. My master gets invitations to those things all the time, but he rarely attends. I'll see if I can get him to pass one of them on to Mr. Wadsworth."

"You pull this off for me, Charlie, we'll do whatever you want."

"Gives me even more of a reason to make sure I succeed." Charlie winked, and Kale just laughed.

Charlie came through three days later. He stopped Kale in the hall.

"I don't have time to talk, but I should have some news for you tonight." Charlie hurried away and left Kale wondering if he dared hope his luck was this good.

That night, Charlie slipped something to Kale as he climbed into bed. "What's this?"

"It's an invitation to the Wyndmar's annual party, courtesy

of my master. Their son is a Thistle Society member, and from what I understand, there will be a lot of them there. You'll have to go, but it's as high class as they come."

"Charlie, I could kiss you right now!"

"I should take you up on that, because you're not going to be feeling that way when you get back. Are you sure you really want to do this?"

"Things have got to change. I swear if he tries to take that crop to me one more time, I'll shove it up his ass."

"Just be careful; these guys are ruthless. They're only interested in using people, and they'll get a lot of entertainment out of you and your country boy master. But if you think it will help—"

"I just need him happy. He'll either get in with this crowd and start socializing with them casually so I can stay home, or he'll realize it's not for him and go back to the way things were. Either way, I'm better off."

"So long as you don't say I didn't warn you." Charlie yawned and rolled over to sleep. Kale tucked the invitation under his pillow. The nerves at having to be on hand at an event that he knew was going to be way over his head were drowned out by the hope that his days of comfort were soon to return.

CHAPTER SEVEN

When Jason's carriage pulled up to the Wyndmar estate, he couldn't help the way his jaw fell open. From the moment the horse-drawn cab passed through the ornate wrought iron gate and proceeded down the long drive, he was in awe. The Wyndmars owned vast acreage, but instead of being used to produce an income, it seemed to have the sole purpose of looking beautiful. Manicured lawns and elaborate topiaries decorated the landscape as far as he could see. Jason was breathless, and this was all before he took the house into consideration.

The Wyndmar estate, however, was not a house—it was a mansion. Jason gawked at the stately building and found it hard to believe that people actually lived in it. When the carriage circled a fountain that was bigger than any he had ever seen and came to a stop in front of the entryway, Jason regarded Kale kneeling on the floor. The formal clothes did nothing to hide the muscle of Kale's chest and arms. He still looked like a farm hand who had wandered too far from home. "Don't embarrass me tonight." If there had been a way to leave Kale behind, he would have done so. At a party of this caliber, everyone would have a personal slave tending them, and Jason could not afford to appear without one.

Stepping out of the carriage, he tried to adopt an air of nonchalance about his surroundings. It was difficult to appear confident when all he wanted to do was look around wide-eyed. Walking through the impressive front door, he felt as if he had finally arrived where he wanted to be.

Jason watched all the people milling about. Everyone was dressed in immaculate formal dinner clothes without a hair out of place or a wrinkle creasing a single suit. Most of the men stood in groups of two or three. Jason didn't see anyone he knew offhand and felt too awkward to walk up to a private conversation. Just as the nerves began to creep into his stomach, he spotted a larger group. There were several men standing together, listening to someone Jason couldn't see. He glanced behind him to make sure Kale was following and then nodded to a table of champagne flutes. Kale seemed to understand and went to get him one. Once Jason's hands were occupied with the drink, Kale fell into step behind him as he made his way over to the group, hoping to blend in.

When he reached the group, he saw that they were all gathered around one man who was in the middle of telling a story about something funny that apparently happened at a polo match. Jason found it hard to concentrate on what the man was saying, and not just because he didn't know anyone in the story, but because the man himself was so captivating. He was tall with jet black hair and clear blue eyes. Jason's stomach knotted up at the sight of them. This mystery man was an expert at working the crowd. They hung on his every word. The easy manner in which he told his story with his whole body, and the way he looked so comfortable being the center of attention impressed Jason. This man's confidence seemed to be inborn. It wasn't like he was confident because of a particular achievement or because he thought himself better than everyone else. He was simply confident because there was no other way for him to be.

Laughter pulled Jason out of his thoughts. Apparently the story was over, and he noticed that the man looked straight at him. The nerves that had retreated came rushing forward. Jason quickly averted his eyes and occupied himself with drinking his champagne and scanning a piece of art on the wall that he didn't really see. If only the man would walk away, he could pretend he hadn't been staring at him.

Aware of a presence beside him, Jason turned to see the intriguing stranger. The man smiled down at him, and Jason worked to maintain his composure.

"I don't believe we've met. My name is Eric Vanderhoff." The man extended his hand toward Jason.

Jason shook the proffered hand. "Eric Vanderhoff, as in the Vanderhoffs?" The Vanderhoff family was the richest in the country; some even said they were richer than the royal family.

Eric chuckled. "Yes, afraid so. But you wouldn't hold that against me, now would you, mister…?"

Jason felt himself go red. "Jason Wadsworth."

"Ah, Mr. Wadsworth. You must be new to Perdana. I feel sure I would have heard of you before now were you not."

Was this really happening? The most popular man in the room was interested in carrying on a conversation with Jason, even after finding out he was essentially nobody? "Fairly new. I started at the university this year."

"Oh, a freshman then. I'm a junior myself." As if Jason didn't already know. Everyone in the capitol knew about Eric Vanderhoff. "Perhaps I could show you around sometime. Where are you from? Who're your family?"

"I'm from Malar County. My family's in cattle. We have some of the best beef in the country."

"Excellent!" It seemed that Eric's response to everything Jason said was positive. "The city must seem terribly stuffy and stifling to you then."

"No, not at all. I rather like it. I've been dreaming my whole life of coming here." Jason stopped himself and blushed again. Damn, could he sound any more eager?

"Ah, you're a true city boy at heart then. So am I. Why don't I show you around, introduce you to some people?"

"I'd like that." Jason smiled and nodded.

Eric took him by the arm and escorted him around the room, introducing him to everyone as if the two of them were lifelong friends. Jason had no idea why Eric would choose to be this kind to him, but he was grateful.

As the night wore on, Jason realized that not only was he smitten with Eric, but he was fostering a slight hope that Eric might return the affection. Anything more than a slight hope was pointless. Jason might like the man, but he didn't want to set himself up for heartbreak, and heartbreak was all he could expect. There was no way someone like Eric Vanderhoff would be interested in him. Just the courtesy of making him feel welcome was more than Jason could have hoped for.

Within an hour, Jason had been introduced to everyone at the party and was beginning to feel like he might actually fit into this world. Everyone seemed nice and acted as if they liked him. Jason had yearned for this kind of validation since his arrival. Not one person here seemed to suspect that he was anything other than an upper class gentleman. Just because he came from the country and his father's money was in cattle didn't mean anything. It was still money, wasn't it? And the people here at this party weren't all old money like Eric. Some of the men were only separated by a generation or two from humble origins. Jason began to feel more comfortable and confident as he realized that this was where he belonged.

"You know, fellows, we might have a new brother on our hands here." The men nearby turned from Eric to look at Jason appraisingly and made sounds of agreement.

Jason's thoughts had wandered away from the conversation, and he hadn't been paying attention. While everyone else was looking at him, he looked at Eric. "What?"

"Come now, I know it's a secret society, but surely it's not that secret. You've heard of the Thistle Society, haven't you?"

In all the excitement of the evening and the thrill of meeting Eric in person, Jason had completely forgotten his objective in coming. "Yeah, I mean yes, of course. That's why

I came here tonight. I'm looking to socialize with a more selective crowd."

"Well, I think you'd be a good fit, Jason. Unfortunately we're not recruiting right now. We only accept new members in the fall. But that gives us plenty of time until then to get to know you better."

"That would be great." Jason had a hard time coming off as anything other than adoring. Was it really this easy? Could he be a member of the Thistle Society by fall? A few hours ago, he had only hoped to meet a member of the secret society, and now here he was, surrounded by the brotherhood and being welcomed into their fold. Everything was finally coming together, and it was happening so fast that Jason was having a hard time keeping up.

Eric smiled and Jason felt his stomach burst into butterflies. "Good. Now that we have it settled that everyone else has until fall to get to know you, I'm sure they won't mind me pulling you away so I can get to know you better now."

"What do you mean?" Jason couldn't help letting his confusion show.

Eric laughed. "You really are a treat, Jason. Come on, let's go outside and I'll show you the grounds. They're really extraordinary. Why don't you leave your slave behind? He and Silas can go help in the kitchen."

Eric's slave stepped forward at his name. Jason was so caught up in the evening that he had nearly forgotten Kale. Quiet and efficient, he had kept Jason in champagne and taken away empty glasses all night. He was as unobtrusive as Eric's shadow. Jason looked back at Kale and nodded. Kale made a small bow and left with the other slave.

Eric turned in the opposite direction, and Jason followed silently. Not only was he puzzled by Eric's apparent interest in him, but he also wondered how they would see much of anything outside in the dark. His mind focused on this second riddle, probably because seeing in the dark seemed much more plausible than Eric Vanderhoff actually being interested in him.

The walk through the house and out to the back was silent, which was nice for Jason because it gave him time to think. However, it also meant that there was no hiding his gasp of amazement when they reached the back of the property. The entire back lawn was lit by torches and strings of colorful electrical lights. Jason was sure the elaborate gardens and hedges would have looked amazing in the daytime, but illuminated at night, they looked as if they were right out of a dream world.

"Pretty nice, isn't it?"

This time, Jason was so stunned he couldn't even be embarrassed by it. The university didn't even have electrical lights yet. "I've never seen anything like it."

"It's Lady Wyndmar's pride and joy. She insists that it be lit every time there are people over. It's old hat now to the dolts in there."

"I don't think I could ever get used to this."

"You will. I know it can be overwhelming at first, but pretty soon you won't be amazed by a fancy garden—or the last name Vanderhoff."

Jason couldn't tell if Eric was teasing or being serious with that last comment. "I wouldn't go that far."

Eric smiled at Jason as they walked, looking as if he were thinking something over. "I like you, Jason. You're new and different, and I like that. I'd enjoy getting to know you better."

"What do you want to know? I've led a terribly uninteresting life."

"I doubt that. What was it like growing up in the country? I was raised in the city. I can't imagine anything else."

As they walked, Jason told Eric about life out in Malar County. Jason felt himself grow more at ease in the conversation. The garden that had seemed surreal only an hour ago began to take on the shape of a new reality for

Jason. All his life, this is what he had wanted, and now it emerged from his dreams into actuality.

On their third turn around the garden, Eric interrupted Jason's description of his first day in the city.

"I'm afraid it's time we headed back inside."

Jason felt his heart sink. The night was too good to last, but he was loathe to leave the garden's magical cocoon.

Eric reached out and gently stroked Jason's face, tilting it to look at him. Between the feel of Eric's skin against his and the smile on Eric's face, Jason was too overwhelmed to breathe.

"I don't want to go inside, but I must. Part of being a Vanderhoff. I'd like to see you again, though. If that's all right."

The look of nervous anticipation in Eric's face made Jason feel like he was flying. It was absurd to think that Eric would worry about whether or not Jason wanted to see him.

"Of course, I'd love to." Jason mentally berated himself. Did he sound too eager? He didn't care, because Eric Vanderhoff was smiling back at him, and nothing else mattered in the world.

CHAPTER EIGHT

Kale looked Silas over as they walked to the kitchen, and he didn't like what he saw. There was the same oily quality about him that his master had. How Jason could want to spend time with someone so clearly full of himself was a mystery.

Once they were in the kitchen, Silas turned to him. "My master had the good sense to introduce me, but I didn't catch your name."

Oh yes, this was one of those slaves. Strange, there was no love lost between Kale and his master, but Silas made him feel defensive of Jason. "My name's Kale."

"Kale, that's a strange name. Has quite an earthy quality to it."

The way this man said "earthy" it was like he meant to say "trashy." Kale acted as though he didn't notice. "I'm a country boy through and through. A simple name for a simple slave."

Silas eyed him up and down, "Yes, so I see."

The cook set them to work arranging little cakes and treats on trays. After a few minutes, Silas stopped and looked at Kale.

"I don't think this is right. There should be more petit fours than this."

"More what?"

"Petit fours, that's what these desserts are. Anyway, the

49

menu is right there by your arm, just read off all the petit fours that are listed."

"I can't."

"What do you mean you can't?"

"I can't read."

Silas looked as if he had never heard anything quite so scandalous. "You mean to tell me that you're a personal slave who can't read? Oh, this is rich."

"Well, I seem to have done just fine without it."

Silas sobered. "No, you're right. Why would you need to?"

Kale felt the color rising in his cheeks. The fact that he couldn't read had never brought him shame before, but the insult was clear. Swallowing his anger, he went back to arranging the trays, and Silas began to talk about something else as if nothing had happened. Kale, however, was not fooled; slaves like Silas were only nice when it came to getting what they, or their masters, wanted.

Once all the little pastries were settled on trays, the cook sent Kale and Silas out to serve them. As it turned out, Kale's concern at standing out from the other slaves was foolish. The people here ignored slaves as much as they did back in Malar. It didn't take him long to relax enough to overhear what was being said around him.

"Did you see the mark Eric picked up?" The mention of Eric caught Kale's attention.

"See him? I know him. His name's Jason something. He was in the group of freshmen I took on tour."

"Is he going to be the one this term, Josh?" Kale discreetly moved closer to the group of four men.

"With all the attention Eric's giving him? Yeah, I'd say so. He's perfect for it. Comes from one of the outlying counties, and I swear he still had manure on his shoes. You should have seen the way his eyes bugged out of his head when I showed them the hall. Eric's going to have fun with this one."

"You think he'll be as devastated at the end as the poor

sap from last term?" The small group of men laughed.

"The higher they rise, the harder they fall. He's already got puppy dog eyes for Eric. I bet he's a virgin."

Kale couldn't stick around without being noticed. Besides, he didn't want to hear more. Charlie was right about these people, and Kale didn't want to see Jason get hurt. He may be a pain, thought Kale, but no one deserves to be treated this way.

When Eric and Jason came back inside, Kale saw Silas offer his master one of those little cakes. As he did, he leaned close to Eric's ear and whispered something. Eric's eyes widened a little and quickly darted to Kale and back again. As Kale approached them, he found it difficult to keep his face blank and not betray the disgust he felt. It was a minor miracle that he didn't get in trouble the rest of the night. Thoughts of whether or not he should tell Jason what he overheard, and how that conversation might go, distracted him right up until it was time to leave.

◆ ◆ ◆

The next morning, Kale didn't understand why he was so worried. What did it matter to him if Jason chose to get involved with a prick? Because he'd have to deal with the fallout. Kale had worked too long and too hard to keep Jason from caring how his only slave spent his time. The whole point of attending the party was to restore that blissful state. When Eric finally broke up with Jason—Kale was sure it would happen, and it wouldn't be pretty—it would be Kale who had to deal with Jason's broken heart. If Jason was as dramatic in his sorrow as he was in everything else, Kale shuddered to think what was going to happen when the inevitable came.

"What's with that look, slave?"

Gods, Jason made it so hard to care sometimes. Kale was

helping Jason get ready to go out with Eric, and it appeared that he wasn't quite as good at schooling his face as he would have liked.

"I was just thinking that you seem to be falling hard for Mr. Vanderhoff."

"It's obvious, isn't it?" Jason raised his eyebrows, and his mouth curved into a little smile.

Kale looked down at the shirt he was buttoning on Jason. "Might it be wise to take things a little slowly? I'd hate to see you get hurt."

"What's that supposed to mean?" Jason's face went stern.

"It's just that Mr. Vanderhoff has a certain reputation—"

Jason jerked his arm free of Kale's hand, which had been buttoning his cuffs. "I suggest you hold your tongue, slave. I won't tolerate you speaking ill of your betters. Now get out."

Kale quickly gathered himself, bowed, and left; Jason was already too far gone if he was that defensive. Kale would just have to wait it out and hope that it wasn't going to be as bad as he thought it was. He expected things to be tense that night when Jason got home, but Jason was so happy after his day out with Eric that he didn't even pay attention to Kale. If it was blissful unawareness he wanted from Jason, he had it.

◆ ◆ ◆

"Where's your master? He doesn't have class this afternoon." Simon eyed Kale over his hand of cards. All four of the household slaves were together playing poker.

"Nope, he doesn't. But Eric does." Kale discarded two cards and waited until Jacob replaced them to continue. "Apparently Mr. Vanderhoff is too busy to attend class, so my master helps him out by going and taking notes for him."

Simon smirked. "You're kidding."

"It gets better," Kale said. "Not only does he go to class for him, he does the assignments, too."

Simon laughed, and Charlie turned a concerned look on Kale. "I told you getting involved with them would be nothing but trouble."

"I know, and I tried to warn him."

Jacob grunted and rearranged his cards. "Bet that went over well."

"What do I care? He's out of my hair and I get to relax around here."

Charlie persisted. "Vanderhoff isn't taking him to any of the high class parties if Jason isn't taking you along. He thinks he's fitting in, but he's not."

"So? He's so happy that even when he is home, he leaves me alone. As long as I get my work done, he ignores me."

"Sounds ideal. I wish I had such an oblivious master," Simon said and then raised his beer. "Let's drink to it. To Kale's good fortune."

"You'd drink to anything," Jacob said, even though he had a slight smile when he lifted his beer to Kale and drank.

As they settled into the game, Kale looked around the table at his friends. In front of them lay the meager stakes of the game. Each slave tried to scrounge up odds and ends that the others would like. There were sweets swiped from the kitchen for Charlie, newspapers and the occasional pamphlet saved from the dustbin for Jacob to read, and discarded clothes for Simon. Kale even spotted some paper and pencils in front of Charlie that were meant for him. After the game, they would distribute their winnings to the people they were intended for, either as gifts or good natured bribes for sex. Life was pretty ideal right now. It was almost too easy for Kale to deceive himself into thinking it would last.

CHAPTER NINE

Jason craned his neck to see the large clock high on the wall. It was three minutes to five. Eric would be arriving any minute. The book in front of him no longer held his attention, but a quick glance at the doors of the library confirmed that he would have to wait a little longer.

It would have been easier to study in one of the wings of the library where there were fewer people, but Jason wanted to make sure he was easy for Eric to find. He had planted himself at one of the many study tables in the rotunda. There were plenty of distractions besides the constant opening of the doors that had Jason turning his head every few minutes. The whispers of students meeting, the ticking of the massive clock, not to mention the beautiful artwork and stained glass that were much more entertaining for the eye than the printed word. It was a miracle he had completed his own work, much less Eric's.

The swish of a door opening called his attention. Three boys entered, none of them Eric. Another glance at the clock. One minute past five. Eric was late. It was hard to mind, though. Eric was a Vanderhoff and Vanderhoffs were busy people. Jason was glad he could help ease some of Eric's stress. Eric had done so much for him.

Eric loved him.

It was still hard to comprehend, and he ducked his head

as the thought went through his mind, even though there was no one around to see. The actual words had never left Eric's mouth, but Jason could tell. If Eric's feelings were only half the magnitude of Jason's, then Jason was well loved indeed.

Eric was kind, generous, and understanding. Jason had hardly expected acknowledgement from him when they first met, but Eric had gone out of his way to make sure Jason felt welcome in his circle of friends. Most flattering was all the time Eric spent with Jason. How could he not feel like the most fortunate man in the world when Eric insisted they spend time alone?

Logically, Jason knew there was little chance this could last. It was common for boys to fool around with each other at university, a way to have some fun before settling down into family life. However, Jason couldn't help hoping that this relationship would stick. It was socially acceptable for a married man to have lovers—there were too many aristocrats stuck in loveless unions for them to look down their noses at one who could find love elsewhere—but Jason was hoping for more than that. Eric hadn't seen anyone else since they started dating. This wasn't the standard fun and games. This was real. Jason was overwhelmed by the feelings he had for Eric, and he had no indication that Eric felt differently. He knew Eric would someday marry, but Jason was confident that he could be Eric's true love.

The warmth of a hand on his back pulled him from his musings. Eric smiled down at him.

"Thinking happy thoughts, I hope?"

"What other kind are there when you're around?" Jason tilted his head up for a kiss, and Eric obliged, as always. It still made Jason a little lightheaded that he could so casually kiss the most popular man in Perdana.

"Are you ready?"

"Yeah, just let me pack up my books." Jason gathered up his books and papers, placing them in his satchel.

"Did you get a chance to finish those notes on ancient

Arine architecture?"

"Oh, yes." Jason fumbled around inside his bag and pulled out two stacks of papers. "These are for your paper, and these are from the lecture today."

Eric grinned and took the two stacks, tucking them away. "Thanks, Jason. I really appreciate this."

Being appreciated for his intellect was a new feeling and Jason reveled in it. "Of course, I'm happy I could help."

The now familiar weight of Eric's arm rested on Jason's shoulder as they walked out of the library. At the street, Eric hailed a cab. The destination was always the same: Eric's townhouse. Unlike Jason, Eric lived alone. The townhouse was one of his father's, and the only other occupants were the staff. Jason felt privileged that Eric brought him there so often.

When they arrived, the elegant butler opened the door for them, and standing in the entryway was Silas. Eric's personal slave was always impeccable in his attentions, always where he was needed, offering devoted service. Jason wished he had such a slave.

"Silas, is dinner ready?"

"Yes, master, just as you requested."

Eric placed his hand at the small of Jason's back and gently pushed him toward the dining room. "I thought you might be hungry after spending all day in class. We'll eat first."

The table was set with china Jason's family would have reserved for special occasions. The first time he ate at Eric's, he thought the setting was a gesture to him; now he knew it was normal fare. For fancy affairs, Eric ate from gilded plates. The formal setting made it difficult for Jason to relax, no matter how jovial Eric's company was.

"There's a concert at the park tonight. I thought we might go." Jason took another bite of his veal while he waited for the answer.

Eric reached across the table and covered Jason's hand

with his own. The warmth of Eric's hand spread through Jason's body. These little casual touches still excited him.

"I wanted to spend tonight alone with you. I've been running around all day, and the only thing that got me through was knowing I had you to come home to. But, if it really means that much to you, we can go."

Eric smiled at him, and just before he pulled his hand away, he rubbed his thumb in a little circle on top of Jason's hand. The touch led Jason's thoughts to what was likely to happen if he chose not to go to the park.

"No, that's all right. Let's stay in." Eric always let him choose. When Jason first came to Perdana, he had wanted to spend as much time as he could at the many social functions throughout the city, but he was flattered by Eric's desire to spend time alone at his home. It was a privilege, and Jason was grateful for the attention.

It wasn't long ago that Jason lost his virginity to Eric. Even though they had slept together often since then, the memory of the first time was still dreamlike. It had been uncomfortable at first, but the mere fact that it was Eric Vanderhoff sent shivers down his spine. To look at Eric's hands and know that they had touched him where no one else ever had was exhilarating. Knowing that those hands could drive him to heights of pleasure previously unknown was enough to keep him in Eric's bed as often as possible.

When dinner was over, Eric extended one of those hands to Jason. Jason slipped his hand inside and felt lightheaded as the hungry look in Eric's eyes sent all the blood in his brain south.

CHAPTER TEN

"I finished beating the rugs, and they're back in their places. Is there anything else I can do for you?" Kale stood in the kitchen doorway and wiped sweat from his forehead. Jason was in such a good mood after his night with Eric that he'd left Kale to his own devices while he was out for the day. With time to spare, he had offered to help Marge with some of the household chores.

"No, that's all right. You can go ahead and draw if you like." Marge was busy preparing for dinner and baking.

His sketchpad waited for him on the large wooden table they used for everything from eating to polishing silverware. Initially he had thought he would enjoy drawing in the garden, but being in the pathetically small plot that people called a yard here was just depressing. Instead, he had taken to drawing in the kitchen.

Turning over his sketchpad, he picked up where he had left off on a drawing of the woods Carter Cartwright used to hunt.

"Here, have a cookie." Before him, Marge placed a plate of not one, but three cookies and a tall glass of cold milk.

"Thanks, Marge." This was another perk of drawing in the kitchen; Marge always gave him treats or portions of whatever she happened to be cooking.

"You're welcome, hon. I like having you here." Marge

went back to kneading dough, and Kale smiled as he took a bite of a chocolate cookie still warm from the oven.

Kale savored the time he had to draw. He helped Marge whenever he was asked, and even when she didn't have anything she needed doing, the other slaves were usually around wanting to play cards, fuck, or simply chat. Right now, though, it was just him and Marge. Charlie was cleaning—he was a habitually good slave—and Simon and Jacob were both out with their masters, who were skipping class.

A rapping on the kitchen door pulled his focus away from his drawing. He considered letting Marge answer it, but thought better of it. She ran around looking like she didn't have enough hands, and it was in poor taste to even think of adding to her burden. Turning over his sketch, he got up, went to the door, and immediately regretted his decision. Staring back at him from the other side of the door's window pane was Silas.

It was tempting to just walk away, but Kale knew that wouldn't achieve anything other than getting him in trouble with Jason. But he didn't have to let Silas in.

"Hello, Silas. My master isn't here."

"I know. My master wished me to give this to you to pass on to Mr. Wadsworth. It's not urgent, but make sure he gets it before he goes to sleep." Silas held out a note and Kale snatched it, eager to send Silas on his way. As soon as he did it, though, he realized his error. Silas smiled, and Kale knew he would now try to prolong the visit just to irritate him. "Can't I come in? I thought you'd appreciate the company."

"Sorry, but Marge is busy, and I'm helping her today. I really don't have time to chat."

"Oh, well, perhaps I can help?"

"Ah, you know how it is; Marge doesn't like anyone she hasn't trained in her kitchen."

"Oh, she's one of those, is she? Such a bother. I guess I'll be going then. Just make sure that note reaches your master tonight."

Kale didn't bother replying before he shut the door. Stuffing the note in his pocket, he went back to the table. When he turned his sketch over to begin working on it again, he let out a string of curses. The paper had landed in some drops of milk and was ruined. It shouldn't really matter. It wasn't as if he ever showed them to anyone, and it would have ended up in the fire in an hour or so anyway. Still, it was one more reason to dislike Silas.

He had no time to start again. Jason would be home soon, and Kale headed to his master's room to tidy it. Before he got to work, he put the note on Jason's bedside table where he was sure to see it before he went to bed.

◆ ◆ ◆

"What's this?"

Kale had just finished dressing Jason for bed, and was putting away his shoes. He looked up. "It's a note that Silas dropped off for you from Mr. Vanderhoff."

Kale's answer wasn't needed, Jason was already reading it. Jason went rigid, and Kale anticipated trouble.

"This is an invitation to dinner tonight. Why didn't you give me this note earlier?"

Kale felt the heat from Jason's gaze. "Silas said it wasn't urgent, to just make sure you got it before bed."

"It says right on it that it's to be delivered immediately. Why are you trying so hard to sabotage me and my happiness?"

"I'm not trying to sabotage you, master, I swear. Why would I do that? I want you to be happy."

"Like hell you do. You've resented my relationship with Eric from the beginning." Jason paced. "Why would you not give me this note as soon as you got it like it says? What excuse will you give me now?"

"None, master, only that I don't know how to read."

Jason stilled. "You what?"

"I don't know how to read. I never learned. Never seemed like much use in me knowing how, so no one ever taught me."

"And you've kept it from me all this time? You lying little wretch."

"I never lied, master. I've just never needed to read anything, and I wouldn't have tonight if Silas had been honest with me."

Jason pointed at him. "Oh no, you don't. Don't go blaming this on Silas. There is no excuse for this kind of deceit. Go get the crop."

Kale hesitated just a moment, which only fueled Jason's anger. "I said go get it, or are you deaf as well as stupid?"

Kale retrieved the crop that had grown so familiar to him in his early weeks in Perdana. He had been naïve to think that he would never have to feel it again. He handed the crop to Jason, but couldn't look him in the eye.

"Now strip and brace yourself against the wall." At this Kale's head snapped up, and his incredulity overcame his shame. He looked Jason in the face, not believing what he heard. "You heard me, I want you naked. If you won't feel shame at your own ignorance, you will feel shame during this punishment. Now go."

Kale did as he was told. He had never heard such danger in Jason's voice before. "This is going to be the worst punishment you've ever received. I can guarantee that. Not only did you ruin my night by not properly performing your duties, you lied to me by not telling me that you can't read, when you should know perfectly well that it would be important to me." That was all the warning before the crop descended. At first, the pain was nothing compared to Kale's white hot shame, but as time passed, the pain steadily worsened. Kale gave up guessing when it would stop. Jason just kept bringing the crop down until Kale could no longer keep quiet and howled, giving up his last shreds of pride. Still, the beating didn't end. What Jason lacked in strength, he made up in endurance. Tears leaked from Kale's eyes.

It wasn't apparent to Kale what stopped the beating—if Jason got tired or figured Kale'd had enough—but it eventually stopped. "Now stand there while I write an apology letter to Eric."

While Kale knew that writing the note couldn't have taken longer than his beating had, it certainly felt like it did. The minutes dragged on with the only sounds being Kale's labored breathing and the occasional scratch of Jason's pen.

"Put on your clothes." Kale bent down to retrieve his pants so quickly he was momentarily dizzy when he straightened. "You will take this note to Eric's townhouse, and if he isn't home, you'll wait. Watch him read the note, and after he's done, you're to show him your backside so he can see that I've properly punished you. If he wishes to punish you further, you're to let him."

Kale wanted to rebel. He had accepted his punishment. Punishment was between a master and his slave, wasn't it? Of course not. He had no privacy. It had been easy the last few weeks to forget that he was a slave, but moments like these were meant to remove any doubt. There was no way that he could avoid doing this. If he tried to get out of it, he'd just end up further humiliated, and he'd still have to do it. He knew Jason wouldn't back down. The best he could do was not let it bother him so much. Jason was trying to take his pride, but Kale didn't have to give it to him. It took him less than a moment to reach this conclusion.

"Yes, sir." He tried to relate with his tone that he was unfazed by this development and took the note Jason handed him with as much aplomb as he could muster. "Is there anything else, sir, or should I leave now?"

It gave Kale a little bit of satisfaction to see the disappointment in Jason's face. Jason was just like a little bully, working to get a rise out of those he terrorized. Kale wasn't giving him what he wanted. "No, that's all, Kale. You're to report back to me once you return. If I'm asleep, wake me."

"Yes, sir." Kale made a little bow and left.

On the way to Eric's house, Kale had time to think over everything that had happened. It was clear that Silas had set him up. Was Eric behind the plan, or did Silas act on his own? A slave getting an afternoon's entertainment? Not likely. Silas wouldn't risk his master's wrath for a little bit of fun. Silas served Eric with devotion. He wouldn't do anything without Eric's knowledge and blessing. Silas was just a puppet; the man pulling the strings was Eric. What an apt analogy: the world really was Eric's stage, and he viewed the people in it as puppets for him to move about for his amusement.

When Kale arrived at Eric's townhouse, he took a moment to steel himself against what was coming. Even more so than with Jason, he didn't want Eric and Silas to have the satisfaction of knowing they had gotten to him. A very formal butler answered the door and showed Kale into a parlor. Silas was the first to appear. Kale wondered if he was sent by Eric, or if it was just coincidence.

"Well, Kale, fancy seeing you here. Is everything well with your master? We were worried when he didn't come to dinner tonight and didn't send word."

Kale focused on making his voice sound as unaffected as possible. "Everything is fine. Thanks for asking."

"Oh, then why are you here?"

Not smacking the smirk off Silas's face was an incredible show of Kale's self-control. "I have a note from my master to deliver."

"Well then, I can take it from you and get you on your way. My master will be a few more minutes."

"No, thank you. I have orders to hand it directly to Mr. Vanderhoff."

Apparently Eric didn't need a few more minutes because he strolled in mere moments later. Kale guessed that he had been standing nearby to hear what Kale said. He hadn't the faintest idea why, but Eric probably wanted to try and trap him again somehow.

"Kale, how wonderful to see you! We missed Jason tonight. I hope everything is all right?" If Kale hadn't known better, he would have thought Eric was genuine. Where does one learn to lie like that? Was he born with such a skill?

"Yes, sir, everything is fine. I'm afraid that his absence tonight was my fault, and I'm sorry. My master wanted me to give you this note with his apologies." Kale held out the note, and Eric took it, not taking his eyes off Kale's face.

"Thank you, Kale. I appreciate your apology. Tell your master I'll see him tomorrow."

Kale knew he was being dismissed, as clearly as he knew that Eric was aware he was meant to stay and watch him read the note. Why else would Kale wait around to give it directly to him? The bastard just wanted to put Kale in the awkward position of a slave who must contradict a free person. "I will, sir. However, my master wished me to stay and watch you read the note in case there is anything further you want from me when you're done."

"Ah, well then, I won't hold you up any longer." He opened the note and read it. Surely he had to know the gist of it before he began, but he did a superb job of acting surprised at the information it contained. Kale thought he knew what was coming, but he was surprised when the next thing Eric said was, "Silas, go up to my room please. I wish to speak with Kale alone."

Why would Eric give up this opportunity to humiliate Kale in front of Silas? Silas seemed to be taken aback, too, and ready to protest when he received a sharp look from Eric. Silas appeared to catch the words that were about to come out of his mouth and sulked away.

"I'm very sorry that things turned out this way, Kale. I should have had Silas deliver the message directly to Jason. I had no idea you couldn't read. Was the punishment very bad?" The concern in Eric's voice seemed all too real.

Kale was caught off guard, and at first, didn't know how

to answer. If he claimed it wasn't bad, then Eric could very well remedy that. If he told Eric it was harsh, he would come off as a whiner trying to curry sympathy. "It was fitting, sir."

"Let me see." Eric made a little circular motion with his finger. Kale turned and lowered his pants and lifted his shirt, keeping his mind as blank as possible. "Tsk, tsk, tsk." Eric came and felt some of the welts. Kale wanted to recoil in disgust at the first touch of Eric's fingers, but held himself in check. "I'm afraid Jason was too harsh on you. You may dress yourself and turn around now." Eric continued to talk. "You have to understand that to Jason, education is very important. He abhors ignorance. He doesn't realize that you weren't given the opportunity to learn to read. Don't take it too harshly. I'll talk to him tomorrow."

What was he playing at? Why wasn't he taking his victory lap and gloating? He had won. Kale didn't kid himself for a moment into thinking that Eric was being genuine. He felt a little cold knowing that Eric could lie and feign emotion so easily. Only someone deeply disturbed could put on this kind of show. Then Kale realized, the show's not over, there's still another act. Taking the long view, Kale could see that Eric was lining him up as a pawn to play him again, possibly against Jason. That was the only thing that made sense. This was the breaking point for Kale, and he let a little crack show. "He also values honesty. Is there any message you'd like me to take back to him?"

Kale could see Eric's eyes harden almost imperceptibly, but that was the only sign that his message had been received. "No, only that I'll be in touch tomorrow. You're dismissed."

Kale bowed and left. At least now Eric knew that Kale wasn't going to be used as a puppet.

When Kale got back to the house, he climbed dutifully up to Jason's room despite his strong desire to just crawl into bed. To make matters worse, Jason was already asleep. A part of Kale was tempted to go to bed and hope that Jason forgot about his orders to wake him. That, however, would be inviting disaster. Instead, he prepared for the worst and whispered "master" until Jason stirred.

"Kale?" Jason's sleep-thickened speech sounded confused.

"Yes, master. I just returned from Mr. Vanderhoff's. He wanted me to tell you that he'll be in touch tomorrow."

"Did you show him?" Jason seemed wide awake now.

"Yes, sir."

"Did he punish you further?"

"No, sir."

"Hmph." Kale was surprised by the hurt he felt at Jason's disappointment.

"Sir, is there anything else you require tonight?"

"No, that's all. Go to bed."

Jason was already snoring again by the time Kale got to the door. He made his way to bed without talking to anyone. Charlie and Simon were already asleep, and Jacob wasn't around. Climbing into bed, Kale hoped that Jason's bitterness was gone by morning.

CHAPTER ELEVEN

Before calculus class, Joshua Sharpton came up to Jason in front of the library. It was still hard to believe that the senior who had so amazed him the day of student orientation by being a member of the Thistle Society was his friend.

"Hey, Jason, I'm glad I caught you."

"I was just on my way to my last class. What's going on?"

"There's a get together at the art museum this evening. Eric wanted me to invite you. Head over after your class lets out."

"Thanks, I'll be there," Jason said. Joshua patted him on the shoulder before heading in the opposite direction.

At least now he would have a chance to make up for last night.

The museum was full of celebrating students. The student art show had gone off well, and it was a great excuse for a party. Jason even noticed that his roommate Phineas was there. He would have gone over to say hello, but he hadn't seen Eric yet.

Scanning the room, he finally found him. Just like the night they had met, Eric was in the middle of a group of people who were hanging on to his every word. Jason made his way over, and as soon as he got close, Eric went quiet and everyone else followed suit. The whole group was watching him as he approached.

When Jason reached Eric, he leaned in for a kiss, but Eric stopped him. With a hand on his shoulder, Eric pushed him an arm's length away.

"Jason, I think it's time we part ways."

"What?" Jason couldn't have heard that right. He hadn't even had a chance to say hello.

"I've been thinking about the way you savagely beat Kale last night for something that wasn't even his fault. And then sending him to me to parade himself naked and show off your savagery? That's a new low. It was humiliating, for me as well as your slave. I just can't be with a man who can't control himself." Eric's voice was loud enough to carry beyond their small group. The other partygoers looked on with interest, and their eyebrows rose at Eric's description of Jason's behavior. As much as Jason was embarrassed by what was happening, he was much more concerned about trying to hold on to the first man he had ever loved.

"I made a mistake, Eric. Please give me another chance. I thought I was doing the right thing at the time. I can see now how I was wrong. Please don't leave me. We're good together." He was desperate. This was his world, and Eric was taking it out from under him.

"Good together? How? We have nothing in common; we come from completely different worlds. I took a chance on you, a country boy. I thought I could treat you like any other city man, but I see I was wrong. You country folk really are backward, and I just can't abide it. I prefer to keep civilized company. Enjoy the rest of your evening, but I can't stay here any longer with you." Eric turned and left with the rest of the Thistle Society members. He was gone, leaving Jason's life as quickly and dramatically as he had entered it.

Jason was left standing in the middle of a group of people who had just seen him shamed. He wanted to disappear, to go into a corner and hide. This was too horrible to contemplate. Jason had been so sure that Eric loved him. He was sure he loved Eric. How could this happen? When two people were in love, couldn't they make it work?

Too depressed to face the people around him, Jason simply fled the party. Once outside, he realized it had started raining and he had no money for a cab. Why would he carry money when he was dating the richest man in Perdana who insisted on paying for everything? He wasn't in a hurry to go home anyway, so he started walking aimlessly, letting the rain cover him as if it could hide him from the world. All he knew was that he was going in the general direction of home and would get there eventually.

CHAPTER TWELVE

That morning, Kale didn't get further than the kitchen before he had to explain what had happened. There was a stiffness to his gait from the whipping that Marge was unwilling to ignore. After she wheedled it out of him, she gave him an extra large breakfast that included bacon, so the embarrassment of having told was worth it. The story had to be repeated twice more, once for Charlie and again for Simon and Jacob. Charlie's pity had been hard to take, but Simon and Jacob had merely nodded and changed the subject, as if it was a common enough occurrence.

That night, only Charlie and Jacob were around. Simon was on campus with his master, and there was no telling when he'd be back. When it started raining, Charlie suggested they play cards, probably in an effort to cheer Kale up, though he didn't need it. Kale was fine, but cards sounded like fun, and they were soon sitting around the table playing. They didn't talk much; Jacob was his usual quiet self, and Charlie still seemed upset about what Jason had done.

After a few hands, Simon came in and leaned over Jacob, giving him a kiss on the cheek. "Mind if I join in?"

"Next hand." Jacob nodded to the empty chair.

As soon as he was seated, Simon turned to Kale. "How's Jason doing?"

"I don't know. Why?"

"You mean he's not home yet?"

"No. Should he be?" Kale honestly didn't keep track of Jason's schedule much anymore.

"You haven't heard?"

"Some of us are trying to play." Jacob grumbled from behind his cards.

Kale ignored him. "What?"

"Eric broke up with him."

"He what?" It shouldn't have been such a great surprise, but Kale had guessed that Eric would get a little more out of Jason before dumping him.

"We just got back from a party, and Eric made a big spectacle of it, calling Jason out for what he did to you last night, practically calling it barbaric. Said he was wrong to take a chance on a country boy."

"That little bastard. He knew exactly what he was doing the entire time." Kale threw down his hand. "Where's my master now?"

"I don't know. He left right after Eric did. I thought he'd be home by now. Everyone was talking about him after he left. It was quite the scene. My master tried to come to Jason's defense, but Eric's story is a much more entertaining one. Phineas said it ruined the party, so we came home early."

"Did he leave with anyone?"

"Not that I saw. I figured he'd grab a cab."

"No, he doesn't carry money. Eric always pays for everything." Kale started to stand. "He's probably wandering around in this weather like a damn fool. I'll have to go out and find him."

"What?" Charlie cried with an incredulous look on his face. He might be the best slave among them, but it was clear he thought Jason was getting what he deserved.

"I can't just let him stay out there. You know how dramatic he is, and now he has a broken heart. He won't do anything logical for a while. The last thing I need is him getting sick in this weather. It's going to be bad enough dealing with him and his broken heart; I don't want to be nursing him back to health at the same time."

"We were at the art museum, so head in that direction and take an umbrella."

"I will. Thanks for letting me know, Simon."

"No problem. Don't make yourself sick looking for him. He may come back while you're out, or he could have run into a friend and be anywhere by now."

"If I don't find him soon, I'll come back and check in here."

Kale set off into the rain headed toward the museum. It didn't take terribly long to get there, and he hadn't seen a trace of Jason, not that he thought he would. Even walking the slow walk of a heartbroken man, there was no way the trip could last as long as he had been gone. No, Jason could be anywhere, wandering aimlessly no doubt. If Kale knew him, Jason'd be wallowing in self-pity, caught up in the dramatic heartbreak he was experiencing. If there was one thing he could say for Jason, it was that the man never did things halfheartedly. If he was going to be depressed, he was going to go all the way. Kale headed back in the general direction of home, searching the side streets and alleys. Still no sign of Jason.

As Kale continued his search in the pouring rain, he began to wonder why exactly he was searching. It wasn't as if it was part of his duties. He hadn't been ordered to come out here and get Jason, and there was no way Jason would even know that Kale was aware he was missing. So why wasn't he at home right now, warm and dry? Because someone had to take care of Jason. He certainly wasn't going to take care of himself. And like he told Charlie, if Jason got sick, Kale would end up having to deal with it, which would be more of a pain than walking around in the rain.

After Kale had covered all the streets he could think of, he decided to try the park. Passing one of the fountains, he spotted movement by the tree line. It had to be Jason. No one else was crazy enough to be out in this weather. Kale rushed over to him and held the umbrella over his head.

"Master, let's get you home."

Jason looked around, startled by the sudden halt to the rain pouring down on his head. At Kale's voice, he tilted his confused face up to Kale's. "What?"

"We need to get you home. This is no weather to be out in."

"He broke up with me, Kale." The lost, sad sound of Jason's voice stirred pity in Kale.

"Yes, I know, sir. Mr. Thalomew was there with Simon and Simon told me."

"I don't want to go home. I'm sure I'm a laughingstock by now."

"No, sir. In fact, Simon said his master came to your defense. Anyone who knows you won't believe anything that Mr. Vanderhoff said."

Jason looked into Kale's eyes. "But it's true. All of it. Everything he said was true. I shouldn't have to remind you of that."

"No, but you were doing what you thought was right. There's no shame in that. Now come on, and let's go home. I'll draw you a warm bath, and then you can get in bed."

"Are you handling me, Kale?"

Jason's voice made Kale think that he probably wouldn't mind being handled for a while. "No, sir, but I will if we don't get a move on; this rain is soaking me to the bone."

It was true. Since he had moved the umbrella to cover Jason, he was completely exposed to the storm. Jason looked at Kale, as if seeing the rest of him for the first time, and started toward home. They walked in silence, Kale shielding Jason from the storm until they got to the house.

As soon as they were in Jason's room, Kale ran a hot bath. When it was ready, Kale found Jason sitting on the sofa, staring blankly ahead.

"Master, your bath is ready."

"Huh?"

"Your bath, sir."

There was still no response. Jason wasn't going to make this easy. Kale lifted him up and supported him to the bathroom. Once there, he peeled off Jason's wet clothes and helped him into the bath. Kale washed Jason's hair and quickly went over his body. The vacant expression never left Jason's face. When Kale was finished, he got up for a towel. When he turned back to the tub, he looked down at Jason.

Sitting in the bath was not the man who had humiliated him. Here was just a boy; a scared and lonely boy who searched desperately for approval. He looked so vulnerable. Jason had really loved Eric. It was foolish for him to have so freely given his love to a man who hadn't earned it, but it was endearing that he loved so completely. It should be admired, not scorned. Even now, Jason was too innocent to suspect that Eric had been lying to him this entire time because Jason would never do something like that.

Kale snapped out of his thoughts and helped Jason out of the tub and dried him. Dressing Jason was another ordeal, and Kale was tempted to just put him to bed naked. The only thing that stopped him was the thought that Jason might be ashamed in the morning, and that would put him in a bad mood.

When Kale tucked Jason into bed and looked down at his master's listless expression, he realized he felt anger. Not anger at Jason, but at Eric. How could he do this to someone like Jason? Kale had his problems with his master, but he acknowledged that the problems were largely due to the fact that he was a slave. Even though it wasn't right, that meant that he wasn't really a person to Jason, at least not as much of a person as a free man. But Jason had never done anything to deserve this kind of treatment. He was just a boy trying to fit in.

Kale had been standing at Jason's bedside absorbed in his thoughts, so it was a surprise when Jason focused on him.

77

"Just go to bed, Kale." Jason rolled over, and Kale could swear he saw his shoulders start to shake.

CHAPTER THIRTEEN

All morning as Kale worked, Jason scowled at him from under his lowered brow. The anger was palpable, and it baffled Kale. He could understand Jason being in a bad mood, needing to nurse the wounds from his first breakup, but why did he direct so much anger at Kale? Kale decided to let it roll off him, and put even more effort into helping Jason and making his morning as comfortable as possible. Still, Jason silently fumed, and the situation just seemed to be getting worse. What could Kale do? And then it happened.

After breakfast, Jason glared at Kale from the table. "Just say it already."

Kale was caught off guard. Jason hadn't said anything to him all morning, and the venom in his voice was a good indication of why. "What do you mean?"

"Quit the act, Kale. Go ahead and say you told me so, that I shouldn't have gotten involved with Eric. If I had just listened to you, this would have never happened."

"That wasn't what I was thinking at all, master. I don't think you're to blame for what happened last night."

"Stop being so damned nice to me, Kale. I humiliated you. I punished you for something that was in no way your fault. You should hate me. I want you to hate me. Go ahead and tell me how much you hate me."

"I don't hate you, sir." Kale was only a little surprised to find that the words were true.

"Stop lying." By now, Jason had stood up and was just a few feet in front of Kale. "I know you hate me; you must hate me. Anyone in your position would."

"But I don't. And I doubt anyone else would either, sir."

"But you must at least want revenge. Hit me. Go on and hit me. I've hit you enough."

Kale tried to hold back a chuckle. This was clearly very serious to Jason. "I'm not going to hit you, sir."

"Why not? It's only fair."

"It's not fair."

"Why not?"

"For starters, I'm bigger than you. And then there's also the fact that you're free and I'm a slave. You had the right to hit me. I do not have the right to hit you."

"I'm giving you the right. There will be no retribution."

Kale didn't believe that for a minute. Jason might believe it right now, but after it was over, his hurt pride would force him to humble Kale once again. "I don't want to hit you."

"Then I'm making it an order. Hit me. Make it hurt." Jason's voice faltered on the last words, and Kale got a glimpse at the pain beneath the surface. Jason was already wounded, and he wanted Kale to hurt him as badly on the outside as he hurt on the inside.

"Sir, there is nothing you can do that will make me hit you."

"Oh yeah?" Jason took a swing at Kale and punched him squarely in the face. It wasn't a great punch, but Kale didn't expect it, and it threw him back a few steps. His fists automatically clenched, and he forced them to relax. That's exactly what Jason wanted, and Kale was not going to give it to him. He certainly wasn't going to indulge a spoiled child who was acting out to get what he wanted.

"Hit me all you want, sir, but I'm not going to hit back."

Something about those words opened the flood gates. Jason pummeled Kale's chest and ribs like a little kid.

Through it all, Kale just stood and took it, trying to look utterly unfazed, as if he were taking Jason's dinner order. Parts of his face were starting to swell, but it would look worse than it was. Bruises would litter his chest by tonight, and there would be stiffness later.

With one swing of his fist, Kale could put an end to this, but he didn't. This wasn't about him. It was about Jason working through his own issues. Kale was just an innocent bystander, and while it wasn't right, this was all that Kale could do for Jason right now. After seeing him last night, he wasn't about to leave him alone. Perhaps, if Jason got this all out of his system, life could return to normal and they could move past this awful time.

The hits weakened until Kale thought he heard Jason's breathing hitch as if he were about to cry. At that point, Jason stopped and hid his face from Kale. He walked over to the far side of the bed and sat down. Without looking up, he said, "You're dismissed. And don't bother coming back here later; I don't want to see you again for the rest of the day."

Taking that to mean Jason didn't want to hear him either, Kale silently left.

The first place he stopped was the kitchen. He really didn't want to face Marge, but he knew he needed some ice, otherwise he'd regret it later.

"Dear gods, what's he done to you?" Marge put her hands on her hips.

"It's nothing."

"Don't tell me it's nothing, I've got eyes. What on earth could have possessed him to do such a thing?"

"Don't worry about it. He's just a heart-sick pup blowing off some steam."

"Well here, let me put some ice on that face of yours." Marge wrapped some ice in a towel and gently pressed it to a bruise. Kale winced at the cold pressure on his cheek. "Should I send for a doctor?"

Kale laughed. "Yes, I'm sure he would love footing a

medical bill. No, I'll be fine. I have the rest of the day off, and I'll rest. I'll be right as rain tomorrow."

"Well, go get yourself in bed. I'll bring your meals to you. I don't want to see or hear of you being out and about, you hear?"

"Yes, Marge. I'll be good, I swear."

When Kale entered his room, he let his exhaustion take over. It was hard to believe he had only been up for a few hours. He knew he should really stay awake to hold the ice to his face, but he couldn't fight off sleep any longer. Tossing the bag of ice aside, he collapsed into bed and was asleep as soon as his head hit the pillow.

◆ ◆ ◆

He woke to the sight of a not very happy Marge looking down at him. "What do you want?" Kale tried to roll over, but the ache that assaulted him convinced him to stay still.

"I brought your lunch. You were supposed to keep the ice on that pretty face of yours."

Kale began to laugh, but stopped when his chest protested. "Pretty, my foot. I've never been pretty a day in my life."

"That may be true, but still, you wasted that ice, and now it's melted all over the floor."

"Sorry about that, Marge, I'll clean it up. I was just so tired for some reason."

"Gee, I wonder why. I hear getting the stuffing beat out of you can be tiring. And don't be silly, you're not getting out of that bed until tomorrow morning. Besides, I've already cleaned it up."

"I knew you loved me." Kale beamed at her.

"More's the curse on me. Now stay awake long enough to eat your lunch. I'll be back down for it later. If you don't finish it, I'll smack you around a little myself."

"You're getting cranky in your old age, Marge. It's not good. I'll finish my lunch, though."

Marge smiled and shook her head at him before she left.

Kale was surprised at what a struggle it was to eat. He really did just want to go back to sleep, and the food wasn't sitting well in his stomach. Now that he was up, though, he found that he couldn't get comfortable again.

Figuring it might help work out some stiffness, he walked around the room. It didn't really help, but at least it was a change. A short while later, he heard someone outside and made a dash for the bed. He was just getting situated when the door opened to reveal Charlie.

Kale caught his eye and saw Charlie wince. He knew he looked bad, but it hurt to have it confirmed by Charlie.

"Marge sent me to collect your lunch dishes. What happened?"

"I didn't finish breakfast, so she walloped me," Kale deadpanned.

Charlie cracked a smile that didn't quite morph into a laugh. He sat down on the edge of Kale's bed. "You want to talk about it?"

"Not really."

"Why would he hurt you like this?"

"So when you asked if I wanted to talk, it was purely curiosity?"

"You need to talk about it, whether you want to or not."

"What's there to talk about? That prick Eric broke up with him, and he's been a pot of emotions since then. He asked me to hit him, and I wouldn't, so he did this instead."

"Bet you're wishing you had clocked him now."

"Well, I didn't know he would do quite this much." They both chortled. When they sobered, Kale continued. "I knew that he needed to get it out of his system. Things would only have gotten worse. Now that he's let it out, we can move on."

"I still can't believe you didn't hit him. After all he's put you through, all the times he's humiliated you, how could you not hit him just once? I would have done it."

"No, you wouldn't have, Charlie, not if you had seen him. Last night when I found him, he was so dejected. I felt like I saw him for the first time. He was like this lost little puppy, and all you want to do is take him in and help him, you know?"

"I know about wanting to help a stray dog. Helping a master that has done nothing but demean you? No, I don't understand that."

Kale grinned and shook his head. "You, the chronically good slave? Is there anything you wouldn't do for your master?"

Charlie smiled. "Not really, not that I can think of."

"But he's punished you before, right?"

"Well, yeah."

"It's the same thing. My master just doesn't know what he's doing. Hopefully, after this whole fiasco, he'll stop trying so hard and just be himself."

"And you're really sure that 'himself' is a good guy?"

Kale considered. "No, I'm not sure, but I have a hunch. The kid has never fit in anywhere. He's never even really lived. Do you know, I think this is the first fight he's ever gotten into?"

"Even more reason for you to have put him in his place."

"He's the master, he is in his place. You know that. Besides, now he'll either feel so guilty that he doesn't want to see me, or my presence will anger him so much that he doesn't want me around. Either way, it looks like things are going to be pretty easy from here on out."

CHAPTER FOURTEEN

The next morning, Jason woke after a fitful night. It was earlier than usual. Jason was nervous at the thought of seeing Kale, and knowing his slave would be the one to wake him made it hard to sleep. Jason knew what he had done yesterday was inexcusable. How had he turned into someone who hit a man who couldn't even defend himself? That wasn't the person Jason wanted to be.

But wasn't that what he'd been doing to Kale all along? All those times he punished his slave, he was beating someone who couldn't hit back. Of course, at the time Jason thought Kale deserved the discipline, and that it was his place to do it. But now, in light of what had happened, he realized that there had never been any excuse for the way he treated Kale. He thought he had been acting the part of the gentleman, but after his experiences with Eric, he realized that was not the type of man he wanted to be. Jason shook his head at himself as he lay in bed. He had been wrong about so many things.

With a start, Jason realized it was just a matter of time until Kale came up, and he felt foolish waiting in bed for him. He got up, put on a robe, and sat down at his desk as if he were going to study. What he really did was keep torturing himself with thoughts of what he had done. Soon, he wondered if Kale was coming at all. Jason pushed that thought out of his head. Of course Kale would come, he always did, and he wouldn't let this stand in his way, if for no other reason than his pride.

Jason laughed bitterly. His slave had more pride than he did. Except Kale's pride was not the kind that was offensive; it was simply the quiet dignity of a man comfortable with himself. Jason had thought he would acquire that same pride once he got away from his father's house and into a world that was more sophisticated. It was only now that Jason realized there was a difference between pride and vanity.

At that moment, Kale quietly opened the door, clearly thinking Jason was still asleep. After he closed the door behind him, he turned to find Jason sitting at his desk, and surprise showed on his face. "I didn't know you were awake, master. Am I late?"

"No, you're not late, Kale. I had trouble sleeping and decided to get an early start on the day."

"I'll just go get your breakfast then, sir." Kale bowed and left.

Jason meant to apologize, but the sight of Kale had so stunned him that he hadn't been able to find the words. There was heavy bruising on Kale's face and some swelling around his left eye. The way he moved belied the stiffness he must be feeling in his abdomen. Yet, he held himself with a certain dignity. None of the men Jason had met in Perdana, not one of them, had Kale's pride.

When Kale came back with the breakfast tray, Jason hurried to speak before he lost his nerve. "I'm sorry for what happened yesterday, Kale. It was uncalled for and inappropriate. I assure you it won't happen again."

Kale's eyes widened a little, and then he shrugged. "You were upset about Mr. Vanderhoff."

That was true, but all Kale's words did was remind Jason that he was oddly unconcerned about what happened between himself and Eric yesterday. He was much more concerned with what had transpired with Kale. Jason decided not to stop and consider why that was.

"That's no excuse for what I did. You were upset about me hitting you, but you controlled yourself and didn't even take a swing at me. You would have been more than justified."

"I'm a slave."

"It was more than that. You're also taller than me, and no doubt you have a good fifty pounds on me, probably more. You didn't hit me because you don't hit people who can't defend themselves. Unlike me."

Kale did nothing. He didn't react at all to Jason's words, and that exasperated Jason even more. "What does it take to rile you up, Kale? I've been nothing but abusive to you since the day I got you. I give you a chance to hit me and you don't take it, and now I apologize, and you act like I've done nothing wrong. Just tell me what a horrible person I am. I know it's true. I know how you must think of me. Yell at me. Get it off your chest."

"If I had hit you, I would have been punished for it later, and if I give you what you want now, I'll be punished for that later, too."

The hurt he felt at Kale's words surprised Jason. He had been harsh with Kale, but he had never purposely trapped him, had he? Did Kale really think that Jason would do that? The answer was obvious: of course he did. Isn't that what Jason had been doing all along, setting impossible standards to trap Kale and give him an excuse to punish him?

"I deserve that, and I know you must think it's true, but it's not. I've behaved horribly from the beginning, and I really am sorry. That's not the person I want to be."

Kale just stood and looked back at Jason, as irritatingly calm as ever. Jason couldn't take the silence. "Well?"

"What type of person do you want to be?"

The words were spoken softly and were so simple they left Jason momentarily speechless. Jason met Kale's eyes and answered the question as truthfully as he could. "I don't know, Kale." Then Jason stood there as if he was expecting Kale to tell him what he should want, what he should be.

Instead, Kale gave a little nod, as if Jason's answer satisfied him, and said, "Your breakfast is ready, sir."

Jason was disappointed that Kale didn't have more to say, but he didn't really know what he had expected. "Go ahead, and take the rest of the day off, Kale. Get healed up."

"I'm fine, sir."

"Well, I'm not. I need to be alone right now. I think I can manage a day on my own."

"Of course, sir. Is there anything else I can do for you before I leave?"

"No." And then as an afterthought, "Thank you."

Kale left, and Jason breathed deep, relieved. He knew it was cowardly, but he just couldn't stand to see Kale, knowing he was to blame for the bruises on his face. Until yesterday, he hadn't thought he was even capable of causing that kind of harm. Now that he had, he couldn't bear to see it.

◆ ◆ ◆

Jason spent much of the day in the park thinking. It had felt too awkward being in the house knowing that Kale was somewhere downstairs, bruised. After a day lost in thought, he was sure of one thing. Somehow, it was vitally important that he get Kale to like him. It was as if that was the standard by which he would measure himself. He wanted to be the type of man Kale could like.

When he came back from the park, he sought out Kale in the garden. When Kale saw Jason walk outside, he rose from where he was seated on the grass.

"No, no, Kale. Go ahead, and sit back down. I want to talk with you." Jason walked to Kale and sat next to him.

The two sat in silence, staring straight ahead, for several minutes. Jason tried to gather his thoughts. There was no way for him to ease into it.

"Do you think I'm a bad person, Kale?" Out of the corner of his eye, Jason saw a flicker of surprise on Kale's face.

"No, sir, I don't. I think you're a good person who lost his way."

"Will I ever be able to earn your trust and respect?"

"I don't know why you would want those things, but yes, you could. I'll never forget the past, but a man can change."

"For someone who's never had an education, you sure are wise."

Kale laughed. "Nah, I'm just older than you."

Jason snorted. "By what, a day? How old are you anyway?"

"I'm twenty-one."

"Hardly the age of sages, is it?"

Kale smiled, and Jason was pleased that he had caused it. "No, but when you're a slave, you learn to learn quickly."

The thought of how different Kale's life had been from his own sobered Jason. "I'm not completely stupid. I know your life has been hard. I don't pretend to understand it. I've just never been much good with people, and I've never really had a slave before. The slaves at my father's ranch all pretty much stayed out of the way."

"What about the esteemed Demetri?"

Jason snorted. "All I knew about Demetri was that he had served in high society. I wanted his experience. I didn't know him well enough to want him."

"And you want me?"

Jason studied Kale and thought about the question. "Yes. You've been good for me. For starters, anyone else would have clobbered me as soon as I threw the first punch."

"Nah, no slave your father would have bought you would have done that."

"Perhaps. But they would have been stilled by fear; you weren't."

Kale quirked an eyebrow. "What makes you say that?"

"You don't get scared. I'm not sure why, but you don't. Or at least I've never seen it."

"I guess when you've got nothing to lose, there's nothing to fear."

"If you had punched me, I could have had you killed. But it wasn't fear of consequences that stopped you."

"You're right. The reason I didn't hit you is because I wanted to be babied by Marge. I got a couple days off, Marge and Charlie waiting on me hand and foot. Not a bad tradeoff for a few bruises." There was Kale's smile again. Jason had never seen him smile before today, and it was a novel thing. It was strange to see his slave's personality.

"Well, it wasn't a good tradeoff for me. Marge has been going out of her way to give me the cold eye. She's been fixing all the meals I hate."

"I'll straighten that out."

"No, it's fine. It's the least of what I deserve for what I did to you. Is there a way that I could show her I'm sorry, though?"

"Tulips. Marge loves tulips. Bring her a bouquet of them and tell her you're loving her meals. Let her know that even liver from her kitchen tastes good. Flash her a smile, and you'll be good as new. Probably even get a special dessert out of it."

"Thanks. You're good with people, Kale. I appreciate that. I promise you, I won't forget how valuable you are again. I'm going to focus on my studies from now on, no more dating or social maneuvering. I've dreamt my whole life of coming to this university, and I'm going to make the most of it. I promise there will be a lot less drama in your life from now on." For a while longer, they sat in comfortable silence. Then Jason turned to Kale. "I've got to go inside. I need to leave for a lecture soon."

Kale stood up, offered his hand to Jason to help him up, and together they walked back into the house.

CHAPTER FIFTEEN

The next week was a mixed blessing for Kale. On one hand, Jason was nicer than he'd ever been. Words like "please" and "thank you" became permanent parts of his vocabulary. On the other hand, since Jason swore off all things frivolous, he was spending an awful lot of time at home studying, and that meant a lot of time with Kale. It wasn't too bad since he was pleasant to be around, but it was boring. There was only so much cleaning that could be done in Jason's small apartment. Once that was finished, Kale had to spend his time sitting around staring at nothing.

It could be worse. He could be kneeling the entire time. Driven, no doubt, by his guilt over his treatment of Kale, Jason had told him he could sit on the furniture, which was nice, but didn't exactly make time fly by. As the days wore on, Kale found himself debating whether or not he should ask Jason if he could be excused, or if there was something he could do. At this point, he would take on extra chores just to be busy. But things were too precarious. Kale was bored, but he wasn't miserable. That could change if he talked to Jason and things didn't go well. Jason was being nice, and Kale liked to think that the change was here for good, but he wasn't that naïve. One wrong word from him, and he risked ruining his good fortune.

As luck would have it, Jason took the matter entirely out

of his hands.

"I think you should learn to read." Kale was sitting on the overstuffed chair in Jason's room, passing the time by counting, for the seemingly thousandth time, the books on Jason's bookshelf. Jason's voice startled him, and Kale thought he didn't quite catch what was said.

"Excuse me, sir?"

"I said, I think you should learn to read."

"If you think it's necessary, master."

"I do. I don't doubt that you could continue to serve me well without being able to read, but you're too intelligent not to learn. It would give you another way to pass the time while I study."

If Jason was concerned about Kale being bored, then why didn't he just dismiss him and call him when needed? Kale didn't think it would be wise to voice this thought. "I'll do my best to learn if you want me to, but I think you're overestimating my ability."

"Well, has anyone ever taken the time to try and teach you?"

"To read? No, sir. The Cartwrights didn't see much point in having a slave who could read, especially when they did so little of it themselves."

Jason smiled at the slight to the Cartwrights. "Reading isn't something you just pick up, Kale. Someone has to teach you how to do it. You won't have problems learning, I assure you. I'm going to get some materials tomorrow, and then we'll start."

"Yes, sir." Kale didn't like the thought of having to learn to read, but he supposed it would be better than his current state of perpetual boredom.

◆ ◆ ◆

The next day when Jason came home from class, he had a bag

of materials for Kale. There were simple children's books and a picture book to teach the alphabet. Kale felt utterly ridiculous looking at a book that had a letter A with a picture of an apple on the first page. It was humiliating being treated like a child, and for a moment, Kale wondered if this was just a non-physical way for Jason to exert dominance. But as they went through the alphabet book together, he glanced at Jason, and there appeared to be no malice in his expression. Quite the opposite, he looked genuinely pleased and excited as Kale progressed through the book.

"Excellent, Kale! See, I told you that you'd learn quickly. Today, just go through this book and memorize the sounds the different letters make. I've got studying to do, but feel free to practice out loud, you won't bother me."

"Yes, sir." Kale spent the rest of the day looking through that dumb book. He felt silly reciting the alphabet and practicing the letter sounds while Jason sat at his desk studying advanced mathematics. At the end of the day, though, when Jason asked him to recite the alphabet, Kale did feel the slightest bit of pride at being able to do it. Maybe he wasn't as inept at book learning as he'd thought. Besides, Jason seemed so thrilled that his pet project was going well that it was worth a little discomfort.

Over the next several weeks, Jason persisted in teaching Kale how to read. Much to his own amazement, Kale learned rather quickly, and it didn't take long to go through all the children's books Jason had brought him. Kale wondered how much of his rapid learning was due to his desire to get through the embarrassingly simple books. There were only so many times one could read about Tom and Mary's adventures with a dog and a ball on a hill without going insane.

A few weeks later, Jason surprised Kale with an announcement.

"I'm really proud of how you're coming with your reading, Kale. I know it wasn't something you were eager to do. I'm going to start giving you a reading assignment each day." Goody, exactly what Kale wanted. "And from now on, after you're done with your chores and your reading assignment, you may entertain yourself however you wish, as long as you stay here so I can call on you when I need you."

Kale stared at Jason in shock. It wasn't much, but it was quite the concession by Jason. "Thank you, sir."

"You've earned it, Kale. I mean it." The sincerity in Jason's eyes warmed something in Kale. Why did this boy's approval mean so much to him? Well, that was easy. If Jason approved, then Kale's life was easier. Hadn't he just proved that? Having the freedom to do what he wanted was a big step in making life more comfortable.

For a moment, Jason stood looking at Kale with warmth in his expression. It seemed the only thing that would make him stop was Kale staring firmly straight back into his eyes. It worked, and Jason looked away. That was one difference between him and the Cartwrights. A Cartwright would never look away first and would tan the hide of any slave that even dared try to stare down a free man.

◆◆◆

The reading assignments weren't bad. Every day, he read a few chapters and told Jason what they were about. Afterward, he would sit at the coffee table and draw whatever items in the room caught his fancy. One day, when it seemed he had drawn everything in Jason's rooms, he took to drawing Jason himself.

Hunched over his desk working, Jason made an interesting subject. Kale tried to capture the concentration in his brown eyes and creased forehead. Little details, like the way he held his tongue just peeking through his lips as he read, amused Kale. Then there was the hair. The dark brown locks were thick on Jason's head, and Kale wondered what it would be like to run his hands through them. He had only ever combed Jason's hair, but imagined that it would feel soft against his fingers.

The scratching of Kale's pencil against his paper must have bothered Jason, because he eventually put his pen down and came to stand behind Kale. Kale froze. He hadn't been told he couldn't draw, but who knew what his master was thinking? Jason might be wondering where he got the supplies. If Kale told him he gambled and won them, he could get the rest of the slaves in trouble. He would have to think up some other explanation if Jason asked.

Once Jason got behind him, he didn't seem angry. In fact, his eyebrows lifted in an expression of surprise. He didn't say anything, just gave a "hmph" and went back to his desk. When it became apparent that Jason wasn't going to do or say anything about the drawing, Kale returned to his project.

The next day when Jason came home from class, he threw a brown paper package on the sofa. "Here. I picked you up a sketchbook and proper charcoal pencils. I also got some pastels in case you want to try drawing in color. Now you can go back to gambling for beer like the other slaves. When you run out, just ask, and I'll get you more supplies. Or if there's something else you'd like, paints perhaps, just ask."

Kale was dumbstruck. He barely pulled himself together to say, wide-eyed, "Thank you, master."

"You're welcome, Kale. Don't look so shocked. You have real talent, and it needs to be encouraged." Jason smiled and cocked his head. "Or did you think I was so clueless that I didn't know about the gambling? Give me a little credit, please. I don't mind gambling, but I won't have your art be dependent on your ability at cards or whether or not another slave can produce what you need."

"Thank you, master, but this is too much. I just sketch to pass the time. I wouldn't call it art."

"Why not? Because you're a slave?"

"No one is ever going to see it because I'm a slave. But it's not very good anyway. Drawing's just a hobby."

"Kale, when I saw that sketch you did of me yesterday, I was blown away. I'm studying at one of the most prestigious universities in the world. I'm surrounded by art every day. Trust me, what you do is art."

Kale didn't know what to say to that, so he just stared at Jason, wondering how he could have changed so much. Drawing had always been a way to amuse himself when there was nothing else to do. It was one of the few personal things Kale had. To hear Jason speak of it in such a way was akin to having Jason's approval of the deepest part of Kale's person. Kale knew that Jason valued him as an effective slave, and that meant something to him, but to know that Jason approved of him as a person made him feel a satisfaction that he had never experienced before. In twenty-one years of slavery, this was something foreign. It was as if they were crossing a line Kale had always taken for granted.

He must have stood there staring like an idiot for some time, because eventually Jason had to clear his throat to get his attention. "Go ahead and read the next five chapters in the book you're studying, and then you may draw."

Over the next several weeks, they fell into a comfortable pattern. Kale would do his reading and then draw. Never before had he been granted the opportunity to draw in color, and he found it fascinating to experiment with the different pigments. One day, a red bird landed on the balcony long enough for Kale to draw him, and the impact of the red on the paper was stunning. Using the pastels, he spent hours trying to accurately portray the world on paper, enhancing it with his own viewpoint.

Whenever Jason needed a break from his studies, he would have Kale read to him, or he would watch over Kale's shoulder as he drew. At first this was aggravating, but gradually Kale came to accept Jason's presence. In the beginning, he waited for Jason to criticize his clumsy reading or laugh at his absurd drawings, but neither happened. Instead, Kale could almost swear that he heard Jason murmur as he drew, and each sound seemed to say, "Yes, Kale, I see you, and I approve." The thought was ludicrous, but Kale couldn't help having it. When Jason stretched out on the bed and closed his eyes to listen to Kale read, he always had a comfortable smile on his face. It was the most relaxed Kale could ever remember seeing him.

It was during one of these reading sessions that the first signs of danger appeared. Kale found himself looking at Jason and thinking of how nice it would be to ravish him. Regarding Jason's lips, relaxed and soft as he lay on the bed, all Kale could think about was how nice they would look and feel around his cock. As soon as he thought it, he was so shocked at himself he actually jolted the book he was reading, sending it tumbling to the floor.

The commotion stirred Jason from his reverie. "Kale, is something wrong?"

Yes, something is wrong, Kale thought. "No, master."

"Why did you drop the book?"

Think fast, think fast. "My hand, uh, cramped, master. That's all. I'm sorry."

"As long as you're fine." Kale was shocked to see concern in Jason's eyes.

The change was too gradual to pinpoint, but he and Jason had gone from master and slave to almost friends, sitting together on the sofa, sometimes lounging on the bed, until the only reminder of the true relationship was Kale's continual use of the word "master." He wasn't stupid enough to stop that convention; it was the only remaining vestige of the world he knew. And now he had actually thought of having sex with Jason, of being the one in control. Things were not fine. Kale was dancing with disaster.

Chapter Sixteen

Kale lounged on the overstuffed chair in the corner, reading. Jason had been working on a paper for hours, which suited Kale fine. He was engrossed in the story of a band of pirates who journeyed to lands Kale knew he would never see. Later, he would take the images the book stirred in his mind and try to commit them to paper.

"Kale, come read to me."

Startled, Kale looked up, his eyes immediately going to Jason's empty desk. From there, he looked to the bed and saw Jason lazily sprawled out on it, smiling at him. He had been so caught up in his book that he hadn't heard Jason move.

"I'm not going to get any further on that paper right now. I need a break. Why don't you come here and read to me?"

"What do you want me to read?"

"Whatever you're reading is fine."

Kale went to the bed. It was big enough for them to lay comfortably side by side. Once he was situated, he asked, "Should I start at the beginning?"

"No, wherever you're at is fine. I just like hearing your voice."

Kale didn't understand that, but it was all right with him. As he began to read, Jason leaned back with his arms crossed behind his head and sighed. Kale was soon absorbed again in his book, and it would have been easy to think that Jason had fallen asleep, except there was no snoring. Kale didn't think Jason ever slept without snoring.

All of a sudden, Kale had the feeling he was being watched. He slowed his reading and glanced to the side. Jason had opened his eyes, and he stared at Kale. Feeling unnerved at being scrutinized so closely, Kale returned to reading and resolved to not look in Jason's direction. A couple of pages later, Kale was still aware of Jason's gaze and couldn't ignore it anymore. He stole another glance in Jason's direction and was surprised to see Jason intently watching his mouth. Even more shocking was the look in Jason's eyes. They were glazed over, and his pupils were dilated. It took only a moment for Kale to realize that Jason was attracted to him. If he had to bet money, he'd say that Jason was thinking of kissing him.

Instead of leaning forward to kiss him, Jason spoke. "Keep reading." His voice was husky and low in a way that Kale had never heard before.

Kale obliged, but he kept sneaking glances at Jason out of his peripheral vision. *If he wants to kiss me, why doesn't he just kiss me?* Kale's reading slowed as he looked away more often. *Just do it already!*

Finally, Kale snapped the book shut and faced Jason head on. The sound of the book closing seemed to make Jason aware of his surroundings and what he was doing. A tinge of pink crept up his cheeks, and Kale guessed it was from embarrassment, not lust. Then, in an apparent attempt to hide his embarrassment, Jason leaned forward and kissed Kale.

Kale's eyes widened in shock. What was he doing? Had he lost his mind? For a second, he expected Jason to pull away, but when he didn't, Kale closed his eyes and carefully let himself feel the kiss. This was exactly the type of danger that Kale had hoped to avoid. In a situation like this, his problem wouldn't be lack of passion; it would be the constant risk of forgetting himself. If he let his guard down, it was likely that he would end up crossing that ever fading line between master and slave.

Suddenly, Jason's lips were no longer on his. "Kale, is this all right? If you don't want to, that's fine. This isn't a service I require of you. I just...I guess I couldn't help myself anymore." Dear gods, he ducked his head and blushed like a damn virgin. "But, I'll stop if you don't like it."

"No!" It came out like a reflex at the suggestion that there might be no more kissing. Even more concerning was how strained Kale's voice sounded to his own ears. Did Jason hear that hint of desperation? "I mean, it's fine. It just took me by surprise is all."

A smile crept up Jason's face, and he leaned in again. This time, Kale was prepared and participated more in the kiss. He'd rather show Jason how much he was enjoying it than have to tell him. Jason's arms crept around him and began to knead the muscles of his back. Traveling down, Jason's hands slipped into Kale's pants, and he released a moan against Jason's mouth. Pulling away, Jason began to mess with the buttons on Kale's pants, but before he could finish unfastening them, he looked up at Kale.

"Are you sure about this? It isn't an order. I haven't done this before because I don't believe a free man should take a slave against his will. I just want you now more than I think I've ever wanted anything. But I'll stop if you don't want it. I won't take you without your permission."

Gods, he didn't want it to stop, but he didn't exactly want to tell Jason that. What was his master thinking, anyway, getting a guy worked up and then backing off? Of course he wanted to continue. Why couldn't Jason just get on with it? Why did Jason have to choose now to have a conscience?

"Do you have any oil?"

Jason looked surprised at the question, and then his face fell. "No."

"I'll be back." Kale scooted off the bed and raced down to the slave quarters, where the boys always had oil available for their frequent fucks. Marge kept them well stocked with extra from the kitchen. When he got back upstairs, Jason had removed his shirt and was lounging on the bed. It was impossible to miss the way his eyes lit up when Kale entered the room. Discarding his own shirt, Kale joined Jason on the bed and placed the oil on the bedside table. As soon as he was situated on the bed, Jason picked up where he left off and continued kissing him. The feel of Jason's hands, so different than the dried, calloused hands of the slaves Kale was used to, was enough to make him shiver.

Ever aware of his place, Kale bit back the desire to take charge. But once Jason got around to removing Kale's pants, Kale reached for the oil. He wasn't about to trust that Jason would think to prepare him properly, especially given his limited experience. Kale doubted that Jason had ever topped before, but he knew he would think the only proper place for a slave was the bottom.

When he set the oil aside, Jason pinned him on his back, Kale's least favorite position. It was too intimate. Jason reached down and brushed Kale's hair back from his forehead as he leaned over him. The look in his eyes was unnerving. This wasn't a recreational fuck. For the first time, someone was making love to Kale. It was a scary thought, and he shut his eyes in an effort to merely surrender to the experience and block out any emotions associated with it.

Closing his eyes intensified the sensations. Kale felt warm breath behind his left ear followed by the soft touch of lips. Had he ever been kissed there before? If he had, he certainly didn't remember it feeling like this. When the tip of Jason's tongue flicked against Kale's earlobe, a tingling shiver traveled down his spine.

Meanwhile, Jason's hands were underneath Kale, digging into his back, pulling him closer. Tight muscles protested the pressure, but the raw desire in the act made Kale yearn for more. More pressure, more kisses, more attention—just more. Their cocks began to rub together with the nearness, and Kale found himself bucking against Jason, trying desperately to increase the friction.

Jason's breath caught, and it was no longer merely lips Kale felt against his skin. As Jason proceeded down Kale's throat, his teeth came into play, nipping their way to Kale's chest. The teeth weren't the only change—Jason began to thrust his penis against Kale's in earnest. Jason moaned, and Kale felt Jason's weight lift from his chest. The air felt cool against his skin, and Kale couldn't help opening his eyes, hoping Jason wasn't somehow done already.

Jason's eyes bore down into Kale, and they were a darker shade of brown than Kale had seen before. Jason situated himself between Kale's legs and lifted one onto his shoulder as he slowly began to enter Kale. It was tight, a little more preparation would have been helpful, but Kale didn't care at the moment. Jason's unhurried attempt to be careful was not appreciated—Kale wanted him inside. He couldn't look up and see the way Jason was looking at him without wanting to consume Jason. Closing his eyes, he exhaled slowly, trying to get a grip on himself. There was no reason this should be any more intense than the sex he regularly had with Charlie.

Once Jason was all the way in, his hands went to Kale's chest and began to alternately fondle the hair there and dig his fingers into the flesh. Every time Jason changed what he did, Kale swore it was his favorite. Then Jason's thrusting hit that sweet bundle of nerves inside, and Kale was corrected once again: this was his favorite.

As Jason sped up his thrusting in a burst of passion, Kale wondered if he had any intention of taking care of his slave's erection. Would Jason be upset if Kale took care of it himself? Each master was different; some allowed slaves their pleasure and others didn't.

"Open your eyes." Jason's throaty voice pierced Kale's thoughts. The moment Kale's eyes opened, the warm tightness of Jason's hand wrapped around his cock, eliciting a moan of pure pleasure. It appeared he didn't need to worry about Jason taking care of him. The eye contact Jason demanded was unnerving, but if it meant he would be permitted to orgasm, it was worth it. At least, at this moment it was.

Jason adjusted the speed of his hand and his thrusting so they both came together. It was as if he was Kale's lover. It was the most thorough fuck Kale had ever experienced. As soon as the last shudders of passion receded, Jason collapsed next to Kale. Before Jason's arm could make it around his chest, Kale was up and headed to the bathroom to clean up.

As he washed himself off, Kale breathed deeply to try and steady his racing heart. He was keenly aware of a desire to go back to the bed and hold Jason, which was baffling. The smartest thing would be to get out of here as quickly as possible. Dampening a wash cloth, he went back out to clean Jason. As Kale worked, Jason sunk his hands into Kale's hair and played with it, causing quite a distraction. Trying to remain distant, Kale got up to leave as soon as he was finished.

As Kale stood up, Jason's hand shot out and grabbed his arm, pulling him down next to him. Jason lightly stroked Kale's face and watched him so intently that Kale felt even more naked. "You're beautiful, Kale. I've always known you were attractive, but the day I saw you drawing that picture of me at my desk, I saw a new part of you. It was like looking into your soul, and it was beautiful. I guess that's when I realized I could fall for you."

What could Kale say to that? Sex was always just sex to him. Tonight had been good, but things like love didn't belong here, especially between a master and his slave. Trust Jason to make things bigger and more dramatic than they needed to be. Jason didn't seem to need a reply; he gave Kale a quick kiss and then rested his head on Kale's shoulder and put his arm over his chest.

As Jason began to drift off, Kale moved to get up, trying not to disturb his master. As soon as he had made it a few inches, though, Jason's arm tightened around him. "Where are you going?" Jason's voice was thick with sleep, and he didn't even open his eyes.

"I was just going down to bed, master."

Jason looked up into Kale's face. "Stay here tonight. Please?"

The thought of staying in bed with Jason curled around him was pleasant enough; it was the thought of how awkward the morning might be that gave Kale pause.

"Please, Kale, I'd just like to lay with you."

The pleading in Jason's eyes made it impossible for Kale to deny him. "Very well, master. As you wish." There was that smile again. Contemplating it, Kale thought that whatever awkwardness morning might bring, it was worth it for this moment. He situated himself back in bed, and Jason nestled up against him, settling in the crook of his arm. As soon as Jason found a comfortable fit, he was asleep again.

Sleep did not come so quickly for Kale. He found himself in an entirely new position. Never before had he spent the night in the bed of someone he had been with, much less a free person who owned him. The blissful after-sex haze had faded, and now the reality of what happened came crashing in on Kale. Was he stupid? Did he have a death wish? There was no way this ended well for him. What was he doing giving in to his feelings? Scratch that, what was he doing having feelings for his master at all? He wasn't that reckless, he couldn't be. There had to be another explanation.

Jason liked to act as if Kale had a choice, but Kale knew better. If he had refused, Jason could have made his life hell. There would have been resentment, and if not outright punishment for the refusal, surely there would have been repercussions. Jason could easily go from the nice agreeable master who suddenly took an interest in making Kale's life easy, to the demanding, domineering man of whom Kale had learned to be wary. That had to be the real reason Kale had surrendered to Jason tonight. There was no harm in allowing himself enjoyment, as long he was clear that he was doing it out of duty. Any other thought was just too worrisome.

Chapter Seventeen

The next morning, the movement of the bed woke Jason. Stretching, he opened his eyes, and they immediately sought out Kale, who was slipping out of bed. Once Kale noticed that Jason was awake, he stopped and Jason smiled. Waking up with Kale like this was different from all the mornings when Kale had woken him up before. The knowledge of what they had shared last night made butterflies go wild in Jason's stomach. Just the sight of those pale green eyes that Jason now knew had flecks of gold in them made Jason want to pull Kale back into bed.

The whole experience with Kale was different than it had been with Eric. Topping had been exquisite, a new sensation after bottoming, but that wasn't it. The whole dynamic was different. With Eric, there had been a kind of hero worship that made Jason turn a blind eye to his true character. With Kale, however, Jason felt true admiration and respect, which made the feelings of affection deeper and more grounded. With Eric, he had felt on edge and nervous, as if the slightest wrong move on his part would pop the bubble. There was none of that here, only a feeling to want to make sure Kale enjoyed himself as much as Jason did.

"Master, I was just going to get your breakfast."

"Bring up enough for yourself as well. We'll eat together." Kale hid his shock well, but Jason could see it in the slight quirk of his eyebrows. "It'll be fun."

"Yes, master."

Once Kale had left, Jason's mind began to wander over the events of last night. It seemed like he had been dreaming about having sex with Kale for weeks now. There were so many times that he had wanted to act on his desire, but he never wanted Kale to feel forced. Even now, Jason wondered if Kale had gone through with it just because his master wanted it. Closing his eyes, Jason replayed the night in his mind. No, there was no mistaking that Kale enjoyed himself and wanted it to happen.

It would be important now to make sure that Kale still felt comfortable. It was disconcerting that he had moved to go down to his own bed. Did Kale think that he was using him? That he wasn't interested in more than sex? Nothing could be further from the truth. It was Kale's character that had made Jason fall for him, and he was sure that he had, indeed, fallen.

Even though he was sure Kale was not unwilling last night, that didn't mean his feelings were the same as Jason's. He had to realize that this transition would be harder on Kale. Regaining Kale's trust would not be easy, and it might not even be possible for Jason to redeem himself. While Jason was falling head first, wanting to immediately change their relationship to one of lovers, there was no guarantee that Kale would ever be in the same place. It was much better to move slowly. Jason would act as if they were just starting out. And in a way they were; until recently, Jason had only ever viewed Kale as a slave. It was time they built a relationship based on more than their legal status. As much as it pained him, Jason was bound and determined to take this as slowly as Kale needed.

When Kale returned with breakfast, it became painfully obvious just how slowly they would need to go. Setting the breakfast tray down on the table, Kale set Jason's place and then looked around in confusion as to what he was supposed to do with his.

"Set your place across from mine." Jason rose to join Kale at the table as he silently obeyed. When Jason seated himself in front of his food, he saw that Kale was once again at a loss. "Take a seat, Kale. Come on; don't tell me you're uncomfortable eating with me after last night."

That got a response. Jason could always count on Kale to defend his pride. "No, of course not, master. I just didn't know if you wanted me to sit with you while you ate. As I recall, that was one of the first rules you outlined."

Not only did Kale remember all the ways in which Jason had been a bastard, but it appeared that he was still bitter about them as well. The subtle jibe hit Jason hard. No matter how happy he was right now, there was still a lot of work to do to get Kale to move with him to a better place. Jason set down his fork and met Kale's gaze. "I was being an ass. I didn't know what I was doing. I was stupid, and I thought that lording myself over someone who had no control and no way to fight back would make me feel big. I was wrong, Kale, and I'm sorry."

It appeared that was the last thing Kale expected. His jaw went slack, and his lips parted slightly. After a moment he looked away. "Thank you, master. I appreciate that."

Jason desperately wished he could get Kale to call him by his name, but it was too soon. When Kale did use Jason's name, he needed it to be because Kale wanted to, because he was in love with him. "Go ahead and eat up. You don't want it to get cold." Jason went back to eating, and when he looked at Kale again, he saw that he was eating, too. Looking down at his plate, though, he couldn't help noticing something was different. "Hey, why is mine fancier than yours?" Jason crinkled his forehead. It wasn't right that they should have different meals.

Kale started to laugh, but began to choke on his dull looking oatmeal. When he had swallowed, he asked, "Fancier, master?"

"Yeah, mine's nicer than yours."

"I'm a slave. Oatmeal is a lot cheaper. It can also sit in a pot waiting for when we have time to eat."

"So? You're eating with me. It's not right. Switch with me."

"Switch?"

"What, you don't think I can eat what you eat every morning?"

"It's not a matter of being able to, master, it's just that you're not going to like it."

"What I don't like is you not eating well. It won't kill me. Pass it over."

When Jason passed his plate to Kale, he noticed the smile that Kale was trying to hide as he handed over the oatmeal. When the plates were settled again, Kale wasn't eating. He was probably waiting for Jason to taste the oatmeal and send it back. Wanting to prove he wasn't the spoiled child Kale seemed to think he was, Jason raised a nice big spoonful to his mouth and looked Kale in the eye.

Big mistake.

If he hadn't tried to keep eye contact, he could have kept the distaste from his face. As it was, he had to turn away to concentrate on swallowing his mouthful. It wasn't that it tasted bad, it was that it had no taste at all, which just left the thick, goopy consistency.

"Care for your poached eggs, master?"

Jason saw that Kale was holding up Jason's original plate and reaching out his hand for the oatmeal. More than that, he had a very satisfied smile on his face. It was the smile that strengthened Jason's resolve.

"No, thank you. I think I'll stick with the oatmeal. It's very filling, really sticks to the ribs."

Kale raised his eyebrows and snorted. "As you wish, master."

Already the honorific was grating on Jason's nerves. One step at a time, though. "I was wondering if you might like to come with me today. I have a couple of lectures, and then I was thinking of going to the library. You could bring a book if you want, and once we get to the library, I'll check out anything you like."

Kale's eyes turned wary. "Would I like to go?"

It was clear Kale was not comfortable being put in this kind of position. Why should he be? Jason knew he had done nothing to make Kale believe it was acceptable for him to make choices and that Jason would respect them. "It's just that I would really like to see you more today, but I can't get away from my classes. Who knows, you might even be interested by the lectures. I have one on philosophy today and one on mythology. Don't worry. I wouldn't invite you to anything too boring."

"I've never been to campus with you."

"No, but it's not uncommon for students to bring slaves. If you'd feel uncomfortable, you can certainly stay home, I won't hold it against you." Jason knew he had him now. There was no way Kale would let him think that anything made him uncomfortable.

"I just wanted to make sure it was appropriate for you, master. Of course, I'll accompany you anywhere you request."

◆◆◆

That day was one of the happiest Jason had spent in classes since he arrived at university. After his humiliation with Eric, it should have been more difficult than this, and it had been. Those first days in class had been nearly unbearable with the looks and whispers he endured from the other students. Then Kale had become an important part of his life. When he was with Kale, Jason felt like they were in their own little world, safe from intrusion.

Kale had opted not to bring a book. He had said

something about not wanting to have to carry it around, but Jason suspected his decision had more to do with his desire to show Jason that he could keep up with the lectures. It was nice to look over and see Kale kneeling next to him. Jason would have preferred to have Kale sitting beside him, but there was no way to do that in class. Even in a massive lecture hall it would cause a scene to have a slave sitting among free men. During his philosophy class, Kale appeared to be interested in the subject matter, and Jason caught him nodding along with what the professor said. Even though that level of enthusiasm was missing in the mythology class, it was easy to see that the lecture amused Kale.

The best part of the day was walking into the library with Kale and hearing his intake of breath. Jason remembered having the same reaction when he first saw the library rotunda. When Jason told him that he could pick any book he wanted, Kale had looked at him as though he was crazy.

"How could I possibly pick one? I don't even know where to start."

"Well, what are you interested in?"

"I don't know."

"Sure you do. You liked that last book you read, with the pirates, didn't you?"

"Yeah."

"Well, what did you like about it?"

"I guess I liked reading about foreign places. All I've ever seen is the old county and here. I've always been curious about the outside world."

"All right then. I actually know a book you'd enjoy. It will just take a minute to find it."

Kale eyed the walls and shelves full of books and looked back at Jason skeptically. A few minutes later, Jason had shown Kale how to find books using the library's catalog and handed him *Voyage of the Sea Strider*, a book about a nautical explorer and his adventures in new lands. It was gratifying to share these things he loved with Kale.

After they finished at the library, Jason strolled with Kale around campus. There was no destination in his mind. Jason simply wanted Kale to see the beauty of what had drawn him to Perdana. The architecture was gorgeous, and there were plenty of grassy areas with beautiful trees where students lounged to study and nap.

Back at the house, they fell into their usual routine. Jason needed to study, and Kale began reading his book. After every few lines that Jason read, he glanced back to watch Kale. After reading the same sentence three times, Jason figured he wouldn't be getting much studying done and went to the bed to lie down.

"Would you mind reading to me, Kale?"

Kale peered at him over the cover of the book with a question in his eyes. "Don't worry. I'm not going to want to have sex every time you read to me from now on. I just like hearing your voice." In an effort to show his sincerity, Jason closed his eyes.

A moment later, Kale began to read aloud. Jason really did love the sound of his voice. It was strong and smooth. Solid would be the word Jason would use to describe it. Even when Kale was unsure about something, his voice sounded like he meant to be unsure. Jason quickly tuned out the words and simply let the rich tones of his voice wash over him. Thinking of how much he liked Kale's voice made Jason think of other things he liked about Kale. The strong arms that were nicely defined, but not too bulky. They weren't as big as they had been when Jason first received him, but they were still nicely muscled. Then there was his flat, firm stomach. And the way his face looked when he orgasmed... this was definitely not a good train of thought to be on when he was trying to prove to Kale that he could just listen to him read. Jason opened his eyes, but just like yesterday, his eyes went straight to Kale's lips, and he began to think about just how much he wanted to taste them again. This would not do.

Jason jumped up and strode toward his desk, hoping that

he could hide the interest his body was taking. "That's good, Kale. I'd better get back to studying. You've done enough reading for today. You may draw if you want." Kale was silent behind him, and Jason couldn't tell if that meant anything. He didn't dare look back and see; he didn't think he could hide his desire from Kale if he faced him.

A few minutes later, Jason heard the familiar scratch of pencil on paper and breathed a sigh of relief. Feeling that he hadn't made a fool of himself, he was now able to study.

When he glanced at the clock, he was surprised to see that two hours had passed. He had accomplished a lot, and it was a good time for a break. When Jason started toward where Kale was sitting in the overstuffed chair, Kale was moving to stand.

"Don't get up. I'm just taking a break. I thought I'd see what you were drawing."

Kale picked up his sketchpad from the table and picked one of the pastels to resume sketching.

"You're using the pastels. Do you like them?"

"Yes, master. Thank you again."

By this time, Jason had made it behind Kale and looked down to see his work. What he saw quite literally took his breath away.

"I know it's not very good." Kale craned his neck to look back at Jason.

"What are you talking about? Kale, this is phenomenal." Before him was a perfect drawing of the library rotunda. Kale had recreated every detail, down to the stained glass windows that had been commissioned from one of the most famous artists in Perdana's history. It was the first time Jason had seen Kale use color, and the result was stunning. Light drifted in through the stained glass windows and settled on bookshelves and tables. The colored light seemed to dance on the page. "I have never seen anything like it."

"You mean from a slave. I know you've been to art shows before, and there are plenty of pretty paintings at your school."

"Kale, I'm telling you, there are not many men who can draw like you, slave or free." At times like this, Jason realized his pre-conceived notions about class were ludicrous. It was a crime to say that a slave was less of a person than a free man when he was capable of producing such art.

"Thank you, master." Kale had begun to fidget and was now putting the drawing back on the table, face down. "Isn't it time for dinner? Will you be eating in the dining room, or should I bring your meal up here?"

Jason wanted to eat with him again, but it was easy to see that Kale was uncomfortable. This morning he had decided not to move too fast, but here he was spending all of his time with Kale. It might do Kale good to have some time on his own. "I'll take my dinner up here. After you bring it up, you're dismissed until nine o'clock." The clear relief on Kale's face was almost comical.

After eating, Jason had planned to go back to studying. On his way from the table to his desk, though, the sight of Kale's sketchbook distracted him. Normally, Kale took it with him when he left, but he had been so flustered by Jason's praise that he hadn't. It was a rare opportunity for Jason to look through his work.

Seating himself on the sofa, Jason took some time to further admire the picture of the library. It was amazing. He flipped to the beginning of the book and looked at the drawings in order. There were drawings of individual knickknacks and pieces of furniture along with drawings from Kale's imagination. Then there were the pictures of Jason. He tried to not let himself feel too flattered; after all, he was the only person available for Kale to sketch. Still, he couldn't help hoping that the flattering way in which Kale captured him on paper was indicative of his feelings. Vain as it sounded, the portraits of himself were the ones Jason liked the most, not because they were of him, but because they captured his emotions so well. Looking at them made him

115

feel something deep inside, rather than just being impressed by an accurate likeness.

At precisely nine o'clock, Kale returned. Jason knew that he wanted to try to convince Kale to stay the night again, not to have sex, but just to talk and fall asleep together. Now that Jason was open with himself about his feelings for Kale, he feared letting him get away. It felt as if everything he had been looking for when he foolishly got involved with Eric was now before him, and he wanted to reach out and grab it before it disappeared. It was a silly thought; Kale was literally his, there was nowhere he could go.

Once Jason was ready for bed and had gone over his schedule for the next day with Kale, he reached out to touch him. Kale looked with surprise at Jason's hand resting lightly on his arm. It wasn't a common occurrence for Jason to casually touch him. "I was wondering if you might stay the night again. Just to talk this time."

"Just talk?" Kale didn't sound like he was looking for a promise, more like he was startled by the request.

"Yes, just talk. And fall asleep with me. I enjoyed having you here last night. It's nice to wake with someone in the morning."

Kale smiled with a mischievous glint in his eyes. "I wake you every morning, master."

Jason groaned. "Don't be coy, Kale, you know what I'm talking about. It was nice having you here this morning. And I'd really like to talk with you."

Kale looked as if he was considering his options. For a moment, Jason wanted to order him to stay. A few weeks ago, he would have. Now he was beginning to see that real strength was in having power and choosing not to abuse it. Still, it would be so nice to just say the words that would get him what he wanted. Except he wanted Kale, not an obedient slave. Kale was going to be a hard enough prize to win. Jason couldn't go making it harder by sabotaging his own efforts.

"Yes, I'll stay the night, master."

Jason couldn't hold in the smile that seemed to bubble up from somewhere deep inside him. The only thing he thought could make him happier now was if Kale hadn't used the word "master" at the end of that sentence.

While Kale began to unbutton his shirt, Jason grabbed the sketchbook and plopped down on the bed. "I looked through your drawings after dinner. I hope you don't mind."

Kale paused in taking off his shirt when he heard Jason speak and then went ahead and removed it. "No, I don't mind, why should I? It's your sketchbook, and they're your drawings."

There was no bitterness in Kale's voice, but Jason felt it anyway, because what he said was true. "Don't be like that, Kale. You know I don't think that way, don't you?"

Kale turned to him after folding his shirt and laying it over the arm of a chair. When he looked at Jason, he seemed to be pondering the question. "If you don't think that way, why'd you look through it?"

Jason felt his skin start to tingle as heat flooded his face. Curses, he was actually blushing. "I just wanted to see them. I like you, Kale, and your drawings are an important part of you. I wanted to feel like I knew you better."

"And do you?"

How come Kale could always stay so calm? Jason envied him the levelheaded way he approached things. There was never anger or malice in his words. Condescension never colored his tone. Yet somehow, Jason often found himself feeling off balance around Kale. It made it easier to see Kale as a person—no owner should ever feel unbalanced around his own slave. "I think so."

"Hmph." Kale moved toward the bed, but just before he climbed in, he looked up at Jason, as if for confirmation. Jason nodded his head and made room. Once Kale was situated, he turned to Jason with a face that clearly said, "I'm here, now what?"

Picking up the sketchbook, Jason flipped to the picture of

117

the library. "I just can't get over how remarkable this is, Kale. The way you captured the light. And the detail! How did you remember it so well? I've been there dozens of times, and I couldn't conjure up a picture this vivid."

"It's not that I remember the particulars, I just remember the impression. From that impression, I can create my own details. Take that drawing with you the next time you go, and you'll see that it is not a perfect representation, far from it. I find that people rarely remember specifics. They're much more likely to remember the way they felt. That's what I was trying to capture here."

"You did a great job. Why did you decide to use color on this one?"

Kale shifted uncomfortably. Jason had noticed that Kale didn't like it when the conversation lingered on him too long. "I don't know. It just seemed appropriate. All the stained glass, it would have been a shame to do that in black and white. It just felt like it should be in color. All those books— some of the greatest words ever written are in that room—it would have been disrespectful not to draw them in color."

"I agree. It's my favorite place on campus. I can easily lose myself in there for hours."

"Exactly. You're there, but the books draw you in to whole other worlds. I mean, I know you study more serious things than the silly stories I read, but when you're there, you can be anywhere. It fascinates me."

How had Jason ever thought that Kale was simpleminded? "Is that why you like reading books about foreign lands? You'd like to see them?"

"Yeah, I suppose. I know I'll never see more than Perdana and Malar County. Perhaps a few other places in Arine. Now that I can read, though, it's as if I can visit anyplace I like. Thank you for that. I would have never learned to read if you hadn't taught me." Kale met Jason's eyes with sincerity before looking away.

At that moment, Jason felt that teaching Kale to read was

the single most important achievement of his life. "You're welcome, Kale. It would have been a shame for you never to have learned."

The rest of the night, they talked about books and the places Kale wanted to see. Jason felt a growing sense of responsibility. If Kale were ever to see anything in his life, it would be because Jason allowed and facilitated it. After Kale had described the places in the book he was reading, Jason asked him a question. "If you were free, would you spend the rest of your life traveling the world?"

Jason turned to look at Kale. They were side by side on their backs, and from this vantage point Jason could see from his profile that Kale frowned. "I don't know. I'd like to see the world, see how other people live, but when it comes down to it, I'd want to have a place that I knew was home, a place I could come back to. In the end, I think I'm really a country boy at heart. Give me a nice patch of land to call my own, and I'd be as happy as could be."

"So if you were free, and money weren't an issue, you'd still want a place back in Malar County?"

"Yeah, it's good land there. There's something so alive about the country that you don't find in the city. If I work it, develop it, build myself a sturdy home, I could be proud of that. It'd be mine."

"You and my father sound a lot alike."

"Is that a bad thing?"

"I just never understood him, I've wanted to get out of there for as long as I can remember, and all he's ever wanted is to stay put, preferably with me there, too."

"And I never understood why you had a problem with Malar County. What's so wrong with it? It was good enough for your father to make a fortune."

"On the backs of slaves."

Kale met Jason's eyes and lifted his brow. "Yes, master, on the backs of slaves. There's no need to lecture me about it. My back's one of the ones you're talking about." He returned

119

to staring at the ceiling.

"I know. I'm sorry. I just don't understand this affinity you have for it."

"There are plenty of common folk who have done well there on their own. There's no reason I couldn't too."

"But there's no reason you couldn't do well anywhere."

Kale turned his head slightly and flashed half a smile. "You're just saying that because you're hoping if you say it enough, I'll be as smart a slave as you wanted."

"You are smart."

Kale shrugged. "So what is it you dislike so much about the county? Master." The last was added as if to soften the forwardness of the question.

"I always thought there should be more to life than fishing and hunting. There's no culture, no real beauty. Everyone is content just being there. It seems like such a waste."

"Perhaps one day, I can show you the kind of beauty that's in the country. It may be different than the art you see here, but it's no less beautiful. And what's wrong with contentment? How many people here are content? They run around, spending money by the barrel, and there's not a content soul in the lot."

Jason rolled onto his side and studied Kale. "How'd you get to be so old?"

Kale responded with a strong belly laugh. "Ah, I don't know, kid. Maybe I'm cynical. Go on, chase your riches, your social scene, just remember to be content when you get what you want, master."

"You know, calling me master doesn't make what you say sound any more submissive."

"Only letting you know that I know my place. Just because you don't have the good sense to tell me to shut up when I should doesn't mean I don't know that you could."

"I don't think I could ever want you to shut up, Kale. I like your voice too much."

"Oh, so that's what it is? You ignore my words to hear my voice, huh? No wonder you haven't tanned me yet."

"No, I listen too. Things are different now, Kale. I'm not going to punish you for something you say. I want to hear you speak your mind. Tonight has been wonderful. You do know that things are different now, right?"

Kale shifted onto his side and regarded Jason. It was unnerving how he always seemed to be looking into Jason's soul and judging the truth of what he saw there. It felt good that Kale took the time to give his responses thought, that he gave honest answers instead of offering words he thought would be pleasing.

Finally, he said, "Yeah, I know." Then he yawned, stretching his arms above his head. "So you were serious when you said no fucking tonight. It must be nearly morning. Unless your plan was to get me all tired out and relaxed so I'd be more pliable."

Jason laughed. "No, just talking and sleeping tonight. I guess it's time to move on to the sleeping part; thank goodness I don't have to be up early."

"So it won't be terribly disrespectful if I turn my back to you now and go to sleep?"

"No, not at all." Kale shifted onto his side with his back facing Jason. "Kale? Do you mind if I cuddle?"

Kale glanced over his shoulder. "What?"

Jason felt that confounded blush again. He felt stupid asking, but what could he do about it now? "I just like feeling you next to me."

"It's not like you need my permission."

"I know I don't need it; I want it."

Kale shrugged and began to roll back over. "Sure, cuddle away."

Jason curled up next to Kale so that they were spooning. With his arm around Kale's chest, he felt content with what he had for the first time in his life.

CHAPTER EIGHTEEN

That was the first of many nights Kale spent talking in Jason's bed. Even though Kale thought it was ridiculous that Jason liked to act as if they were lovers, it was nice being able to sleep in his bed. It was far more comfortable than Kale's own bed in the basement, and he didn't feel like he had anything to talk about with the other slaves anymore. He even grew accustomed to Jason's snoring. Sometimes they would have sex, others they would just lay together until sleep overcame them, and still others they would talk until the first rays of sunlight peeked through the crack in the drapes.

It was nights like those that worried Kale. Sex was one thing, cuddling up together like they were lovers falling asleep in each other's arms was tolerable, but staying up all night talking? That was an entirely different matter. The intimacy was disconcerting.

The second time they had sex, Kale was sprawled on his stomach afterward when Jason propped himself up on an elbow and began running his hand up and down his back. The sensation was nice, but Kale had always been the type to sleep after sex, and any display of interest or—gods forbid—love afterward was unwelcome and awkward.

"What are these scars here?" Kale had been almost asleep, enjoying the feel of Jason's hand on his back, when Jason's question pulled him back to wakefulness.

"What do you think?" He was in no mood to have this discussion. If Jason was going to insist that he stay awake, couldn't he insist on a conversation that wasn't so damn awkward?

"I've never seen them before."

"You've never looked hard enough. They're old, ancient by now. They're mostly from the Cartwright's."

"What happened?"

"James Cartwright isn't known for his restraint with the whip. I'm mouthy, you know that. And anytime Carter got in trouble, it was me who was punished. Said I was a bad influence. Besides, he didn't need a reason. Wanting to was good enough."

"That's horrible."

"Could have been worse." Kale moved onto his back, hoping that if it wasn't in view the conversation would stop, and put his arm over his eyes to block the light. All he really wanted was to go to sleep.

"That's all you have to say? It could have been worse?"

"I'm tired, master, please."

"How can you be so cavalier about it?"

"What?" Kale's brain was too foggy with sleep to try and figure out the meaning of unfamiliar words.

"You act like it's nothing."

Kale removed his arm from his eyes. This was going to be one of those times when Jason decided to get righteously indignant in the way of the truly young and naïve. Kale took in a deep breath, summoning the strength to stay awake and talk. He sat up. "What do you want me to say? That it was unfair? That it hurt like hell? Do you want details, like how much blood there was? I can tell you all that. And then, afterward, I'll still have the scars, and you'll know things you'd rather not. It won't make anything better. Or, we can go to sleep, and when I wake up I won't be so damn tired that I talk to my master so disrespectfully that, if you were James Cartwright, I'd be getting a beating that would make these

124

scars look like a slap on the hand."

"You know you can be honest with me, Kale. If you'd rather not talk about it, that's fine. But it's time you realized I care about you, and what James Cartwright did wasn't right. I know you've been through things that I can't imagine, but if you lived through them, then I can at least hear about them. I'm not a child."

The earnestness in Jason's expression softened Kale. "I know you're not a child, master. I'd just rather not talk about it."

"All right, then. Let's go to sleep."

Jason turned off the lamp, and they fell asleep in what was becoming their usual position, with Jason's arm over his chest, holding onto Kale like he was claiming him.

◆ ◆ ◆

A few days later, tired of being cooped up in the house, they went to the park. The day was beautiful with the cool breeze curtailing the heat of the sun. The only thing Kale missed about his old life was being outside. There was something invigorating about it: the sun heating his skin, the slightest of breezes cooling his sweat, and that smell that let him know all around him the earth was alive.

Marge had packed them a lunch, and they settled under a giant oak. Jason brought a novel he was reading, and Kale his sketchpad and charcoal. Their spot was perfect. The shade from the tree provided a haven from the sun's heat, but rays of sunlight filtered through the branches and leaves, making a beautiful dancing pattern on the grass. After they had eaten, Kale settled on his back to try and draw the canopy of the tree while Jason read.

In the cool grass, Kale felt at peace. For him, nature was home. He knew that any place he lived would never belong to him, but this—the raw earth—was as much his as anyone's.

After drawing the tree, he sat up and looked around. Jason appeared to still be absorbed in his book, so Kale looked for another subject. Right outside of the tree's shade, a single flower grew. Actually, it was a weed. It appeared that the city gardeners were not keeping up on their work, or maybe they thought it looked too pretty and noble standing by itself to pull it. Funny how one of the most beautiful things in the park was deemed a weed simply because it wasn't planned or planted.

Kale lay down on his stomach with his body still shaded by the tree, and began to draw. The flower was beautiful from a distance, but up close he could see its texture and smell the sweet fragrance. If he was especially quiet and still, holding his breath, he could almost imagine that he saw it growing.

As he drew, he heard Jason mumble in irritation. Looking back to make sure he wasn't needed, Kale saw Jason swat furiously at a bee. It was hard not to laugh, but Kale didn't want to draw attention to himself. He settled for rolling his eyes. Turning back to the flower, he continued to sketch. A little while later, a bee buzzed by, probably the same bee that bothered Jason. It hovered over the flower, landed for a short time, and took off, heavy with pollen. Barely even realizing it, Kale had drawn the bee into his picture.

As Kale was putting the finishing touches on the flower, he heard Jason shut his book and walk over. This time Kale didn't look back, knowing Jason just came to watch. It was annoying the way Jason liked hovering over his shoulder while he drew. It made Kale aware of everything, even his own breathing. All his life he could breathe just fine, but when Jason peered over his shoulder, it was as if Kale needed to pay attention to make sure his breaths came at the right intervals.

Jason sat cross-legged by Kale's side and asked, "Why are you drawing that weed?"

"It's pretty." Kale answered without looking up.

"But it's a weed."

Kale sighed. This boy was incorrigible. Instead of answering, he looked up at the skyline. They were right at the edge of the park, and the street was less than a hundred yards away. Kale began to fill the background of his picture with the nearby buildings. Quick, almost angry, strokes formed the smoke coming out of kitchen chimneys. Though the sketching was rough, he included such details as the sewage on the side of the road, the broken window shutters, laundry hanging between buildings. In front of this dreary background, the quiet flower sat, small and simple, shaming what the wealth of Perdana had built around her.

Kale turned to Jason, who still stared at the picture, his mouth slightly open and his eyes roaming over the page. "That's why I draw the weed, master."

Jason closed his mouth. Kale held his breath, wondering if he was out of line. Holding out his hand, Jason asked, "May I see it?"

Kale relaxed. He knew that he would eventually ruin the good fortune of being in his master's favor, but apparently today was not that day. Silently, he handed over the sketchbook and watched Jason turn the page to look at the picture of the tree. Jason pondered it for a moment, making no indication of what he thought. Then he flipped back to the picture of the flower. Back and forth he went a few times. Finally, he sighed and looked at Kale.

"How is it that you see things I don't? I've come to this park often enough, but it's never looked as beautiful as you make it out to be in your drawings."

"We just notice different things, I suppose." Kale shrugged. He didn't know if he would ever get used to receiving praise, no matter how much he enjoyed it. He knew he couldn't really be that good, but it still felt nice to hear what Jason had to say. The look that came over Jason when he saw one of Kale's drawings delighted Kale.

When they got back to the house, Jason took the picture of the flower and ripped it from the sketchbook. Apparently he hadn't liked it that much. Even though Kale knew that his drawings weren't good enough for anything more than burning, he still had let a little part of himself believe Jason's praise. He felt foolish for ever letting himself think he was better than he was. Jason was just being nice and overcompensating for the way he had treated Kale in the past.

Jason handed Kale back the sketchbook, and Kale just wanted to burn the whole thing. He threw it on the table as he strode to the sofa. It hit the wood with a resounding thud.

"What's wrong?" Jason asked.

Kale turned to see Jason watching him with a concerned look in his eyes beneath a brow drawn in confusion. Behind him was Kale's drawing, propped up against some books on Jason's desk. When Kale saw it, his eyes widened, and he looked back at Jason, who smiled. "I know it should be framed, but that'll have to wait. I was going to ask you first, but then you would have given me one of your 'do what you want, I can't stop you' responses, and I just didn't want to deal with that right now."

Kale didn't know what to say.

◆ ◆ ◆

Weeks later, Kale knelt by Jason's side in his astronomy class. The professor described a meteor shower that would be occurring that night. It was supposed to be the biggest in a century. Immediately, Jason's hand came down to Kale's shoulder and squeezed. Jason's face glowed with excitement, and Kale knew where they'd be later.

Sure enough, several hours after class, they were riding two horses out of town. They found a hill several miles from the city lights and made camp.

"I didn't think you were the camping type, master." Kale was at the tree line building a makeshift lean-to. Jason didn't have any camping supplies, but Marge had helped Kale put together two bedrolls that would be sufficient, and he had found a hatchet and some rope in the garden shed. Jason set up his telescope in the clearing several yards away.

"There's usually nothing interesting enough to make me want to go camping. My father always tried to get me to go, but what's the point? This camping trip has a point."

"For some people, camping is the point." Kale joined Jason in the clearing, and they sat around the campfire Kale had built when they arrived.

"I never saw the appeal. I used to wish I had a little brother that my father could take out camping and fishing and all those things I never had any interest in. That way he could have just left me alone."

"Trust me, you wouldn't have liked a younger brother running around the house, being loud, playing pranks. And if you think it was hard turning down your father, you've got no idea. A little brother would have been far more persistent, and there's no way you could have seen him looking up at you and not given him whatever he wanted. At least that's how it was with me and my brother."

"You have a brother?"

"Yeah, kid had me wrapped around his little finger, and he knew it."

"What happened to him?"

"I got sold to the Cartwrights. Never saw him or my mother after that."

"Wait, you weren't born to the Cartwrights?"

"No, I was sold to them when I was fourteen." Kale tossed a few more sticks onto the fire and watched as the flames danced across Jason's face.

"I never thought of you having a family. It must have been dreadful having to leave them."

"What, you thought the stork dropped me in?" Kale smiled. Things were getting a little serious, and he wanted to lighten it up before he said anything too personal.

"No, I guess I just never thought about it."

"Yeah, well, you don't think about a lot of things, including why we're out here. Isn't this meteor shower supposed to start soon?" It was a stab in the dark, but fortunately his timing wasn't too far off, and it started almost immediately. They sat cross-legged, leaning back on their hands and peering into the sky.

It was an astonishing sight. It appeared as if a wave of stars fell from the heavens. From the astronomy lectures Kale had attended, he knew these were meteors passing on their way through space, but he couldn't help thinking of what his mother used to tell him when they saw shooting stars. As a child, he would listen to her weave stories of messengers who flew around on stars doing the business of the gods. Higher class people tended to put more emphasis on the saints than the gods. Their religion was much more dour, and they believed it sacrilegious to talk about heavenly beings. Kale didn't put much stock in religion one way or the other, but as he watched a spray of diamonds blow across the sky, he couldn't help believing that his mother's stories were closer to the truth, and Kale was happy Jason had brought him to see it.

Eventually he couldn't help noticing that Jason glanced his way every few minutes with a look of curiosity and concern on his face. Kale knew his master was itching to talk more about his family, and he wasn't going to let himself be sucked into it again. Family was off limits. Jason didn't have a right to that, and it wasn't something Kale wanted to discuss with the man who owned him.

When the meteor shower ended, before Jason could say a word, Kale got to his feet and went to his bedroll, murmuring about being tired. By the time Jason put away the telescope and joined him, Kale was under the blankets feigning sleep.

The next morning they made it home without any more personal questions, and Kale thought that was the end of it.

◆ ◆ ◆

It was beginning to get too cool for comfort, so on the rare days when the weather was nice, Jason would sit in the back garden with Kale. Kale had a strong suspicion that this was a kind gesture toward him. Jason rarely chose to be outdoors. For Kale, it was an especially relaxing time, and he was grateful to Jason for making the effort, even though Jason often used these times for awkward conversation.

"Would you ever run away, Kale?" Where did this boy come up with these questions? They were in their usual position, side by side on their backs, eyes closed, trying to absorb as much heat from the sun as they could.

"No."

"Are you just saying that because I'm the one asking?"

Kale kept his eyes closed, but he smiled. "It is a dangerous question."

"No it's not. I can understand why you'd feel that way, but I'm just curious. It's hard to imagine what it's like to be you. If I was in your position, I think I'd try to run away."

"No, you wouldn't. You had parents who love you. The first thing they would teach you if you were a slave is that hoping for freedom is the quickest way to get yourself killed. Focus on what you can change, on what you can control—which is precious little—and don't let yourself worry about the rest."

"Your mother teach you that?"

"Yeah."

"What else did she teach you?"

Kale opened his eyes and looked at Jason. All his life he had kept his personal thoughts secret. Why was it so easy to surrender them to Jason? He tried to summon the healthy apprehension that kept him safe, the instinct that told him to keep his mouth shut. It was nowhere to be found. He wanted to share with Jason. "To act more like a gentleman than a slave. She wanted me to be a valet from the start."

"What did your dad want?"

Kale turned his face back to the sky and closed his eyes. "Never met him."

"What?"

"Most slaves don't know who their fathers are. It's hard enough keeping a mother and child together; no use making it harder on a kid by introducing a father they'll hardly ever see and will most likely be separated from."

"I'm sorry."

"Don't be. That's the point: I can't feel bad over something I never had."

"Still, no one should have to go through that. Especially a child."

Kale could feel the intensity of Jason's stare. Opening his eyes, he met his gaze. "Thank you. I appreciate your concern, really, but don't worry about it." Kale knew Jason did worry about it, and it baffled him. "Believe me when I say I never think of it."

"What about your mother? And your brother?"

The familiar pinprick hit his heart, and he pushed the feeling away before a similar pricking hit his eyes. Any other time, Kale would have immediately withdrawn, but that was before he saw the sincerity in Jason's face. This was not idle talk. Jason was reaching out to him, and a part of Kale that he had thought buried with his childhood wanted desperately to cling to what Jason offered.

"I miss them. The worst part is not knowing whether they're even alive, not knowing what work they put my brother to. But that's one of the things I can't control, so I don't think about them much."

Jason reached over and grasped Kale's hand. Before he even realized it, Kale squeezed back. The silence between them was peaceful, but Kale didn't like the way his personal thoughts lingered in the air. He wanted the conversation to turn back to Jason. "What about you? Do you ever think of your mother?"

"Yes, all the time. The woman was pure love. The way she acted with me, you would have thought everything I said was genius. I always knew I could tell her anything, and she would understand. She'd get as excited as I was about whatever idea or story I told her. I often wonder what she would think of me now."

"She'd be proud."

A few moments passed as Jason pondered something. Then he focused back on Kale. "Thanks, I hope so."

When the chilly air chased them back inside, their hands were still warmly interlocked.

◆ ◆ ◆

A week before Holy Saints' Day, Kale sat in the kitchen helping Marge. It wasn't often that Jason went places without him now, but when he did, Kale came to the kitchen. He claimed it was because the kitchen was the warmest spot in the house, but really he felt most comfortable there. It was odd to go back to the slave quarters when he never slept there anymore.

As Kale sliced potatoes, Charlie came whistling into the kitchen. "Well, look who we have here. I'm sorry, sir, but do I know you?"

Kale looked up. "Stop it. I'm here all the time."

Charlie grabbed a piece of bread and sat next to Kale. "Really? All the time? It's been over a week since I've seen you. Of course, some of us keep busy doing actual work."

"Hey, I work too."

Charlie snorted. "Yeah, I wish my master considered fucking me enough work on my part for the day."

"I'm cutting potatoes, aren't I?"

"That's different. You don't have to, and you're only doing it so Marge will give you a treat. Which reminds me:

you are looking a little pudgy. I hear your master's feeding you like a free man."

"Pay him no mind, Kale. I think someone's just jealous." Marge shot Charlie a stern look.

"Jealous? Not on my life, Marge. Everyone knows I love everything you fix."

Kale knew Charlie was joking, but he had noticed lately that he wasn't as firm as he once had been. A little padding had appeared on his abdomen, but he wasn't pudgy, was he? "That's what happens when you're a good slave, Charlie, you get rewarded."

"A good slave? You? No, this is what happens when your master falls in love with you."

Kale stopped cold and dropped his knife. He looked up at Charlie and saw his usual smile. Did the other slaves think the same way Charlie did? "He's not in love with me."

"All right."

"He's not. You don't think he is, do you, Marge?"

"I'm staying out of this one. It's none of my business."

Charlie chuckled. "Are you blind? Or just stupid? He's got it for you worse than he did for Eric."

"No, he doesn't. He just feels guilty for what he did while they were dating, and he's overcompensating. I'm going to enjoy it while it lasts."

Charlie sobered. "You don't really believe that, do you? Kale, that boy is completely in love with you. He'd probably buy you a pony if you asked for one."

"Charlie, you really don't know what you're talking about."

"I don't? I guess you're right. I would have thought it would have been easy for you to spot the signs since you're in love with him, too."

All of a sudden, it was hard for Kale to breathe. How had Charlie gotten that idea? More importantly, if Charlie thought that, then did the others too? "I'm not in love with him."

"Really? So why haven't you had sex with anyone else

134

since you started sleeping with him?"

"Because I'm sleeping with him, Charlie. When the hell am I supposed to have sex with someone else?"

"I can think of dozens of times we've had sex in the middle of the day. Do you want to have a go now?"

Kale didn't have to think about it; the immediate answer was no.

"Come on, you can top. I doubt he's been letting you." There was a glint of mischief in Charlie's eyes.

It was true. Kale had never topped with Jason. But that didn't change his answer. "No thanks, Charlie."

"Why?"

"Because. He fancies we're lovers. If I were to sleep with someone else, he would see it as cheating. I'm not about to throw away this cushy life just to plow into your scrawny ass."

"My scrawny ass was fine before you started sleeping with him. But you're right. It doesn't sound like you two are in love, not at all." Charlie gave Kale an incredulous look that matched his sarcastic tone.

Kale decided not to rise to the bait, and they lapsed into silence as Charlie finished eating his bread, and Kale continued to cut potatoes. The steady mindless work was easy to get lost in, and Kale could let his mind go blank.

"So how do you think things are going to go when he takes you back home?"

Kale shook his head. It took him a minute to comprehend the question. "What are you talking about?"

"Holy Saints' Day? Everyone's going home. Didn't you know?"

No, actually, he didn't. "I guess I never thought about it."

"They do celebrate Holy Saints' Day where you're from, right? You're not that cut off from civilization."

"Yes, we celebrate Holy Saints' Day, Charlie. My master just hasn't mentioned it at all. I suppose he's planning to wake up the day he wants to leave, and I'm supposed to have magically packed all of his trunks."

"That sounds about right. He'll probably want to leave the day after classes get out."

"Thanks for the heads-up."

"Sure." Charlie rose from the table. "I've got to go. But listen, watch yourself back home. I know you say this thing between you and your master is nothing more than the usual, but you could have fooled me. You'd better hope his father's more dense."

"I'll keep that in mind." Kale could see the concern on Charlie's face, and his words did nothing to alleviate it.

After Charlie left, Kale sat at the table staring at nothing. Had he gotten too comfortable? Mr. Wadsworth was a fair slave master, but he wouldn't tolerate any kind of impropriety between Kale and his son. There was no reason to worry, though. There would only be cause to worry if Kale had developed feelings for Jason, and despite what Charlie said, that simply was not the case. Everything should be fine. Really. It had to be.

CHAPTER NINETEEN

Jason watched Kale sleep through the jostling of the carriage. Jason was usually the first one asleep and the last one up, so it was nice to be able to watch Kale. It was interesting how much a person's appearance changed in sleep. Kale retained his look of confidence and surety, but he also took on a look of tranquility, as if during the day he had the weight of the world on his shoulders and handed it off to someone else while he slept. It would be easy to look at him and think of him as a powerful businessman, commanding the lives of thousands of workers, or a politician running the country. Kale would be good at both those things, but he would never be allowed to venture into those worlds.

Jason desperately wished he could free Kale, but no law or legal procedure provided for it. Freedom would change so much in their relationship. Of course, Kale would then have the option to leave, and Jason couldn't help thinking that he would if he could. As things were, he didn't doubt that Kale wanted to be with him. But Jason wasn't naïve enough to think that if faced with other options, Kale wouldn't run to any of the better opportunities that would present themselves.

A few months ago, he would have thought it sad that his only significant relationship was with a slave. In that time, he had come to a keen awareness that Kale was a better person than he in every way. When it came to character, Jason knew who was master in this relationship. He had done too many terrible things in his life to ever hope that he could measure up to the man sitting across from him.

Jason didn't realize just how long he had been staring until Kale began to stir. Seeing Kale's face undergo the transition from sleep to wakefulness made him smile. Before long, the restfulness was gone, and the responsible slave with the weight of the world—or at least one inadequate master—on his shoulders stared back at him.

Jason couldn't help the attraction he felt to Kale. While Kale slept, it had been easier to keep his physical desires at bay. Now that Kale was awake, Jason found it hard not to pull him across the carriage and kiss him. Kale, still rubbing sleep from his eyes, probably wouldn't appreciate it. "Did you have a nice nap?"

"Yes, master."

Jason's desire wavered, and he grimaced. "I wish you wouldn't do that, you know."

"Do what?"

"Call me master."

"It's who you are." Kale was so matter-of-fact that it irritated Jason. Of course it's who he was, but he didn't go around calling Kale "slave," did he? It was so irritating trying to argue with Kale; he was always so damn logical.

"I wish there were other words you thought of me as first."

"Yes, well, it seems like a dangerous habit to get into, calling you something else, when we're on our way to see your father."

Jason sighed. "I suppose you're right."

"Of course I'm right. Next thing you know, you'll be telling me to sit with the two of you at dinner. It's almost like you want your father to skin me alive."

Jason shuddered at the picture. His father wasn't a cruel man, but having a slave sit in his presence, much less at the dinner table, would push him to use a whip. "You know that's not true. I just wish you were free. It feels as though I'm taking my intended to meet my father more than it feels like traveling with a slave."

Kale smiled. "Thank you for the compliment."

"You do know that I'd free you if I could?"

Kale pursed his lips as he did when thinking things over. Jason appreciated that Kale always gave careful thought to his answers, but it made him want to kiss him even more.

"Yes, I do."

"Good. I don't think of you as a slave anymore, but I can understand it's dangerous for you to behave like a free person." Dangerous was an understatement. There were laws on the books to keep slaves from impersonating free citizens. It was acceptable, and even common, for owners to become close to favored slaves, but there was always a distinct boundary between free and slave, no matter how casual the relationship. If an owner was caught violating the slavery laws, he was required to pay a fine and forfeit the slave. The thought made Jason nauseous. He didn't know what happened to the slave; he had never thought to ask.

"Speaking of that, it's probably best if I'm on the floor when we arrive at your father's house."

"Sure. You're right, as always." Jason was sulking. He knew it, and he didn't care.

Kale reached over and turned Jason's face to meet his. The gesture itself was comforting. At least Kale was willing to touch him without a direct order. "Hey, don't be like that. Say the word, and I'll bound out of the carriage and grab your father in a bear hug and call him dad. He'll probably die of a heart attack, and then we won't have to worry anymore."

Try as he might, Jason couldn't contain his laughter, no matter how much he wanted to indulge his desire to sulk right now. "As much as I'd like to see that, I think having you behave is safer."

"You are very wise, master." Kale said it with such a

solemn face that Jason surrendered himself to laughter once again.

CHAPTER TWENTY

When they pulled up in front of the house, Kale knelt appropriately on the floor of the carriage as Jason carded a hand through his hair. There was a part of Kale that despised himself for the amount of comfort he drew from Jason's gesture. It wasn't right for him to want his master's touch this badly. Then again, his knees screamed from the hard floor, and there were nerves in the pit of his stomach. Any gentle touch was welcome.

The loss of Jason's hand when he stepped out of the carriage made Kale realize just how effective Jason's touch had been at keeping his nerves in check. His stomach filled with butterflies as he followed Jason outside.

Standing in the open, Kale felt lost. What should he do? Should he follow Jason, or was that too presumptuous? Should he help unload the carriage? Over the last several weeks, he had gotten sloppy. The line between slave and free blurred, and he found himself questioning every action. How should he behave around Jason's father? The boys in Perdana wouldn't raise a fuss about the way Kale and Jason interacted, but he wasn't so stupid as to believe that Mr. Wadsworth would feel the same. Charlie's warning from a week ago was ever-present in the back of his mind. Just as Jason had calmed him with his touch, he saved Kale again.

"Kale, follow me." Jason said it without so much as

looking at Kale. It felt cold, and Kale noticed Jason dropped the "please" that had become so habitual between them that Kale had stopped noticing until it was absent.

Thank the gods it's fall, Kale thought as they entered the house. That was clearly the reason they hadn't been greeted outside, because here in the entryway the entire staff assembled to welcome the young heir home. It would have been much worse without the small amount of time outside to gather himself and get direction from Jason. He stood behind, off to the side, and respectfully lowered his head.

"Welcome home, son. Was the ride from town agreeable?" Kale, keeping his head lowered, saw Mr. Wadsworth come forward and slap his son on the back in a perfunctory hug. The man seemed happy to see his son, and Kale wished he could see the expression on Jason's face.

"It was good. We made excellent time." Gods, Jason sounded so formal. Couldn't he warm up a bit around his own father?

"Glad to hear it. I'll let you freshen up for dinner; we eat in thirty minutes."

"Thank you, father."

With that, the joyous reunion of father and son was over. Mr. Wadsworth went off to some part of the house while the slaves dispersed. Kale followed Jason to his room. In the space of thirty minutes, Kale got them unpacked and ready for dinner. There wasn't time for talking, and Jason seemed preoccupied.

Downstairs, Jason went into the dining room and Kale to the kitchen to prepare for the first course. The hustle and bustle of the kitchen immediately put Kale at ease. Even though he had only spent one morning in this house, he felt comfortable in this kitchen. The cook had been nice to him and, as always, the kitchen was clear of any masters.

"Well, what's this? Looks like you've survived all right." Darlene was as jovial as she had been the last time he'd seen her.

"Yes, ma'am. I've been lucky."

"Indeed you have. It looks like he feeds you well."

"Better than I deserve." Kale gave her a smile and headed to the stove. "I'm to serve him tonight. How can I help get things ready?"

"A kitchen full of slaves, and not one of them ever asks how they can help. Everything's ready to go, thank you, sweetheart. Why don't you just sit here and eat some soup while we're waiting for the master to be ready?"

"Thank you, ma'am." It never fails, Kale thought. Act like you want to take the weight of the world off of a cook's shoulders and she'll make sure you never go hungry. It looked like he wouldn't have to worry about getting enough food while they were here.

The dining room was new to Kale. He never had reason to enter it the last time he was in this house. The table was big enough to seat twelve comfortably, but there were only four people present. Besides Jason and Mr. Wadsworth, there were two other men who bore no familial resemblance. Kale guessed that they must be business associates.

Kale performed his duties flawlessly and unobtrusively. After serving Jason, he took his place against the wall behind, with an easy view of Jason's glass to know when he would need a refill. Fixing his face with the blank look free men seemed to love on their slaves, Kale settled as comfortably as he could and listened to the conversation.

"I thought we'd keep this dinner small. You're probably exhausted from your trip. We'll have everyone over tomorrow night to really celebrate your homecoming." Mr. Wadsworth began to eat his soup.

"Thank you for the consideration, father." Kale wondered if he was the only one who could tell from Jason's tone that he had no desire to see everyone tonight or any other night.

Throughout the soup course, the conversation consisted mainly of Mr. Wadsworth and the other two gentlemen telling Jason all the news of what had happened since he was last home. Jason didn't act interested in any of it, but that didn't seem to deter them.

Abruptly, the conversation took a turn that caused Kale to perk up his ears.

"How's this slave working out for you, son? I'm a little surprised you brought him with you."

"He's great, father. Thank you. I never thought to leave him behind. His service has become invaluable to me. I'm so glad you didn't give me Demetri as I had wanted. Kale was the perfect gift."

Was it Kale's imagination, or did Jason's voice warm when he talked about him? Kale saw the curious glance Mr. Wadsworth gave Jason, and he feared it wasn't his imagination. Robert did not look happy with his son's sudden animation at the mention of his slave.

"It's good to hear that you like him. I had hoped he would be good for you."

"Oh he has been, father. If it weren't for him, I doubt I would have gotten such high marks this semester. He keeps my life running smoothly."

Kale wished that Jason would shut up already. He knew his master thought only to compliment him, but this was not the way a man talked about a man he owned. Kale found himself staring at the back of Jason's head, willing him to be quiet.

"Really? Well, I'm glad I got my money's worth. I hope you're keeping him on a short leash, though. You've got to remember to show him who's master." Robert glanced in Kale's direction, and Kale made sure his eyes were lowered and that he looked the picture of submissive servitude.

"I know how to handle my slave, father." Now there was a dangerous edge to Jason's voice that worried Kale. There was no reason for him to get defensive, except Jason never could tolerate anyone speaking ill of those closest to him.

Looking for a way to break the sudden tension, Kale refilled Jason's cup, even though it wasn't necessary yet. When that didn't appear to ease the stiffness in Jason's posture, Kale decided to risk speaking, even though it wasn't appropriate without having been addressed first.

"Is there anything else I may get you, master?" Kale kept his voice soft, as if the thought of him ever being forceful or manipulating his young master was the most outlandish idea.

The sound of Kale's voice seemed to have the desired effect on Jason. Immediately, he relaxed. "No, thank you."

Kale returned to his station. When he faced the table, he caught Robert looking at him and felt the pit of his stomach drop. Instead of helping, he had made the situation worse. Kale had calmed Jason, and possibly prevented him from saying something he would regret, but his influence on Jason had been noted and was not appreciated. Kale mentally kicked himself. He had stupidly confirmed Mr. Wadsworth's suspicions.

Jason either didn't notice or just acted as though he didn't, and the conversation continued. Kale took care to make sure his service was impeccable, but every time he approached the table, he sensed Robert's scrutinizing gaze. Made more aware by the observation, Kale couldn't deny that Jason relaxed whenever he was near, that he always turned his body toward Kale when he approached to refill a glass or remove a plate. Kale felt like he watched Jason seal his own doom and couldn't call out a warning. Kale wanted to tell him to stop it, to stop acting like he cared for his slave, but even if he could, it would be useless. Kale knew that Jason had no idea what he was doing.

After dessert was cleared away, Robert tossed his napkin on the table and stood. "Jason, why don't you join us for drinks and cigars in the lounge? Go ahead with John and Stefan. I need to speak to the cook, and then I'll join you."

"Very well, father. Kale?" Jason turned to Kale, bidding him to join him.

"Why don't you let Kale stay and help clear the table? I know the kitchen staff would appreciate the help. He can come to you when he's done." Robert looked at his son with a smile, as if everything was fine, but Kale knew that he didn't intend to talk to the cook.

"All right." Jason looked at his father and then back at Kale. "Come to me when you're finished."

"Yes, master." Kale bowed his head in acknowledgement.

Once Jason and the other men were gone, Robert dismissed the other slaves. When he turned to Kale, all pretense of friendliness was gone. "Don't think I don't know what you're doing."

"I don't know what you're talking about, sir."

"Don't play with me. You've manipulated him, and I won't stand for it. I won't have a slave taking advantage of his inexperience."

The comment riled Kale, and he met Robert's eyes with cool control. "If you think my master is inexperienced, then you don't know him very well, sir."

The crack of Robert's hand against his cheek was more of a surprise than it should have been. Dammit, was he really this careless and stupid? This wasn't Jason he was dealing with. Tacking a "sir" onto the end of a sentence didn't make it respectful, and he damn well knew it. Still, it took all of his effort to do no more than clench his fists.

"Watch your mouth, slave."

"If you have a problem with my behavior, sir, I suggest you take it up with my master."

"Your master is my son, boy. I gave you to him, and I can take you away."

Kale was caught off guard. Did Robert still hold his title? The thought chilled him. If that were the case, he could take Kale from Jason, and even worse. Without Jason as a safety net, Kale felt the indignation leave him to be replaced by dread. His first instinct was to beg. It took every ounce of self-control to keep from falling on his knees, bowing his head to this man, and begging him not to take him away. The picture of it disgusted him, but there were more important things to think of than his pride. If he let Robert know how much he wanted to be Jason's, it would be a sign of weakness, an admission that there was something inappropriate between them. Kale knew that how he handled this could very well determine the course his life would take.

Lowering his eyes, Kale spoke in a soft submissive tone, careful to sound acquiescent while trying to keep any trace of desperation out of his voice. "I assure you, sir, there is nothing inappropriate between myself and the master. He has simply become accustomed to me; he went through a terrible bout of homesickness, and my presence comforted him, reminded him of home. He was just nervous tonight. He's been anxious about coming back here. I serve him with complete loyalty, sir, and he appreciates it, that is all."

"You better hope it is. If I find out differently, I won't hesitate to beat you senseless before I sell you off."

"Yes, sir." Kale kept his eyes lowered. He felt more than saw Robert step back and change his entire demeanor.

"Well, get to cleaning up. You don't want to keep Jason waiting, do you?"

"No, sir." The light tone of Robert's voice put him even more on edge. The change from cold ruthlessness to calm composure was unsettling.

CHAPTER TWENTY-ONE

For Jason, the night dragged. It was nice to only have to talk with his father, the overseer, and foreman, but he didn't have anything in common with these men. More than anything, he wanted to go up to his room and fall asleep with Kale. He hadn't realized how used he was to spending all of his time with him until he couldn't. It felt wrong to have Kale standing so far away and acting like a slave when he was so much more than that.

After dodging the cigars and nodding his way through a glass of port—he didn't much care what had been happening in the county since he left or the state of his father's business —he was finally able to take Kale and go upstairs. The urge to put his arm around Kale and draw him close was strong, but Kale was carefully composed and kept a proper distance. No one would be able to tell they were anything more than master and slave.

Once the door to his room was closed, Jason broke out in a grin, feeling as if he had gotten away with a great deception, and put his arm around Kale's waist, pulling him close. As soon as their bodies touched, Jason kissed Kale as if they had been separated for days rather than hours.

"Saints alive, Kale. I thought they would never let us leave. It's been so hard seeing you there, so close and yet not being able to touch you. You're mine, for gods' sake, you'd

think I'd be able to do whatever the hell I want with you."
Kale's eyes widened slightly. "What? I can curse when I want
to."

"Apparently. I've just never heard you use anything other
than all that saints crap you and every other free man seem to
swear by."

"You're rubbing off on me." Jason was all smiles, but he
saw a cloud pass over Kale's face. "What's wrong?"

Kale jerked slightly, as if his mind had been elsewhere.
"Nothing."

Jason looked closer, trying to see the problem, but he was
never good at reading people. With scrutiny, he did see
something he didn't approve of. "Kale, did someone hit you
tonight?"

"No, sir." It sounded like the truth, but Jason saw a faint
mark on his cheek. Brushing his finger over it lightly, he
watched for a reaction. There wasn't much, but Jason did
catch a slight twitch.

"You're lying."

"No, I'm not. When I was cleaning up in the dining
room, I had to bend down to get some silverware that had
fallen on the floor. I turned and whacked right into the table.
Not my proudest moment."

Jason frowned. "Oh, you poor thing. Well how about I
take care of it for you?" Jason leaned forward and brushed
his lips lightly against the faint mark. When he pulled away, he
grabbed Kale's arm and began to drag him toward the bed.
"Now come on. I've been waiting all night to get you here."

Kale smiled. "You sure you don't want to tie me to the
bed, master?"

Jason groaned. "Gods, was I stupid. I feel like such an
idiot. Do you forgive me?" Jason sat on the bed and had Kale
standing between his legs. He looked up at Kale's face, not
completely teasing in his request for absolution. Kale merely
sighed, as if he were thinking it over. "How about you tie me
to the bed?" Jason asked.

Kale laughed, "Don't tempt me."

"I'm serious."

"You are, aren't you?" Kale sobered. "No, I don't need to tie you up to forgive you. I was just teasing, anyway. I never really think about that. You were disappointed and drunk that night."

"And you are far too forgiving."

"And you're crazy thinking that you need to ask for forgiveness for anything from your slave."

CHAPTER TWENTY-TWO

The next morning, Jason felt better about being home. It must have been the time with Kale, but he felt like he might just be able to make it through this trip unscathed. It didn't take long to be proven wrong.

Breakfast was a small affair, just him and his father. Jason found himself counting how many more breakfasts he would have to endure without Kale sitting opposite him. What exactly were he and his father supposed to talk about? As it turned out, his father had ample conversation material in mind.

"I noticed that your slave slept in your room last night." Robert said it casually as he ate his eggs, but Jason had a feeling that this wasn't going somewhere pleasant.

"Yes, he sleeps in my room in Perdana."

"There aren't slave quarters at the house in town?"

"Yes, there are, but I prefer him in my room, available whenever I need him." Jason hated the way he automatically got defensive whenever his father spoke to him.

"Ah, using him to warm your bed then? There's no need to blush, boy, I was a kid once too, you know. Just make sure you're keeping him in his place. You invite a slave into your bed, and next thing you know he's putting on airs."

Jason didn't know whether he blushed from the implication that he and Kale were having sex, or from the

153

implication that he was using his slave for sex. "I know what I'm doing, father."

Robert made eye contact for the first time. "Yes, of course you do." Jason wondered if his father's words were mocking. The way his father held his eyes made him feel inadequate. Why was it that nothing he said or did ever satisfied this man?

"Kale, come here." Robert's tone was firm, and his eyes never left Jason's. When Kale silently appeared between himself and his father, Jason looked at him for a clue as to what was about to happen. Kale looked as docile as Jason had ever seen him, and something didn't feel right.

"You taking advantage of my son, slave?"

"No, sir." Kale's voice sounded soft and timid in a way that Jason had never heard before.

Robert finally looked at Kale, and Jason could see that he didn't view him as a person. Had he once looked at Kale the same way? "Good. You'll be sleeping in the slave quarters from now on."

"Yes, sir."

Jason felt anger boiling up inside him. He didn't know what was more disturbing: his father giving his slave orders or Kale so humbly accepting them. What had happened here?

"No. Kale, you'll continue to sleep with me." Jason was looking at his father when he spoke, but looked up at Kale when he didn't get any kind of confirmation. Kale's eyes had a look of desperation in them, as if he were begging Jason to see or understand something.

"I don't have a problem with him servicing you—fuck him all you want—but it's inappropriate to have a slave sleeping with you. I've seen the way you react to him, like you're lovers. Are you lovers, Kale?" Again, he didn't take his eyes off Jason's.

"No, sir."

"What are you?"

"His slave, sir."

"Did you tell him that I slapped you last night?" Before Jason knew it, he was on his feet. Somewhere in the back of his mind, he registered the sound of his chair crashing to the floor.

"You what?" Jason couldn't remember a time when he had raised his voice this loud—and certainly never to his father. "You hit him?"

"Yes. Is there a problem?"

"Yes, there's a problem. He's mine. You don't touch what is mine."

"Seems like quite the reaction for a slave. You were raised in this house. You know how slaves are treated here. I'll take a whip to his back if I want to."

Jason lunged at his father. Kale moved to stop him, but he was too late. Jason grabbed his father by the front of his shirt, hauling him up and ramming him against the wall. "If you ever touch a hair on his head again, I swear I will have the law down here and charge you with destruction of property so fast you won't know what hit you."

"I suggest you take your hands off of me, boy." Robert's voice was dangerously cool, but Jason didn't care. The only thought going through his head was that Kale had been threatened. Jason had been threatened, and there was little he could do about it. He couldn't protect Kale here.

"Master, please." It wasn't the words so much as the pleading tone in Kale's voice that brought him back to himself. He let go of his father and stepped back.

"If I can't be assured of my property's safety while I'm here, then I'll have to leave."

"You're missing the point, son. This slave has an unhealthy effect on you. Right now, you should be courting lovers or potential brides. As I said before, fuck all you want with however many slaves you want, but this has gone way past that. If I've noticed his effect on you in less than a day, then you can bet others have too. Think about your reputation, son. Think about your future."

155

"I'm happy, father. Why can't you be happy for me? I thought that's what you wanted."

"You have the shortsightedness of youth. I want you to grow up and be a man. Stop disgracing yourself like a spoiled little boy."

"I'm not being shortsighted. I'm focusing on my studies, doing what I went to Perdana to do."

"No, you went to Perdana to climb the social ranks. University was just a good excuse to get there."

"Just because you can't understand the appeal of learning and improving yourself doesn't mean I don't. You may be satisfied being an ignorant hick, but I'm better than that."

Robert's hand rose to backhand him, and Jason braced for the blow, closing his eyes. When it didn't come right away, he opened them to see Kale standing between them, his hand gripping his father's raised wrist. The look of pure shock on his father's face would have been funny if the circumstances were different.

Gone was the docile slave who had quietly shuffled to and fro this morning. Now Kale was as Jason was used to seeing him: strong, steady, and eerily calm as he stared Robert down.

"Release me." The mere tone of Robert's voice would have compelled instant obedience in anyone but Kale. Jason was a little in awe of how he could stand up to Robert like that. But now it was his turn to plead.

"Kale." Jason didn't need to say more than that. As soon as the word was out of his mouth, Kale released Robert and moved to kneel. Before his knees hit the floor, Robert's hand had closed around his neck and jerked him up and against the same wall that he had been held to only moments before.

"You've done it now. See, Jason, I told you. Give them a little bit of freedom, and they start thinking they can do whatever they want. It's time we beat some sense into this one."

"Father, no. Let him go or I'm going to go get the sheriff

and bring him back here."

"To do what? I should kill him for raising his hand to a free man."

Fear gripped Jason's mind and paralyzed him. His father was right, and he knew it. In the silence as Jason tried to figure out what to do, Robert let go of Kale, and Jason watched Kale fall to his knees, bending his forehead to the ground. The sight made Jason's stomach roil.

"Don't worry, son. I'm not going to kill him." There was an edge of softness to Robert's voice, but Jason wondered if it just seemed that way because of how he had sounded earlier. "But I am going to have him beaten. It will do him some good, and you too. You could both use a reminder of what he is."

"No, father. I meant what I said; you harm him in any way and I'll have you charged."

"Master, please. I deserve it." There was something broken about Kale's voice.

"You'd best listen to the slave, boy. I've made allowances because I know you're young, and you don't always think things through, but I suggest you stop threatening me in my home."

"No, Kale, you don't deserve it. And father, it's not a threat. You're right, this is your home. It's no longer mine. Kale and I are leaving."

"So you're going to let him get away with what he did?"

"With protecting me? Yes, I think I will."

"You're my son. I'll slap you if I want. A slave has no business interfering. If you're going to choose him over me, then I'm no longer your father."

"I'm not going to let you hurt him."

"Fine, go get your things and get out of here. You're dead to me."

"Father, please." But it was too late. Robert had turned his back on his son and left the room.

Chapter Twenty-Three

Kale was in shock. What had possessed him to physically assault a free man? Kale found it difficult to restrain himself when anyone threatened Jason. Still, it was a stupid move to let Robert unnerve him like that. After Robert left the room, Jason had tried to comfort him. If there was anything more confusing than Kale's own craziness, it was his master's choice to be disowned by his father rather than allowing the man take a whip to his back. They had both let their feelings of protectiveness toward each other get the better of them and cloud their judgment. The difference was that Jason was full of young drama, and Kale expected this kind of thing from him. Kale, on the other hand, was more practical than that. He knew better than to put his own ass on the line. What would have happened if he hadn't interfered? Nothing. Jason wouldn't have been mad because he wouldn't have expected it.

Kale knew he was being the shortsighted one this time. If he had seen Robert strike Jason, when all Jason had ever tried to do was please the man, Kale would have snapped. If he hadn't interfered when he did, things would have been much worse.

When had he become willing to risk himself for this man who owned him?

Sitting next to Jason in the carriage—there was no need

for pretense now—Kale turned the situation over and over again in his mind. All he could think was that this was not good. If Robert did have his title, and Kale had no reason to doubt him, he could legally send someone to take him away. The thought was enough to increase his heart rate. Knowing that he couldn't think straight in a panic, he willed himself to calm down. Jason had said once that Kale wasn't afraid of anything. That wasn't quite true, he had just learned to distance himself from the fear and examine the problem to find out the source and face it head on.

If Robert sent men after him, they would take him away.

Calm. Breathe. In and out.

Then what? They'd beat the shit out of him, that's what. He'd taken pain before—a lot of it when he belonged to the Cartwrights. There was nothing new or scary there. He would either survive it or he wouldn't. There wasn't much he could do about it, and that helpless resignation was also nothing new. Then what? They would either take him back to Mr. Wadsworth's and he would serve there, or he would be sold. He'd been through both experiences before and there was nothing earth shatteringly frightening about either. A lifetime of experience had taught him that it was futile to worry about things he couldn't control. His mother had taught him to not let free people scare him, it was one less power they could hold over you.

So why did he still break out in a cold sweat every time he thought about being taken away? It didn't make sense.

It must have been hours before he realized they had been sitting in silence the entire time, and that it was comfortable. Kale glanced at Jason, trying to discern his thoughts. His face gave nothing away. There was no indication that this boy— could he really still be called a boy?—had just abandoned everything he knew.

"Why did you do it? Why did you turn your back on your father? On your home?" It came out in a rush. Kale hadn't realized how much he wanted to know until it all came bubbling out of him.

Jason started and turned to Kale, a faint smile gracing his lips. "Actually, he was the one who turned his back on me, if you recall."

"You know what I mean." Kale was not in the mood for jokes. This was not a laughing matter, didn't Jason see that? Was that his problem? Did he really not understand what a big deal this was?

"Yes, I do. I suppose this must be awkward for you, but it's not your fault. That place was never really my home. Perdana is my home now."

"Of course it's my fault. And you're pretty dumb for being so nice to me after what I've caused, if you don't mind me saying so, master."

"You never much care whether I mind or not."

"See, and that's the point. What were you thinking bringing me here? We both know I'm a shit slave. Or at least I am now. I used to be pretty decent at it, if I remember. You should have just left me back in Perdana."

"Well, for starters, you're not a shit slave. I happen to think you're the best. Why else would I have you? You know I only get the best." Jason smiled. How could he be humorous at a time like this?

"Which is why you wanted Demetri."

"Which is why I kept you instead of selling you the moment we arrived in Perdana."

"You didn't sell me because you couldn't. Stop playing these games. Your father told me he still holds my title. And what do you think he's going to do now? He's going to take me away." Damn, did his voice actually catch? That's exactly what he needed right now, to let Jason know his fear. "So what exactly did you accomplish back there? You didn't save me. All you did was get yourself in a world of hurt with your stupid sense of loyalty." When Kale finally got it all out—it felt like it had all been in one breath—he saw that Jason was trying, rather unsuccessfully, to hold back a laugh.

"Are you done? No, my father does not hold your title." Jason's face went from humorous to furious frighteningly fast. Kale marveled that he had inherited that skill from his father, though instead of changing to ice, Jason was hot fire when angry. "That sick bastard was just trying to scare you. I wish you had told me the truth about it when it happened." Jason paused to glare at Kale.

"If what he said was true, it would have been a colossal mistake telling you."

"You should have trusted me, Kale. Do you really think I'd put you in harm's way?" Kale didn't know. It was an interesting thought to file away for later. "And as for my stupid sense of loyalty, as you call it," Jason smiled, and Kale was glad to see he wasn't upset, "how do you know that's why I did it? It's entirely plausible that I went through this whole act to get out of seeing everyone at the party tonight. As if I would have anything to say to Carter Cartwright."

Kale couldn't help it; he needed to laugh too badly and he let it out. Soon they were laughing together, and when they finally calmed down again, they settled back into that comfortable silence. Only now, it was peaceful as well.

A little while later, Kale heard the telltale snoring and envied Jason's ability to sleep no matter what was going on around him. Questions Kale had been holding at bay came forward. Did he trust Jason not to put him in harm's way? Obviously not, otherwise he wouldn't have believed Robert. But was that just instinct? Some part of him knew that Jason would never hurt him. A stupid part, Kale thought, because Jason had already hurt him plenty. But that was before.

Before what? Before Jason's guilt started to eat him up. But that didn't make any sense. Guilt didn't last this long. There was more to it than that, but he didn't care to think on it too much. No reason for him to go diving into that well as long as he knew that he could trust Jason. With the sense of loyalty that kid had, Kale knew he could.

There was the matter of this ridiculous fear he had of

162

being taken. Kale had lived the last twenty-one years knowing that every aspect of his life was controlled by the whims of the men who owned him. He had never had a say in his life and never expected one. The best he could hope for was some semblance of comfort if he performed his duties well, but even that was not guaranteed. What had changed?

Jason had said this was home now. Perdana was home. Except Kale didn't give a crap about Perdana. He had never been made for city life. So what was it then? If that townhouse with the drafty basement, the cramped hallways, and the balcony that overlooked a pathetic plot of garden wasn't home, then why did he fear being taken from it? Why did he feel like he was home for the first time since being separated from his mother?

Kale felt like he had been punched in the gut. That couldn't be it, but it had to be; and even though it was an uncomfortable thought, he knew as soon as he thought it that it was right.

Jason was home to him now.

Home was not a place for him like it was for Jason. It was a person, because that's all Kale could have.

That's why he had been willing to risk himself for Jason. Somewhere along the way, things had changed. Kale's happiness was no longer dependent on Jason's the way every slave's happiness depended on his master's; Kale's happiness had become intertwined with Jason's.

As uncomfortable as these realizations were, Kale knew that they were true. Once he accepted them, his mind eased, and he began to drift off, only slightly aware before he fell asleep that not only was he comfortable and safe with Jason as his home, he was also incredibly vulnerable.

CHAPTER TWENTY-FOUR

Back in Perdana, life settled right back into its usual rhythm as if nothing had happened. Except something had happened, and even though the actions were the same as before, Kale couldn't deny that a thick fog of sadness hung around Jason. Being disowned was a big deal to anyone, but to Jason, who was always keenly aware of how others thought about him, it was devastating.

"Why don't you just apologize to your father?" They were in Jason's room on the bed. Jason had tried studying and then reading, but nothing held his attention, and he had taken to laying in silence.

"What?" There was indignation in Jason's voice. "What for?"

"Whatever it is he wants you to apologize for. Tell him you're sorry for interfering, for talking back to him, for defying him. It's killing you not to have his approval."

"I'm not apologizing to him. I don't even like him. I never did. We've never gotten along."

"That may be true, but he's still your father. And like it or not, his opinion matters to you. Try to make things right. I want you to be happy."

"I am happy."

"No, you're not. You're not as good an actor as you think you are. You came here to climb the social ladder, to be part

165

of the elite, and now all you do is spend time in your room or in the park with your slave."

"Dreams change, Kale."

"All right. Well, what about money? Now that you're cut off from your father, how are you going to afford to stay here?"

"My mother had her father set up a trust for me. She left me enough money for us to live on for a few years, at least to get me through school." A hint of laughter entered Jason's eyes. "What, were you scared that I'd resort to selling you to survive?" Jason was smiling, and Kale liked seeing it.

"No, although that isn't a bad idea. I am the one who caused all of this."

"Stop it, Kale." All mirth left Jason's face, and he knelt in front of Kale, grabbing his chin and forcing eye contact. "Stop it. I don't want to hear that from you again. You want me to be happy? Stop blaming yourself for something that's not your fault. You think if you weren't here that my father and I would get along swimmingly? You're not naïve, Kale. The problems between us go back much further than that. I was never going to be his pride and joy." Jason let go of Kale's face and turned away, but not before Kale saw a glint of pain in his eyes.

Kale would never understand it. Despite Jason's dislike for his father, he would always want his approval. Even now, he seemed to loathe himself for needing it so badly.

◆ ◆ ◆

After several days of Jason moping around, trying to act happy and failing miserably, Kale finally had enough. He couldn't stand seeing Jason like this. As much as he hated the thought of going to any of the uppity parties that were going on all over the city, he knew something like that would be just the thing to cheer Jason up. Charlie was gone—his master had gone back home for the holidays—but Simon and Jacob were still around. Their masters preferred to stay in the city and attend all the local festivities. One of them might be able to help.

Kale timed Jason's dinner so that he had a chance of running into one of the other slaves in the kitchen. He was rewarded when he found Simon preparing his master's tray.

"Simon, what's going on this week that I could get my master to?"

Simon didn't even look up from where he was arranging silverware. "Nothing that wouldn't require you to go with him."

"That's fine, I don't mind."

"Oh, has the princess decided to actually start serving?" Simon glanced at Kale and cocked his eyebrow.

"Stop it, Simon. I need to get him out of this house. It's depressing seeing him up in that room all day. I can't persuade him to go out anywhere, but I figured if there was something good enough happening, or something he would feel obligated to go to, it might help."

Simon went back to his work. "Well, there is an engagement party the day after tomorrow."

"All right, whose?"

"My master's cousin."

"How come I didn't know about it?"

"Come on, Kale, really?" Simon looked at him. "Why would anyone tell you or your master anything? Everyone knows he prefers to spend his time with you. None of us mentioned it because we knew you wouldn't want to go. My master didn't invite him because he's not really part of his social circle. Besides, you two were supposed to be out of town."

Kale didn't realize that others talked about them like this. Had people really stopped inviting Jason places because he spent all of his time with Kale? It didn't surprise him, now that he thought about it, but he didn't like that he hadn't noticed. Why should it matter if he wanted to go to this party or not? Mr. Thalomew was from a well-known family; this party would be the perfect opportunity for Jason to not only have a good time, but to socialize with the people he came to the city to join.

"Can you get us an invitation?"

"This late? Normally, no. But since Jason's his housemate, I guess I could let it slip that it would be the polite thing to do now that he's back in town."

"Thanks, Simon. I owe you one."

"Yes, you do." Simon eyed him suggestively and left.

❖ ❖ ❖

Kale tried not to be too obvious as he shifted his shoulders. This formal clothing was too restrictive for his tastes, and the boredom of the party made it hard to focus on anything else.

"Another glass of champagne, please." Jason's voice reminded Kale that he was here for a reason and was shirking his duty. It was easy to forget; slaves at this sort of thing were like accessories, people brought them to show they could afford them. When Kale stepped forward to take away the empty champagne flute, Jason leaned in and whispered in his ear, "I'm going to need it." Kale and his master shared a smile. Nice to know that he wasn't the only one bored.

Walking to a refreshment table, Kale felt like he was being watched. Peering discreetly around, he saw that people were indeed throwing glances his way and going back to their conversations. Kale tried to overhear what they were talking about, but he only caught bits and pieces.

"Did you see how he looked at him?"

"Spends all his time with him."

"It isn't right."

Were these people really talking about Kale and his master? It was probably just paranoia. Returning to his master's side, he handed Jason his champagne and stood back to observe. While Jason played the part of high society gentleman well, there were little subtleties that gave away that he didn't quite belong. For one, he had little to talk about with a lot of these people and spent most of his time listening. For the last several weeks, he had not made any social appearances and was left out of all the latest gossip. It was important to Jason to be a part of this world. Kale knew that, but he had been more than happy to push that knowledge aside when Jason offered him a comfortable existence devoid of any real responsibility.

"To the happy couple." Jason raised his glass of champagne in a toast.

"It's been a while since I've seen you, Jason. How do you know Cordelia?" Kale didn't recognize the young man speaking.

"I'm housemates with a cousin of hers, Phineas Thalomew."

"Ah, good fellow. A bit wild, but I guess that runs in the family, as Cordelia has shown." The unknown man laughed at his own joke, but Jason's expression showed that he was as in the dark as Kale was. "Oh, come now, don't tell me you haven't heard that story?"

"Like you said, it's been a while. I'm not up to date on my gossip."

"Well then, let me tell you that sweet Cordelia is nothing of the sort. Her fiancé, Mr. Pinkerton, is barely more than a servant. Her father forbade her to see him, but she snuck around with him anyway. When dear father found out, he was furious, and she went on and on about how she would simply die if she didn't marry Pinkerton. It was quite the scene from what I heard. Then, when it still didn't look like she would get her way, Cordelia threatened her father with a bastard child."

"She didn't," Jason said, aghast. "Her father couldn't have taken kindly to that."

"To make matters worse, she's his only child. So what did

he do? He opened his arms to Pinkerton, gave him a position with his firm, and here we are at their engagement party pretending everything's respectable."

Kale didn't listen to the rest of their conversation. The idea that all this pomp was hiding a scandal intrigued him. Though he should hardly be surprised, the aristocracy in Perdana was known for money, not discretion. Still, what else could a good marriage hide, he wondered?

The rest of the evening went by in a haze of champagne refills and dull conversation. Although Kale did notice that every time his master moved on to a new group of people, the other partygoers clearly sought Kale out with their eyes. From people who normally ignored slaves or regarded them the same way they would a utilitarian piece of furniture, that betrayed a deep level of interest and curiosity.

CHAPTER TWENTY-FIVE

Jason had a good time at the party, but it was different than he remembered. Since falling for Kale, he was much less interested in society. All of the socialites' gossip and drama seemed shallow and vapid. While it was nice to get out of the house, Jason wished that Kale could have accompanied him as a free companion so he could have gotten away with talking to him all night. Still, it was probably wise to start making himself a part of the social scene on occasion now that his father had disowned him.

"Isn't it interesting, master, how a marriage could solve their problems?" Kale helped Jason undress for the night.

"Yes, well, you know these people are more concerned with appearances than anything else. It doesn't matter what the truth of the matter is, as long as it looks decent and respectable."

"I imagine there will still be gossip about them, but that will just make people love them more for providing entertainment."

"That's quite the high opinion you have of the aristocracy here." Jason smiled. He knew Kale didn't have any patience for these people; it was nice to be privy to his real thoughts on the matter. Still, Jason knew that a part of him would always want to be invited to the party.

"Well, they could be useful for one thing," Kale said.

171

Jason raised his eyebrows in question. "If it works for them, why not for you?"

"As much as I'd like to, I can't exactly marry you, Kale."

"I'm not joking."

"That has me worried."

"Why don't we find you a nice, upstanding bride?"

"What?" Jason jerked his hand out of Kale's grasp where he had been unfastening a cufflink and began to do it himself.

"You heard me."

Why did Kale insist on trying Jason's patience with silly things? By his tone of voice, Jason knew that Kale was not going to back down until they talked this out. "Yes, I heard you, but what would possess you to say something like that? I've got you, Kale. What possible need do I have for a wife?"

"Oh, I don't know. Money, social standing, entry into the club. You know how it is. A good marriage would do wonders for you right now."

"I told you, I have the money my mother left me. We're going to be fine."

"Yes, but you don't have enough to buy the place you want in society."

"No, but that doesn't matter to me anymore."

"Yes, it does. You just deny it for my sake. It's bad enough that you've split with your father over me. I'm not going to let you give up all of your dreams. Besides, you're going to grow bored of me sooner or later, and then it's going to be awful for you to not be able to get an invitation anywhere."

"First of all, I will never get bored of you." Jason stepped close to Kale and stroked his cheek. He would spend the rest of his life reassuring Kale if he had to. "Second, I'm not giving up anything being with you. I don't care about all that stuff anymore, and you should know that."

"Really? So what would you think if you knew that the real reason you didn't get an invite to the party initially was because everyone knows you spend all of your time up in your room with your slave? Or that people talk about the way you look at your slave when you're out with him? Hmm? What then?"

"Are they really saying such things?" Jason couldn't help the feeling of loss when he heard what Kale said, and he stepped away so that Kale wouldn't see it. It felt like his stomach dropped to the floor. He didn't mind people knowing about his feelings for Kale, not really, but it hurt to know he was being excluded because of it.

"Yes." Kale's voice was close to his ear, and he felt Kale's hands on his shoulders, turning Jason to face him.

"It doesn't matter."

"Yes, it does. You're not thinking long-term. Remember, I'm older than you, I know what I'm talking about."

"Yes, three months older, and I'll never get to be the wiser one because of it."

"Just think about it. Having a good wife might make your situation a lot better. Matters are only going to get worse once it gets out that your father disowned you. If you want to have any type of future, you need to be thinking of these things."

It was strange how their positions had reversed. Jason didn't like the idea of getting married, but he wouldn't dismiss what Kale had said. "Fine, I'll think about it. Can we just go to bed now? It feels like we're arguing, and I don't like it. If anything, I never thought I'd have to convince you to step back from the social scene."

"Oh, you don't. If I never get back into that ridiculous getup, it will be too soon. I just want to make sure you're thinking about the future. I want to do what's best for you."

"I know, and I think it's sweet." Jason leaned forward and kissed Kale on the tip of his nose. When Kale rolled his eyes in response, Jason caught his lips in a much more passionate kiss, dragging him backward to the bed at the same time. When the back of Jason's legs hit the bed, he broke away. "Speaking of that getup, seeing you in it again is reason enough to start going out more. Here's a little hint from someone who has studied battle tactics: you go for a man's weakness in order to get what you want." Jason didn't give Kale a chance to reply before he dragged him down onto the bed and into another kiss. If this was going to be a battle with Kale, then he was going to fight dirty.

CHAPTER TWENTY-SIX

Having sex probably hadn't been the best way to get Jason to agree to find a wife—wasn't there some saying about a cow and milk that applied?—but Kale had never been great at turning down sex. What had seemed like harmless sex the night before, though, looked like a colossal mistake in the light of day. He knew from the look Jason gave him when he rolled over in the morning to kiss him that he had his mind made up. It was going to be a tough battle, but Kale knew it was important. There was no way a disowned man who preferred the company of his slave to anyone else stood a chance in this world. But all that could be changed with a simple engagement and wedding ceremony. That would be the easy part. The hard part was getting Jason to let go of his idealistic notions long enough to agree to it.

Kale decided to wait until breakfast to talk about it again. In bed in the morning was just too domestic, too blissful, to be effective. This was really a business proposition, and it seemed rich people always conducted business over food.

"Did you think about it like I asked?" There hadn't really been much time for Jason to contemplate it, but Kale knew he would think he had.

Jason sighed and put down the fork that was partway to his mouth. "Yes, Kale, I thought about it. After making love with you, it was abundantly clear that I can't even consider

175

what you're suggesting. My heart is yours; how can I give it to another?"

Kale wanted to roll his eyes. He could always count on Jason to be overly dramatic, but the sheer intensity of Jason's gaze and the sincerity of his words prevented him. He knew Jason believed it, and it made Kale's stomach feel weird. "Who said anything about romance? I'm talking about marriage."

"Really, Kale? I knew you were cynical, but I didn't think it extended that far."

"You know as well as I do that marriages in this city are more like business contracts than anything else."

"All right, yes, I know that. But what do I have to offer a woman who could grant me the kind of social standing you're proposing?"

"Freedom. You wouldn't care what she did, wouldn't try to manage her life. You don't have it in you. Plus, you'll still have me, so you won't mind when she pursues her own interests. Not to mention you're quite the catch; any woman would be lucky to have you."

"Thanks, Kale. But I think you're overestimating my appeal. The fact of the matter is, I would be betraying you if I got married."

"That's your concern?" Kale hoped his tone sounded as incredulous as he felt. "Ridiculous. How is setting yourself up for a better life betraying me? You think I would care if you lived with a woman?"

"Well, even if you wouldn't, how can I betray some woman like that? I would be entering into marriage with her knowing full well that I didn't love her, not the way I love you."

Kale kept silent long enough to let the heat from Jason's speech dissipate. "Let me know when you've got the dramatics out of your system and we can talk about this some more." Kale didn't want to sound mean, but he couldn't reason with someone who wouldn't even acknowledge the reality of the situation. He knew damn well that marriage was not a proposition of love in this day and age.

"They're not dramatics, Kale. I won't betray you, and I won't lure some poor woman into marriage under false pretenses."

"Who said anything about false pretenses? You think you're going to shove me in a closet somewhere until after the wedding? It took your father less than a day to figure out how you feel about me; you think a woman wouldn't figure it out long before you got around to proposing? I think you're underestimating the intelligence of women."

"That's not what I mean, and you know it."

"What would be so different in our day-to-day lives? We'd move into a different house, but I could still sleep in your room with you, and your wife can have her own room. You'll visit it every once in a while to fulfill your marital obligations, and that's that. At social occasions, you'll have someone at your side to introduce as your wife. She will take the attention off of me standing behind you, but I'll still be there. You wouldn't be misleading anyone. Most marriages in this city are between people who can barely stand the sight of each other. There isn't a married woman alive who would dream of insisting that her husband not take a slave to bed. Everyone does it. If nothing else, she's going to want to keep her own options open, and it's hard for her to justify having a slave warm her bed if she's making an issue over the fact that you do. There is absolutely no downside to this. You have everything to gain."

Kale stared Jason down. He was going to get him to see reason, no matter what it took. Jason had never yet been able to stare him down, and Kale was betting today wouldn't be the day that changed. Jason blinked and sighed. "I suppose you're right. Not much would really change."

Kale had to contain his smile to one of mere happiness rather than gloating. "Of course I'm right. Just let me try. I'll help you find someone suitable. All I'm asking is that you give this idea a chance."

"Fine, I still don't like it, but I'll give it a chance for your sake."

"Why, thank you. The things you suffer for your slave."

"No, I would never do this for a slave. But for you, I'd do anything."

Why did Jason have to say things that made Kale uncomfortable? Yes, he had come to terms with the fact that their relationship was unique among masters and slaves, but hearing things like this made him feel funny. He could never think of anything to say, so he returned to eating his now-cold breakfast.

CHAPTER TWENTY-SEVEN

Three days later, they were at an art gallery. Jason hadn't expected the search for a bride to begin so quickly, but he supposed that this was as good a place as any to start. Besides, he liked the art, so at least the night wouldn't be a complete waste.

It still irked him that Kale had convinced him to take part in this ridiculous idea. When it came down to it, though, Jason knew he didn't have an income and his mother's money was finite. It would still be some time before he would need to bring in any more money to sustain them, but Jason did feel responsibility toward Kale. He understood how it could be unsettling to be in his situation; a slave was valuable and easy to sell if the owner needed money. He had thought about looking for work, but what was he qualified to do? And any good jobs that would pay the kind of income he would eventually need to support himself and a slave would require that he have good connections and be a family man. Neither of those were available to him unless he was married.

"Master? There's Mr. Isaishin over by that landscape. Why don't you go say hello?" Kale whispered in his ear—which made it hard to concentrate on anything else—but when Kale stepped back, Jason saw Hector Isaishin standing with a group of people. Jason knew him from philosophy class, and it would be good to catch up.

"Jason, how good to see you! I didn't know you were still in town."

"Yes, I decided to cut my vacation short. There's much more going on here than back home."

"I never knew how people could stand to live that far from civilization." Hector turned to a girl by his side. "Jason comes from one of the outlying counties. Just came to Perdana this year." The girl nodded politely and eyed Jason with interest. "Oh, you haven't been introduced, have you? Jason Wadsworth, it's my pleasure to present my cousin, Miss Lillian Seville."

"How nice to meet you, Miss Seville." Jason took her hand and placed a kiss on it. She was quite beautiful, petite with blonde hair and blue eyes. She looked almost like a porcelain doll and just a hint of blush rose in her cheeks when Jason kissed her hand.

"Oh please, call me Lillian."

"Very well, Lillian."

Jason joined Hector's party in touring the gallery. He was surprised that he didn't feel awkward around Lillian. He had never been one for socializing with women and was nervous to begin with. It turned out to be rather easy though, since he didn't really care what Lillian thought of him. On the other hand, she seemed to care quite a bit. She took his arm as they proceeded and did plenty of giggling and fluttering of her eyelashes. Perhaps this was why he had never been attracted to the fairer sex. Any comments she made about the art were along the lines of, "This one's pretty," or, "I don't get this one," or, "I like the colors." There was no level of understanding or inquisitiveness in her comments. As the day wore on, he was convinced that there was nothing behind the pretty façade.

When it was finally time to leave, Jason felt a pang of regret and irritation. This exhibit was one that he had been looking forward to seeing with Kale, to hear his insights. Jason already knew that Kale could make better art than anything he had seen today, and his insights and thoughts would have been enriching. Instead, he got to listen to some insipid woman coo about the pretty blues and puzzle over why some of the paintings didn't look anything like their subject matter. The whole day had been a waste.

"How did you like her, master?"

They were still standing on the steps outside the gallery where the group had parted. "What was there to like? I wanted to see this exhibit with you, Kale. I don't like how you got me wrangled into spending the whole day with that woman."

"Oh come on, master. We can see it again together if you like. She was beautiful, wasn't she?"

"Yes, and that's about it."

"No, that's not about it. She also happens to come from one of the richest families in the country, and she couldn't take her eyes off of you. Haven't you heard of the Seville mines?"

"Yes."

"Well, who do you think the heir is?"

"Kale, I don't know if any amount of money is worth having to spend the rest of my life with a woman who reacts to some of the greatest art in the world the same way a toddler reacts to a rattle."

Kale's laughter brought Jason out of his sour mood. "You're not going to make this easy on me, are you, master?"

"I don't think it's too much to ask."

"To find an attractive, highborn woman who is also intelligent?"

"Who said anything about attractive? Just get me a woman with whom I won't be embarrassed or bored out of my mind."

"Very well, master. One unattractive, rich girl with a brain coming right up. Anything else you'd like with that?"

"Don't get cheeky."

The walk home was quiet. It wasn't far from the gallery to

the house, and it was nice to have companionable silence after the incessant chatter from Lillian and her friends. As they ascended the front steps, Kale spoke.

"You have to admit that she fawned over you quite a bit. A man could get used to that kind of attention."

Jason couldn't help smiling. Did he imagine the hint of jealousy in Kale's voice? No wonder he had stayed silent for the walk home. If he could have Kale with him, he supposed he could suffer through almost any woman. "You're right, she was. I guess I could resign myself to her lack of intelligence. I'm sure she had other ways in mind for keeping me entertained."

"I wouldn't get your hopes up about that. The dumb ones tend to be boring in bed."

Jason couldn't keep the surprise off his face. Part of him knew that Kale was more experienced than he was, but it was still somewhat of a blunt shock to hear him reference it so casually. "Oh really? Have much experience, do you?"

Jason had hoped to embarrass Kale a little. It bothered him that Kale so easily put him off balance, but he hadn't yet been able to retaliate. In this instance, he was sorely disappointed. Kale looked at him straight on and said with his usual equanimity, "Wouldn't you like to know."

Instead of Kale blushing, it was Jason who turned red. He wasn't sure why. Was he feeling a twinge of jealousy now?

CHAPTER TWENTY-EIGHT

The next few weeks were insufferable. Kale had Jason going out to every event in Perdana where there was a chance of meeting a suitable young woman, and while Jason was happy to be going out again, he was quite frankly tired of the matchmaking. Kale had made it his personal mission to secure Jason's place in society. It was frightening, really, how much Kale knew about the women of Perdana. Jason didn't know where Kale got his information, but he knew slaves gossiped any chance they could. Looking around at the clustered groups of people at the party, he realized the same was true of the upper classes. People really weren't all that different no matter where fate had borne them. The thought made him smile over his champagne glass.

"What has you smiling? You've done absolutely nothing to advance your prospects tonight. Unless you're smiling at that girl across the way. In which case, you can save yourself the trouble. She doesn't have any money to back up her name."

Frightening. That's what it was. It was also a little adorable how perturbed Kale sounded with him. "No, I wasn't smiling at her. I was just thinking that you have more in common with these people than you'd care to admit." Kale furrowed his brow and drew his lips together in a line. "Don't give me that look. You know far more about high society women than any person should. I bet you could gossip with the best of them."

"Nah, they wouldn't like my brand of gossip. Much too honest, not enough dramatic embellishment. Besides, they do it for enjoyment. I do it because it serves a purpose. If I had a master who could even pretend to care about getting married, maybe I wouldn't have to stoop to gossiping to get the necessary information."

"Well, maybe I'd take more interest if you ever arranged for me to meet someone interesting."

"Picky, picky, aren't you, master? That's what I don't understand about you. You're so particular when it comes to finding a woman, but you took the first slave that your father threw your way. Is it just that you're not picky about ass? Don't really need me for my brain, do you?"

Kale was grinning, but Jason didn't like that those thoughts were in his head to begin with. "You might want to get your facts straight before you start lecturing your master, slave." By the flicker of surprise in his eye and the chagrined look on his face, Jason guessed that his effort at a stern tone had paid off. "I'm picky because of you. After engaging with you in everything from philosophy to sex, it's hard to content myself with just a pretty face, even if it is only for a marriage of convenience."

"Maybe if you stopped spending all your time talking to your slave at these things, you would find more than a pretty face. Hard to find a good woman if you don't actually talk to any of them."

Jason looked around and saw people stealing glances their way. It was hard for Jason not to talk to Kale like he would anyone else. Scratch that, it was hard for him to talk with anyone here the way he did with Kale. Still, Kale was right. Being seen shying away from the company of aristocrats for that of his slave wasn't going to help his position. Downing the last of his champagne, he handed the glass to Kale.

"Here. I've had enough champagne to last me a lifetime. I

want something stronger."

"Is there something you'd like me to get you?"

"No, I have something else in mind. We're leaving."

"But you haven't met…" The words faded from Kale's lips when he saw the look on Jason's face. He shifted to a more submissive stance, bowing his head slightly, as if he just remembered that he was, in fact, a slave. "Yes, master. I'll get your coat." Jason didn't enjoy seeing him like that, he much preferred to keep his illusion of Kale as a social equal intact, but their difference in station did hold some benefits, including being able to decide when it was time to get away from the inane banality of his life.

◆ ◆ ◆

"How did you even know about this place, master?" Kale spoke loudly to be heard over the din in Flannigan's. The bar smelled of cheap cigarettes and dried beer. Jason had never been in an establishment that didn't require a suit coat. Seeing the patrons here, wearing stained shirts, trousers that looked as if they had been worked too hard, and boots that tracked in mud and any number of other things Jason didn't care to think about, it was apparent that the proprietor here had no such dress code. It was a thrill and Jason wanted, more than anything, to forget for a moment who he was and what his life meant.

"Don't call me master. No one here could possibly know you're a slave, unless you act like one, and I'm telling you not to. Dressed the way you are, these people probably think you're a minor noble or a successful businessman."

"All right then, how'd you find this place?"

Jason smiled. Everything in Kale's stance had relaxed. Jason hadn't even noticed how tensely Kale held himself at formal affairs. Here, though, he looked almost as if he were at home. There was a spark of excitement in his eyes, and

Jason knew he had made the right choice coming here tonight. From the looks of it, the marriage situation had been taking a toll on Kale as well, even though Jason doubted he'd ever be able to get Kale to admit it.

Jason led them through the bar to a table in the corner. He didn't answer until they were both seated and he had taken off his coat. "I heard the other slaves in the house talking about it one day, and I asked around for directions."

"It doesn't seem like your kind of place."

"Obviously. I thought it would be fun to get away. I told you, I'm tired of champagne."

"I can always get you something stronger."

"No, it's not really that. I suppose I needed to see people act differently. I couldn't help thinking at that party that everyone resembled stuffed animals, holding themselves stiff and never really moving other than to nod or laugh in that restrained way. I want to laugh tonight, Kale."

"I think I can arrange that. What do you want to drink?"

"Whiskey."

Kale cocked an eyebrow at him. "Have you ever tried whiskey before?"

"Yes, the night I got you." From the look Kale gave him, Jason could tell it wasn't an experience he was eager to see repeated. "Will you calm down? I'm not tying you to the bed, am I?"

"It's not me I'm worried about. You could barely make it from the parlor to your bedroom that night. We're going to have to go across town after this."

"I've got money for a cab. Humor me. I want to get drunk out of my mind, and I want you to get drunk with me."

"That's going to be a bit of a problem."

"Why?"

"I don't get drunk."

"What are you talking about? You've never gotten your hands on enough alcohol at those gambling sessions you like to think I don't know about?"

"It's not that. I just hold my liquor well. You kind of have to when your life depends on how well you perform your work. You'd be passed out before I ever started to lose control."

"Well good, then you won't have any problems making sure we get home. We'll both have whiskey. Where's the damn waiter?" Jason looked around for someone who could take their order. When he turned back to Kale, he saw him biting his lower lip, and the sides of his mouth were twitching. "What? Oh, there are no waiters here, are there?" Kale shook his head. "How am I supposed to know?"

Kale released his lip and smiled as he stood up. "You're not. I'll be back with the drinks."

When Kale returned, he carried two glasses and a bottle. Kale pushed the fuller of the two glasses toward Jason. "Why do I get more? I thought you said you could take more liquor than I can."

"I can. The extra is water. You wouldn't like it straight."

"How do you know?" Jason felt he was being treated like a child. Kale wasn't helping his feeling of independent manhood.

Kale merely looked back at him with raised eyebrows and barely disguised mirth. He held his own glass out to Jason in invitation.

Taking the glass, Jason kept his eyes on Kale. When the glass came under his nose, it was hard not to flinch at the smell of the alcohol. It was stronger than he remembered. Then, remembering the disaster the first time he tried Kale's breakfast while attempting to maintain eye contact, he broke off his gaze and looked down at the glass. Closing his eyes, he lifted it to his lips and tried to take a swig of the pungent liquid.

Much of it came right back out on the table.

In the back of his mind, Jason was aware that Kale was laughing, but all he could focus on was the liquid fire making

187

its way down his throat. He rubbed his shirt sleeve across his mouth out of instinct. When he realized what he was doing, he paused. This was an expensive shirt, and he had just ruined it. Another moment and he realized he didn't care. It felt good to soil clothes that were always meant to look perfect at picturesque occasions. He resumed wiping the liquid off his face. It was also on the table, and figuring he had already ruined it anyway, he took his shirt sleeve to that as well.

When he felt a little more composed, he turned to Kale, who appeared to be at least making an effort to control his laughter. "That's not like what I remember."

"I thought not." Kale took his glass back, replacing it with the one he had originally put in front of Jason. "I would guess that the whiskey you tried was watered down. And even if it wasn't, you weren't drinking whiskey when I saw you that night, so you were probably already on your way to getting drunk when you switched from the champagne. Whiskey's easier to take when you ease into it."

"How can you remember that so well? I have a hard time remembering the details of a book I've just read for a class."

"Again, if your life depended on it, I bet you'd remember a lot more details."

"But how could your life depend on what I was drinking the night I got you?"

"Maybe not my life, that's a bit of an exaggeration, but certainly my comfort. You were my new master. I needed to be aware of the details. It helped me gauge what kind of mood you would be in when your attention settled back on me. It's always best to know as much as you can about the man who holds your life in his hands."

"We didn't get off to the best start, did we?"

"No. I'd say that seeing fury on the face of your new owner, and knowing that you're the cause of that fury, is about the worst way to start. But you've made up for it since then."

Jason had taken to sipping at his watered-down drink. Better to appear a cautious drinker than an inept one. "Do you ever get nervous around me anymore? I mean, are you still afraid of me?"

Kale chuckled. "And this is why slaves know better than to get drunk; we might answer a question like that with something stupid."

"I want the truth, Kale." Jason tried to look as sober as he could. "You don't have to worry about saying the wrong thing. I hope you know that. Or is that my answer right there? If you're too scared to answer me with some alcohol in you, if you really think I would hold that against you, then I guess I really haven't changed that much."

"No, it's not that, I was just illustrating a point." Kale paused and considered Jason. His lips came together in that slight purse that always meant he was weighing his words carefully. Jason always felt when Kale took his time like this it was because he was trying to discern the truth of what he was about to say, not trying to think of the most diplomatic response. "No, I'm not scared or nervous around you. If I was, nothing short of a threat would have gotten me to drink with you here tonight."

"I thought you don't get drunk."

"I don't, but you do, and I've seen my fair share of mean drunks. If I worried about you, I wouldn't allow myself to relax enough to drink."

"Oh. Well, I'm glad to hear it. The last thing I want is for you to be afraid of me. Now what's the beer for?"

"I thought you might like it more. If you want to stay for any length of time, you're not going to be able to keep drinking liquor. I thought you might enjoy a more leisurely evening."

"Good thinking." Jason pushed the whiskey out of the way—even watered down, he didn't much like it—and took a swig of the beer, more because he knew he could than for any affinity for ale.

189

"We've got to talk about these girls you keep trying to match me with. They're dull, Kale. They are beyond dull. I would sooner marry a goldfish."

Kale smiled the beautiful smile that always made Jason forget what they were talking about for a moment. Was it the alcohol that made him want to fuck Kale after just seeing that smile?

"Hey, if it was legal and the goldfish had a fortune, I'd be all for it."

"That's good to know. But what are we going to do?"

"Why is it so important to you that she be interesting?"

"Because I'm going to have to last long enough to at least propose to her. Besides, I'm not going to just ignore this person. You should know me better than that by now. I couldn't do that."

"Yes, I know that, but you used to take to these people well enough."

"That was before you. You have yourself to blame for this."

"That's good, blame the slave, master."

Jason watched as Kale continued to sip from his drink, trying not to let Kale's use of the word "master" perturb him, especially since it was said playfully. Why couldn't they just be two people having a drink together? He had come here tonight to get away and pretend that all the other expectations of him didn't exist, to feel what it would be like to be with Kale as just another man. But Kale would never let him forget. There was no escaping what they legally were to each other.

After the silence had dragged on for longer than was comfortable, Kale finally spoke. "What is it?"

Jason hadn't realized he'd been staring, and he shook his head and looked away, back at his drink. "Nothing." He lifted the bottle to his lips and took a long drink. He wanted more than ever to get drunk. Perhaps that would make him forget that he couldn't have things his way.

"No, you were thinking about something. What was it, master?"

Jason gave a humorless chuckle. "Even now you won't call me by my name?"

"What?"

"You heard me. Here we are, having a great time, drinking together in a bar, I've told you not to treat me like your master, and still you won't call me by my name. You're the only slave I know who has the audacity to demand things from his master, yet you insist on calling me by that stupid title, as if that makes a difference."

"You're my master. No amount of alcohol is going to change that."

"I know, but why can't you just indulge me?"

"You know I will if you order it. Are you ordering it?"

Jason felt disgusted, and it was hard not to lash out at Kale, but that would only prove that he was right. "No, you know that."

"Then as long as you give me a choice in the matter—and I am grateful for that, I hope you know—as long as you give me a choice, I'm going to call you master."

"Fine. Then avoid calling me anything tonight. Do you think you can do that? Or is too much to ask that you just let me forget that you're my slave for a few hours? You're sitting here demanding that I find a woman to marry and pretend like I don't feel anything for you when we both know that's a damned lie. I'll do it. I'll do it because I feel responsible for you and because I love you. I'll take a wife and go work for her daddy and even have a couple of kids to keep the in-laws happy. I'll do it all, Kale, but for the love of all that is holy, I'm going to get so drunk tonight that I forget how fucking unfair this all is. And you're going to sit there and let me. And if you call me master one more time tonight, love you or not, I'll beat the shit out of you." Jason hadn't meant to sound so nasty. He hadn't even been fully aware of just how bitter he felt until it all came pouring out. But now that it was out, he felt good.

As he looked back at Kale, keeping his eyes steady to see the reaction to his outburst, Jason was agitated, but not surprised, that Kale took it all in, face as calm as if he were chatting with a casual acquaintance. Why couldn't Jason have that kind of equanimity? When Jason was confronted with anything, he always felt awash in a sea of emotion. Everything seemed so large and significant to him. How did Kale manage to always appear so tranquil? It was an even more agitating thought when Jason remembered that in Kale's life, he actually did have occasion to fear, more than Jason ever had, and still he was steady. Only a man like that could stand to be with Jason after all he had done to him.

After Kale had absorbed what Jason had said, he nodded. "I understand, and I'm sorry. It won't happen again tonight. If that's what you want, you have it."

Jason released a breath he hadn't realized he'd been holding. "Thank you, Kale. I'm sorry I snapped at you. I just don't know how to cope with all this."

"I know. There's no need to apologize." Miraculously, Jason saw that he actually meant it. "I'll do a better job. I won't try and push you toward anyone who isn't suitably interesting in the future."

Jason nodded and went back to his drink, but he didn't know if there was enough alcohol in Perdana to ease the ache he felt.

CHAPTER TWENTY-NINE

Getting Jason home had been something of a project. Kale was right in his first impressions of Jason: the boy couldn't hold his liquor. As Jason grew more and more drunk, he got boisterous, telling Kale exactly what he thought of all the girls he had met over the last few weeks. Thinking back on it, Kale laughed a little. At one point, Jason had flailed his arms about as if it helped him make a point about just how shallow Meredith Cartilliard was. At the time, though, it just seemed sad, because in his eyes, Kale didn't see humor, just a sort of lost and confused pain.

It would get better. Kale had underestimated what this undertaking would entail, that was all. He was naïve to think that Jason would be happy with merely the money and position that came from marrying into a wealthy family. He wanted someone who would be a good companion. Kale was foolish to think that Jason was so wrapped up in him that he wouldn't want companionship, and he deserved it. Thinking back to when Eric dumped him, Kale knew that the pain he had seen in Jason was not from missed opportunities, it was from something much more substantial. Kale needed that substance to help Jason be happy. And hopefully that happiness would be connected to a substantial fortune.

It was easy for Jason to be romantic now, but Kale knew that, in time, Jason would come to resent him. When the novelty has worn off and he remembers all his dreams, he'll be bitter, Kale thought. And then it would be too late. Kale wasn't going to let that happen.

While Jason slept off his hangover, Kale slipped downstairs. When he reached the kitchen, he stopped for a moment in the doorway and took in a deep breath. The smell of something baking wafted up to his nose, and he couldn't help the happy hum that left his mouth. As he exhaled, all the tension left his body and he remembered why he'd always loved kitchens. Opening his eyes, he caught sight of Charlie sitting at the table with a cup of tea reading while Marge pulled biscuits out of the oven.

"Marge, my master won't be eating breakfast this morning. He's got a bit of a hangover, and I'm letting him sleep it off."

"Thanks for letting me know, hon. How nice of you to let him sleep in." Marge flashed a grin and Kale winced. It was said in jest, but at the moment, he felt that he was getting above himself and losing perspective about his relationship with Jason. Marge noticed and laughed. "It wasn't meant as a reprimand, hon. You want a biscuit?"

Kale shook himself out of his thoughts and smiled. "That'd be great. I'm starved."

"You always did know how to get what you wanted out of me, pulling that hurt puppy dog act when you know I've never reprimanded you before."

"Aww, come on, Marge, that wasn't it. I'm just a little preoccupied is all." He came up behind her at the counter and planted a kiss on her cheek as he reached over her shoulder and grabbed two biscuits off the pan. "Don't worry about fixing me anything; the biscuits will hold me until lunch."

"What, no oatmeal? Can't handle the mush after what you're used to getting?" Charlie asked.

"I don't know what you're talking about, Charlie. Marge's oatmeal is divine."

"See, some people around here appreciate me." Marge shot a not too serious glare at Charlie and turned to Kale. "I'll dish some up for you, go take a seat."

"So what are you up to?" Kale asked. He was glad to see Charlie; he was the easiest to talk to, and he wasn't sure he could have handled the others at the moment.

"Just reading. Carl's visiting his sister, and he didn't want to take me. It's been a while since I've seen you."

"I've been busy. I'm trying to find my master a wife."

Charlie made like he was choking on his drink. "You what?"

"You heard me."

"Yes, but what are you doing that for? Wives can be bad news for slaves, especially slaves that share their master's bed."

"He's looking for a marriage of convenience, not love. All the men around here have slaves in their beds."

"Yes, but don't you think your situation is a little different?"

"How?"

"Dear gods, Kale. Sometimes I wonder if you're playing dumb or if you really are that dense. Never mind. What's with the urgent wife hunt?"

Kale decided to let Charlie's comment go. "You know there are rumors going around about him. His reputation's suffering, and he doesn't seem to care. He had a falling out with his father, and if he doesn't get married soon, he may lose his chance for a good match altogether."

"What do you care?"

Kale glared at Charlie until he realized that it was a fair question. "He wants to be a part of that world. After what happened with Eric, his reclusive behavior, and now the problems with his father that I can't count on staying secret for long, I don't know what's going to happen to him when the money he has runs out. And you know the cardinal rule: if the master isn't happy, no one is. The last thing I need is him resenting me because he spent the best years of his life thinking he was in love with me when he could have been living the life he wanted."

"What he wants could have changed," Charlie said. His soft tone and pointed stare stopped Kale for second.

"No, not him. I know him better than you do. He's still hurt over what happened with Eric, but he's not ready to be out of society. Not really."

"If you say so. What's the problem then? You two have been going out regularly. You've been to every highbrow event that's happened since you came back."

"I was dumb, that's the problem. I thought he'd be happy with a pretty face with a daddy who could offer him a good job, maybe even an inheritance if we were lucky. But no, of course nothing can be simple with him. Apparently, all the girls in this town are too dumb for him."

"Why don't you try getting him introduced to Renee Arlington?"

"Who?"

"Renee's an old friend of my master's, a real intellectual. I'm surprised you haven't heard of her yet. She's made quite a few waves. Spends a lot of her time at the university library. Insists she's entitled to as good an education as a man, and since they won't let her take classes, she uses their library."

"Really? What about her family?"

"Her father's in steel, and she's an only child. She's not too shabby to look at either. Real nice girl. You should try to arrange a meeting."

"I'll do that. Do you know where I might find her?"

"Well, she's been out of town the last couple of months. She studied in Calea. Just got back into town a week ago. She should start being at the same social events my master attends. I'm sure I can get him to introduce you. He likes Jason quite a bit, as much as he likes anyone. They'll get along great."

"That'd be wonderful. I'd owe you if you could work it

out."

"Yes, you would. As I recall, you owe me for quite a few things and have yet to pay up." Charlie leered at Kale.

"I know, Charlie. I just haven't had time lately, you know that."

"Seems like you haven't had time for anyone but him."

"Look, I'll make it up to you some other way, I promise."

"Promises, promises. Of course, you know I'll help you."

"Thanks, Charlie, you're the best."

"That's what all my lovers say." Charlie winked and Kale laughed, shaking his head.

◆◆◆

Charlie made good on his promise, and a few nights later, Kale was with Jason at a poetry reading at the home of a wealthy lord. They had accompanied Charlie and his master, and as they walked into the expansive ballroom, Kale caught Charlie's eye and gave a silent dramatic sigh. Charlie had to work not to laugh, and Kale was glad he'd at least have a friendly face around.

Mr. Bonham led Jason to a group of waiting friends. Kale's eyes immediately found the one woman he didn't recognize. Dark red hair, sort of an auburn color, crowned her petite frame and rich blue eyes contained a spark that bespoke a fiery personality.

"Jason Wadsworth, I'd like to introduce you to Miss Renee Arlington." The girl Kale had pegged extended her hand. When Jason went to place a kiss on it, she instead latched onto his hand in a firm grip and shook it. Nothing delicate there.

"It's a pleasure to meet you, Mr. Wadsworth. I've heard a bit about you."

Oh gods. It had been too much to ask that she not indulge in gossip. "Really?" Jason was fidgeting now. This was not going well.

"Yes. I hear you're quite studious. It's nice to see that some people take their chance for a university education seriously." There was hope after all.

"I take it very seriously, Miss Arlington. Mr. Bonham has told me that you are quite the intellectual yourself."

"I believe we all have the responsibility to educate ourselves as much as possible. I try to make use of the university library whenever I can."

Jason snapped his fingers. "Yes, I remember you now. I saw you in the library the day of my orientation."

"It must have been one of my last days here before I went to Calea. I left around the start of term."

"And how did you enjoy Calea?"

It was at this point that Kale stopped listening. Charlie had wandered off with Carl after making the introduction, and Kale was looking around the room for him when a quick motion caught his eye. Charlie was discreetly waving his hand. Once he had Kale's attention, he pointed toward Renee and tilted his head, looking at Kale as if to say, "Well?"

Kale lifted his eyes to the heavens in a look of thanks and Charlie smiled. When Kale turned back to Jason and saw the smile on his face and the way he looked at Renee, giving her his undivided attention with interest bubbling in his eyes, Kale could have very well kissed Charlie for suggesting they meet.

A clinking sound echoed through the room, and everyone quieted down. Looking around for the source of the sound, Kale found an older gentleman holding a knife and glass. "Excuse me, ladies and gentleman, the reading is about to begin. If you'd please take your seats."

Without even looking at Kale, Jason walked with Renee to the seating area, talking the entire way. Standing suddenly alone, Kale started to feel a little empty. It was as if Jason had completely forgotten him. Not that Kale expected his master to check in with him, but he always had. Shaking off the feeling, he walked to the back wall to join Charlie. This was the part of the night that Kale always dreaded. It was bad enough enduring what rich people seemed to think was entertainment, but he couldn't even entertain himself watching how enthused Jason got over these sorts of things.

Kale never even saw who performed. His eyes were riveted to Jason and Renee, noting every time their heads leaned in together. Every once in a while, they whispered in each other's ears. What were they saying? Why did it bother him that he wasn't there? A pinch on his leg distracted him, and he looked to his side where Charlie made funny faces. It was so unexpected that Kale had to choke back a laugh, which made Charlie smile.

When the reading was done, the audience broke out in polite applause, the most fervent, Kale noted, coming from Jason and Renee. Kale spent the rest of the evening refilling his master's drink and fetching him finger foods. The happy couple was thoroughly enjoying themselves, and it couldn't be going better if Kale had wished it. Still, Kale knew that Jason wouldn't have noticed if someone else had replaced him all night, and it was an odd feeling.

After what seemed an interminably long time, Jason finally motioned for Kale to get his coat. When he brought it to Jason, his heart leapt when he heard their conversation.

"This was great, Renee." Renee? So they were on a first name basis. "I hope I can see you again."

"I'm here for good now, so I suppose we'll see each other around."

"I was hoping we might see each other sooner than that."

Renee smiled and bit her lip. It was the one bit of girlishness Kale had seen out of her all night. "I'd like that too."

"There's a debate at the university tomorrow. Would you care to join me?"

A debate? Tomorrow? Kale didn't know anything about it. If he didn't know, how did Jason? Of course, he probably heard about it tonight. Besides, who was Kale to assume that he was involved in every bit of planning in his master's life?

"Yes, I was hoping to attend."

"Good, I'll see you there."

CHAPTER THIRTY

When tomorrow came, Jason left Kale at the house while he went to the debate. "This isn't the kind of event you bring slaves to," Jason had said. Kale used to be ecstatic at being left at home—it wasn't like he had any interest in the debate —but it had been months since Jason had gone anywhere without Kale. Most of all, it was strange because it was the only time Jason had ever left him at the house when Kale actually wanted to go.

He should be there to keep an eye on Jason and help him. The kid wasn't the most socially adept person, and his history in the courting department left something to be desired. Renee was the only girl out of dozens in whom Jason had shown the least bit of interest. If he messed things up with her, who knew how long it would be before he found another acceptable young lady? Here at home, Kale couldn't do anything to help, and he felt powerless, waiting to see what would happen. He didn't like the feeling at all, though he should be used to it by now. It had never bothered him before that he had no control over his own life. In the last few months, though, the illusion of control had spoiled him.

Jason's room was spotless. Kale looked for anything to clean or straighten, but he was at a loss. Three turns around the room left him with nothing else to do to pass the time. Kale picked up his sketchpad and sat on the sofa, hoping that his nervous energy wouldn't prevent him from losing himself in a sketch. There were pastels on the side table, but Kale passed over them for charcoal. The subtlety of expressing feelings and perceptions through the absence of color resonated with Kale, and he needed the outlet. The result was a series of sketches made up of quick strokes all depicting his master surrounded by scenes of dark sadness. Sometimes Kale was in the picture himself, but always as a despairing figure. The sound of steps in the hallway brought his mind out of his drawing, and he closed his pad and stashed it away just as Jason came through the door.

Jason unwound his scarf and threw it on a chair with a blissful sigh before heading to the bathroom, all without looking at Kale. It was so unexpected that it took Kale a second to gather himself and go get the scarf to put it away. Jason came out of the bathroom a moment later with the goofiest smile Kale had ever seen on him.

"Did it go well, master?" Kale ventured, needing to both snap Jason out of it and hear what had transpired.

Jason looked at Kale as if he had forgotten he even existed, and then his smile widened even more, if that were possible. "Kale, it was amazing! She's so engaging and intelligent and the things she cares about actually matter." Jason paced as he talked, becoming more animated by the second.

"So I take it she's smart enough for you."

"She's the smartest person I've ever met, man or woman. And her looks! Have you seen her?"

"Yes, master."

"She's certainly nice to look at."

"Yes, master."

"Who would have guessed that this woman existed? I didn't think I'd ever find someone who I'd actually like to see again, much less start a relationship with."

This was the happiest Kale could remember Jason. It reminded him of those first few days when he was dating

202

Eric. It was fun seeing him so excited, and he couldn't help smiling when he looked at the kid. Everything was coming together, just as Kale planned. Jason had tried to make him believe that he didn't need this, but how could a person not need the type of happiness Jason was showing? This had been the right move. In fact, it was hard to see why Jason needed him at all.

That thought lingered in his mind, and he didn't realize Jason had stopped pacing and was looking at him until he spoke.

"What's bothering you, Kale?"

Kale startled out of his thoughts. "Oh, nothing, master."

"You know, you've never once made me believe you when you've said that before. I don't know why you think it'll work this time." Jason placed his hand on Kale's arm. The warm pressure of his hand was welcome, and Kale gave him a faint smile. "I had thought you'd be happy. Renee's just what you wanted."

"And she's perfect for you. I am happy. I guess it all just seemed too easy. I'm hoping it lasts."

CHAPTER THIRTY-ONE

Kale glanced at his hand and back to Jacob who was leaning back in his chair, staring at him. As usual, his dark eyes gave away nothing.

"You going to fold, Kale?"

Something inside him bristled. Jacob had figured out how to play him. Jacob had never asked Charlie and Simon that, but he knew Kale's pride hated the idea of folding.

"Check. Whatcha got?"

"Full house, queens over eights."

"Damn." Kale threw down his cards. After all this time, he knew every one of Charlie's and Simon's tells, but he still didn't have a read on Jacob.

Between laughs, Simon said, "Give it up, Kale. You're never going to be a better card player than Jacob. None of us are."

"Someone's got to humble him, it might as well be me." Kale took a swig of his beer as Jacob cleared away the pot.

"Yeah, well, your master keeps gallivanting around with that skirt of his and you'll have plenty of opportunity."

"How is Miss Arlington?" Charlie's question sounded casual enough, but Kale could see his concern. The last time Kale had this much time to play cards was back when Jason was dating Eric, and that had been a disaster.

"Oh she's perfect. Perfect breeding, perfect manners,

perfect looks, perfect social standing. Perfect."

"She sounds like a bitch," Simon said.

Kale laughed. "Nah, she actually is nice. Smiles at me and says please and thank you, even when we're out. As far as free women go, he could do a lot worse."

"A woman gets a man in her thrall and she could convince him to get rid of a slave if she has a mind to. You're not worried?"

"Of course he's not." Charlie looked incredulous. "You've seen the way Mr. Wadsworth looks at him. No way he'd ever get rid of Kale."

"And I'm telling you that a woman can change things."

"I'm not worried, Simon," Kale said. "Really, she's a great girl. In fact, she seems to like me. She's always appreciative. If anything, she likes that I take care of him."

"Yeah, well, she may want to be taking care of him herself."

After the game, Kale left to wait for Jason like he always did. On the way up the stairs, he thought about Renee. He believed everything he had said about her tonight. So why, when Jason slept, did a lump of dread deep in his stomach keep Kale awake?

Chapter Thirty-Two

Jason made sure his schedule was clear for the evening. Renee had wanted to go to the planetarium, but she could wait; this was more important. Kale seemed unhappy, and he wondered how long it had been going on. Admittedly, he spent a lot of time with Renee, sometimes away from Kale. At the time, it didn't seem like a bad idea. Kale had always appreciated being left at home rather than going to events he found boring. But perhaps he felt neglected. How selfish could one man be? Here he was, basking in the glory of a life that seemed to be blessed all because of Kale, and he hadn't paused to make sure Kale was getting what he needed. That would all change tonight.

When he walked into his room after class, Kale was sprawled out on the bed with his sketchpad. It was a sight that made Jason sigh with contentment. At times like these, he could picture them as two lovers without a care in the world. Kale certainly looked the part, here in the early afternoon lying on the bed, face intent on his latest sketch, clothes comfortably askew. And when he looked up at Jason, a smile instantly on his lips—not a wide grin, but a comfortable lift of the lips, as if that was the natural pose his face took when he saw Jason—Jason thought life must be perfect.

"Hello, master." And the illusion burst. "I didn't expect

you home so early."

Jason strode in and closed the door behind him, shedding his coat on his way to the bed. Kale was already gathering up his sketchpad and sitting up, making room for Jason to join him. Unfastening his cuffs, Jason sat on the bed and leaned over to give Kale a kiss on the lips. It was solid and reassuring in a way that Renee's kisses could never be. Like it just made sense that they should kiss, like Jason belonged with Kale. It was a feeling that Jason didn't think he could live without. And from the slight hesitancy he felt in Kale's lips before he surrendered himself to the kiss, Jason knew Kale was unaware of just how important this was to him.

"All this time with Renee has left me pining away for you. Tonight I want you," Jason said.

"Hmph." Kale pulled away and flopped back on the pillows. "More like you're wanting a lay. I know little Miss Arlington isn't letting you have your way with her. She's much too noble for that. You just want some tail. Fine. It's yours, take it."

Kale stared at the ceiling, and it looked to Jason like he was fighting not to look at him. Jason sidled up along Kale's side and put his arm across his chest. "Don't be like that, Kale. You know you're the first in my heart. Or at least you should. We don't even have to have sex tonight if it's not what you want. I just want to be here, with you."

"Sure you do. What with all I have to offer."

Self-pity was not attractive on Kale and hearing him speak about himself like that burned something inside Jason. He lifted himself up so he loomed over Kale, not giving him a way to escape his gaze. "Stop that right now, Kale. You know I don't like you talking like that. I'm in love with you. I only ever started seeing Renee to make you happy, to secure our future."

Kale sighed and rolled over, forcing Jason to settle back on the bed as they faced each other. "I know. I'm sorry I'm being an ass. I should have known that you would attack this whole courting thing with the same enthusiasm you do everything. I'm not being fair, and I know it. I guess all this free time on my hands has made me indulge in self-pity." Then he reached out and grasped Jason's hand. "Thanks for taking tonight with me."

The warmth of Kale's hand atop his own spread through Jason as it always did when they touched. "Of course, and if you ever need me, you know you only have to ask. I'm in love with you, Kale, you know that."

"Yeah, but you love her too."

Jason trod carefully. There was no point in lying, Kale knew him better than anyone, but a little tact would go a long way. "Yes, I do love her. Do you not want me to?"

Kale looked at him intently, and Jason knew he could see that it was a genuine question. "No. Of course you love her. That's part of what makes you you. You could never marry someone you didn't love. You're too much of a romantic."

Jason felt himself blush, which made Kale smile, so it was worth it. When Kale's hand reached up and cupped his cheek, it only made him hotter. "Thanks, Kale. I knew you would understand. And I'm sorry for neglecting you. You're the most important person in the world to me, and I won't let you forget again."

"Don't worry about me. I'm fine. It's just a transition, that's all. I'll be better once things are settled, once the future's more certain. Everything is going so well right now, I just worry that something's going to go wrong, that the wind's going to blow a little differently one day, and this will all come tumbling down."

"And so what if it does? I'll still have you. I'm not letting you go anywhere. I know you set this all up to make me happy, and I am. But if Renee left me tomorrow, it would hurt—I'm not going to lie—but I'd still be happy. I really don't need all this, but you've given me the courage to go for it, so I'm going to try. But even if it doesn't work out, I would still be happy with you." Then, to illustrate his point, he

209

began kissing Kale and didn't come up for air until they were nothing more than a sated sweaty tangle of limbs on the bed.

CHAPTER THIRTY-THREE

Jason walked through the park with Renee, both so bundled up they didn't feel the chill that caused their breath to mist in the night air. An eclipse was going to occur, and people gathered in the one place in the city where it was possible to pretend that they were in nature. It reminded Jason of the time he had gone stargazing with Kale outside the city. Kale had stayed home tonight. He was concerned that Renee might be losing interest. Ever since Jason had noticed that he was neglecting Kale, he had been spending more time with him, and he needed to learn how to balance the two. Glancing over at Renee walking next to him with her neck craned upward looking at the sky, he knew that she was a woman he could marry.

"When I was a little girl, I once took a diamond necklace of my mother's and separated all the diamonds from it," Renee said as they walked. "I pasted them to some craft paper and hung it over my bed so I could look at it and pretend I was looking up at the stars."

Jason laughed and Renee looked at him with a childlike grin on her face. "You were a terror, weren't you, darling?"

"Not a terror, just stubborn. Whenever I wanted something, I didn't stop until I had it."

"An admirable quality."

"Thank you. I'm not sure my parents agree."

"Come now, I know they're proud of you. You're making a difference. You know, a lot of the fellows at school admire you for the stand you're taking on education."

"I think most people would rather I shut up and sit at home. I'd never be able to stand it, though, being a trophy wife whose only value is in being a good hostess and producing children."

"That would be a waste."

"I'm glad you think so."

They walked for a while in silence. Once they reached a nice quiet spot, Jason spread out the blanket he had been carrying for them, and they got comfortable to watch the eclipse.

"I've always dreamed of being here, in the city," Jason said once they were settled. "It's quite a surreal feeling now. I'm going to the university I always admired, attending the events I'd always fantasized about, socializing with people who I used to only read about in the papers, and now I've met a woman I never thought existed." Jason felt the blood rushing to his face as he looked at Renee, gauging her reaction. Why did he have to blush so easily?

"I feel the same way. Of course, you know what it's like being an only child. Your parents force all of their hopes and dreams on you. They all have their own expectations for what your life should be, but they never stop and ask if it's what you want."

"Exactly!" This is what he loved about Renee. She understood parts of him that no one else ever had.

"My mother nearly fainted when I told her that I would be traveling abroad for an education. She's always wanted me to be content with the role of dutiful wife. She thinks education for a woman of my standing is pointless."

"It's never pointless to better your mind."

Renee smiled. "You try telling her that."

Jason made a show of gulping. "No, I don't think I will."

"See, you play the part of my dashing prince charming,

here to save me, but then you bolt at the first sign of a challenge." Renee moved as if to get up, and Jason grabbed her around the waist, pulling her back down.

"No, you don't, I'm not letting you get away. I'm just surprised you want me to face the fiery dragon. Where would you be if I didn't return? You'd be heartbroken."

"Yes, that's true. I suppose I shall just have to make do with you loving me." Renee's eyes widened, as if she was surprised at what she had said. She looked nervously at Jason, waiting for his response.

Jason sobered and returned her gaze with as much affection as he could. "I do love you, Renee."

Her face transformed so quickly into a smile that Jason was momentarily stunned. Matching his soberness, she said, "I love you too."

Jason didn't know which one of them leaned in first, but they came together in a passionate kiss. Just as Jason began to want to do more than just kiss, Renee spoke against his lips. "Look, it's started."

Opening his eyes, he saw that she was looking into the sky and pointing to the moon as it slowly succumbed to darkness.

Chapter Thirty-Four

Renee hummed to herself as she sat down for tea with her old governess the next day. Cora had been with her since she was five years old, and even though Renee was past the age of needing a governess, she remained steadfast friends with the woman who had been her only confidant through childhood. The woman's tall, austere frame hid an understanding heart, and her gray eyes could go from cold and stern to warm and compassionate in an instant.

"And what has you so cheery this afternoon?" Cora asked as soon as Renee picked up her teacup.

"Nothing." Renee hoped she didn't look as silly as she felt when her face burst into a wide grin. "Well, something."

"This something wouldn't happen to be a Mr. Jason Wadsworth, now would it?"

"There's no point trying to hide it, is there?" Renee placed her teacup down without taking a sip. "He told me he loved me last night."

"Ah, that would explain it. You look like you're walking amongst the clouds today. I didn't think I'd ever see you get this way over a boy."

"I didn't think I would either, but he's different."

"That's what they all say." Cora fixed a stern glare on her. "I thought you were going to hold out until your parents forced you into a marriage."

215

"So did I. But that was before—"

"Yes, before Mr. Perfect entered the picture. I understand."

"No, you don't, Cora." Renee had a feeling she was being teased, but this was important, she needed Cora's understanding. "With him, I wouldn't be just a trophy wife. He cares about what I have to say; he values my intellect. And he really does love me. I think he's going to propose soon. Do you think my parents will approve?"

"Of a young man with hardly any prospects? I don't think he's exactly who your parents dreamed you'd marry."

"I know. But he makes me happy. Doesn't that count for something? This whole time I thought that marriage was a death sentence. The most I let myself hope for was a little respect, but now I have a chance to have it all, and I don't want to let it go." If only she could convince Cora how important this was to her, then perhaps she could gain her as an ally in dealing with her parents.

"Well, your previous stubbornness toward the idea of marriage will help your cause. With your father's health being in the state it is, I think your parents will be so grateful you've finally decided to settle down that they'll approve," Cora said. "So he's really the one?"

"Most definitely." Renee couldn't help smiling so big that her cheeks began to ache. "He doesn't want me to change, Cora. He loves me just the way I am. I know he'll support me in my educational and women's rights activism. He would never want to shut me away in the house. All the parts of me that I've always been told are unattractive—my talkativeness, my strong opinions—he loves them all. I know he'd do an excellent job managing papa's company; he's brilliant. Everything's perfect." Or as close as possible, she thought as she gazed off into space.

"Except?"

Renee glanced at Cora and saw her old governess looking back at her expectantly. "Except what?"

216

Cora gave an exasperated sigh. "There's something you're not telling me. I've known you since you used to hide in your wardrobe to avoid going to church, and you're hiding something now."

"It's just that he has this slave, Kale, who he's close to."

"And it bothers you?"

"At first it didn't. But now that our relationship is moving toward marriage, I can't help wanting him all to myself. I know that's unrealistic."

Cora gave a mirthless chuckle. "You know he's going to take other lovers, all men do."

"But not him. Jason's fiercely loyal, I know without a doubt that he would never have an affair. That's what makes it harder in a way. The only reason he is involved with Kale is because he obviously loves him."

"Ah, so it's not the physical affair that bothers you."

"Yes…no…I don't know." Renee dropped the scone that she had worried into multiple pieces. "I accepted a long time ago that I would be in a loveless marriage. It seems silly now to worry about this, but that's part of Jason's charm. I never thought to dream that I could be this happy, but he's also made me realize that I deserve it all. Now that this perfect life is so close, I can't help reaching for it. I can't bring myself to settle."

"So tell him to sell the slave."

Renee let out a heartfelt sigh. "I wish I could, but I'm scared. The same loyalty that assures me he won't have an affair also makes me believe that he won't sell Kale. I'd be devastated if I asked him to and he didn't. I'd lose it all. I'm already getting more than I've ever wished for. I just wish I could be content with it."

"Perhaps what you really wish is that he would be content with just you."

Looking at Cora's questioning brow, Renee felt winded. Before she had known what being in love was, she had hoped for nothing more than respect from a husband; now she wanted to be the center of his world the way he was quickly becoming the center of hers.

Chapter Thirty-Five

Kale was eager for Jason to propose so they could settle into some sort of normalcy, but there was still one obstacle to overcome. The plan had seemed so simple in the beginning, but how would Jason convince Renee's family to agree to let him marry her? Did Renee really hold enough sway with her parents for them to overlook the fact that he was disowned? She seemed in love with him, and she did have a penchant for taking dramatic stands, but would it work? Kale wished he had his own plan in place to ensure success, but he couldn't think of one. Luckily, he didn't have to.

The solution to their problem came wrapped in a plain envelope one Saturday afternoon. Kale was in the middle of reading a novel, something he loved doing now almost as much as he loved drawing, when the hurried scratch of Jason's chair against the wood floor startled him. He looked up to find Jason standing in front of his desk, a letter clutched in his hand.

"That son of a bitch!"

Kale forgot his book, dropping it without marking his place. Jason rarely cursed, or at least rarely cursed in a way not in vogue with the wealthy. "What is it?" Kale rose, stood behind Jason, and placed his hands on both of his shoulders, trying to ease some of the tension so he could find out what was going on.

"Here, see for yourself." Jason shrugged out from under Kale's hands and flung the letter at him. He stormed to the sofa and sat down, but it was only a moment before he was back up and pacing, running his hands through his hair while murmuring to himself.

Kale straightened out the crumpled letter and glanced down to see the signature. When his eyes lighted on Robert Wadsworth's name, his head snapped up to look at Jason.

"Oh yes, it's my father. Read the whole thing." Jason never paused from his frantic pacing.

Kale focused back on the letter. As he read, his heart rate sped up. Could it really be this easy? Robert was extending a peace offering. Word had travelled back to the county that Jason was courting Renee and Robert took it as a sign that he had lost his fascination with Kale. Apparently the prospect of a respectable marriage was enough to erase the disgrace of what Jason had done.

"This is great news! What are you so upset for? I think we should celebrate; I'll go get a bottle of champagne." Kale headed for the door, grinning from ear to ear, reading over the letter again as he walked. It was hard to believe it was real.

When he opened the door, his arm was jerked forward as Jason slammed it shut with Kale's hand still on the doorknob. Looking at Jason, Kale was overwhelmed by the emotions on Jason's face. Anger, confusion, and a hint of betrayal, but mostly anger.

"What do you mean, this is good news?" The words came out hard between tight lips.

"He's taking you back. You're no longer disowned. How is this not good news?"

"Well, let me see. First of all, he's only doing it because he thinks I'm over you, and I'm not. Second, he's not taking me back; he's taking Renee Arlington."

Kale backed into the room, and Jason followed. They stood facing each other, Jason looking like he was geared up for battle. "Who cares what your father believes about us?

He's not taking Renee Arlington. He's just using her as proof that you're not being controlled by a slave. If you think about it, getting disowned worked in your favor. Before this, he would have never approved of you marrying anyone other than a nice country girl with freckles who would churn out a litter of babies. Now he's so happy that you're not in love with me that anyone looks good."

"But I am in love with you, and that's not going to change."

"So?"

"I'm not going to pretend that I've discarded you." Jason grew more agitated and stepped closer to Kale, his confused eyes pleading for understanding.

"This romantic notion of noble love doesn't do anything. It doesn't prove anything. Take his money and be happy. With his blessing, you'll be able to marry Renee and get everything you've ever wanted. You'll be playing with the big boys and living the life you dreamed of." Kale grabbed Jason's shoulders, staring him in the eye. "You want to stick it to your father? Take his money and his blessing knowing you're your own man."

Jason relaxed. The fire slowly ebbed from him, but Kale wasn't sure if he was convinced or if he was just tired of fighting. Closing the remaining space between them, Kale took Jason in his arms in a tender embrace. He spoke into his ear, "I'm flattered at your righteous indignation, but it doesn't serve me, and it doesn't serve you."

Kale felt the rest of the tension melt from Jason as his master lifted his arms to return the embrace. "I just wish he could like me for who I am. I wish that I was good enough for him."

Kale pulled back and gazed steadily into Jason's eyes. Shaking his head, he sighed. "Did you ever stop and think that maybe he knows you're too smart for him? That it terrifies him that he has a son that never fit into the simple world he belongs to? He'll never understand you, but I do think he loves you. Otherwise, why would he care so much about our relationship?"

"Thanks, Kale." Jason rested his head on Kale's shoulder for a moment. "How about you go get that champagne you were after? I'll need to unwind some more if I'm going to answer his letter in a respectful manner."

"Of course. Just relax on the bed, and I'll be back with some champagne and whatever I can wheedle out of Marge."

CHAPTER THIRTY-SIX

Jason was lying in bed with Kale. Butterflies assaulted his stomach. Tonight he'd been on another date with Renee, and he was feeling more and more like now was the time to propose. Of course, Kale had waited up for him, and even though it was late, Jason needed to talk. He had hurried to bed, not wanting to start this discussion before he was comfortable. Now that they were side by side, Jason turned to Kale. Calm and steady eyes stared back at him. In that moment, Jason felt doubt. Was it betraying Kale to feel this way about Renee? Would he be all right with the new developments in their relationship? There was only one way to find out. Jason took a deep breath and dived right in.

"I think I should propose to Renee, and I want to know if you're all right with it."

Kale smirked and shook his head. "Is that what's got you all worked up tonight? Of course you should propose to her. I believe that was the whole point."

"We've both said 'I love you.'"

"Good. I already told you, you could never marry someone you couldn't love, and it's all the better that she loves you back."

"Are you just saying that because you don't want to disappoint me? Because if you don't want me to, I won't. I love her, and I know I would be happy with her, but you

223

come first."

"And what kind of jackass would I be if I told you no? This is great news. I've been rooting for you two all along. If you remember, I'm the one who introduced you."

Jason smiled. "Yes, you are. So how do you think I should go about it?" When he realized what he said, he dropped the smile and looked harder at Kale. "Or do you not want to talk about it?"

"And let you mess up all my hard matchmaking work? I think not." Good. Jason knew he needed Kale's help in this, but he hadn't wanted to make him uncomfortable if talking about it was a bit much.

"All right, so what are your ideas?"

"Well, don't do all that asking the father crap. Go straight to Renee. She'll appreciate not being treated like a commodity changing hands. Her father's either going to agree to the marriage or not, and I think he is; going to him first is not going to change his mind one way or the other."

"You're right. She'll like that I respect her enough to get her agreement first. What else?"

"What do you mean, what else? That's all I have. You're the one who's all romantic, not me. Just be honest with her. It's not like she's going to say no. You two are perfect for each other. Be sincere."

"When should I do it?"

"Tomorrow. Definitely tomorrow. I'd tell you to do it now, but I don't want to risk her saying no just because you woke her up. The last thing I need is to deal with your nerves. Quick and painless. You'll only make things worse if you wait."

"Tomorrow. I can do that." The park would be the perfect place. It was romantic, was feasible at the last minute, and it would be appropriate to ask her where they'd said, "I love you" to each other. There was no need to tell Kale all those details; Jason couldn't imagine that he would like hearing them.

"Thank you so much, Kale. I know I didn't give you an easy time with this, but I am grateful you pushed the issue. I really think we're going to be happy. I would never have believed this was all possible if it weren't for you." Jason stared at Kale until he began to shift uncomfortably.

"Stop it. All I did was introduce you, it's no big deal. Besides, if I hadn't been here, you would have ended up happy anyway. Stop making me out to be more than I am."

"I'll never understand how someone who is as wise as you are could be so utterly stupid when it comes to some matters."

Kale merely grunted as Jason cuddled up behind him.

CHAPTER THIRTY-SEVEN

Kale helped Jason get ready the next day as usual, except there was nothing usual about it. Today would change their lives forever. This was the last time Kale would help Jason get ready as an unattached man. When he came back through those doors, he would be engaged.

"Will you stop it already? You'll never get out of here if you don't just let me do my job." Kale batted Jason's hands away from the buttons on his waistcoat. After three tries, Jason hadn't been able to get his shaking hands to do the job.

Jason let out a nervous laugh. "You're right. Sorry. I just don't know what to do with myself."

Kale finished buttoning the vest and looked into his eyes. The uncertainty he saw staring back at him told him there was more to that statement than the obvious. "I've told you already. I told you a hundred times. This was my idea, and I'm fine with it. Just don't botch the proposal. I don't want to have to find you yet another girl. This one was hard enough to come by."

Jason's face and shoulders relaxed. Kale knew this wasn't easy for him. In truth, it wasn't easy for Kale either, but he couldn't let it show. If Jason saw one chink in Kale's armor, he would call the whole thing off. They would get through this time of transition. Kale knew it would be awkward, but it was only change, and once it was past, things would be better for Jason. If Kale could get these two married, he would prove to himself that he could contribute something to Jason's life and that he wasn't just holding him back. If only he could get Jason out the door.

"You really think she'll say yes?" The uncertainty was still there, but not the stress.

"I know she'll say yes, master. What else is she going to say? You two are nauseatingly perfect for each other. You think she'll give you up to go decorate the arm of one of the thousands of pricks in this city? Renee's smart; she'll make the right choice." Kale straightened Jason's tie, which had gotten crooked during the activity with the vest. "Not to mention the fact that she's in love with you and you love her back." Finished with the tie, he looked at Jason again and choked back a gasp at the look of love in Jason's face.

"I don't deserve you, you know. I can't help feeling that this is the worst kind of betrayal. The fact that you're willing to let yourself be hurt just so that I can be happy makes me feel even worse for doing this. How can I answer that level of devotion with this kind of disloyalty?"

And here Kale thought he was doing such a good job of hiding his pain, but Jason saw right through him. He always did. That wouldn't stop Kale from trying, though. "Pshaw, what pain? You think I want to stay in this boardinghouse when I could be living it up in one of her father's homes? I've got to be the luckiest slave in the world, convincing my master to marry so I can have a nicer place. You obviously don't know much about being a slave if you think this is painful. So you start fucking her, what do I care? It's not like you haven't fucked other people before, and the gods know I've fucked my fair share."

Jason's eyes narrowed, and he grabbed Kale's wrist where he had been straightening Jason's collar. "What?"

Kale sighed as if he was dealing with a spoiled child. "Not since we started doing it. But nice to know where you stand on the matter."

Jason released Kale's wrist, and he began fastening Jason's cufflinks. "You know how I feel about such things. I'll perform my familial duty with Renee, but you'll still be in my bed."

"Please, save some of the romantic talk for the proposal."

"I just want you to know that you're first in my heart."

Kale finished with the cufflinks and then looked Jason in the eye, all humor gone from his face. "I do know it."

"Good."

The two men stood in silence for a moment. Life was about to change forever, Kale knew it, and he knew Jason did, too. With their eyes locked, Kale saw what Jason seemed desperate to let him know: some things would never change. It was an easy message to recognize; it was the same one Kale hoped Jason could see in his face. In a split second, the wind was knocked out of him as Jason leaned in swiftly and grabbed the back of his neck, pulling him into a kiss that was hard, fast, and rough, showing Kale that these were not just empty words he had spoken tonight.

Jason broke the kiss, but kept his hand on Kale's neck, forcing them to stay touching forehead to forehead as they caught their breath.

"You better get going," Kale whispered.

Jason let go and straightened up. Kale keenly felt his absence, but Jason met his eyes one last time before he turned and walked to the door. After opening it, he looked back at Kale, his hand still on the doorknob. "Wish me luck." Jason smiled, but Kale could see how important it was to him to leave on a happy note and with Kale's blessing.

"You don't need it, but if you think it will help, good luck."

Jason's smile widened, and he closed the door behind him.

CHAPTER THIRTY-EIGHT

"Renee, there's something I want to ask you." Jason turned toward her and took both of her hands in his. Looking into her eyes, he noticed an expectant look on her face. Her mouth had the beginnings of a smile on it, as if she were scared to hope for too much. "I've really enjoyed the last few months with you. I never thought I'd find a woman who would make me feel this way. I had given up on ever finding someone, and then you came along, perfect for me in every way. That's why I'd be honored, Renee Arlington, if you would agree to marry me." Jason held his breath and only released it when he saw that the hints of Renee's smile had given way to a full sized grin that looked like it would break her face.

"Yes, of course I will."

Jason swept her up in his arms and held her to him. The relief he felt surprised him; he hadn't realized how worried he was. Now that she had said yes, he saw that his life was going to drastically improve. The best part was he knew he would be able to take care of Kale. With a respectable marriage and the sizable fortune that came with it, he would never have to worry about being able to keep Kale.

"Jason?"

Jason looked down at her. He hadn't realized that he had been staring off behind her as he thought about the changes this entailed. Renee's eyes narrowed. "You were thinking about him, weren't you?"

Jason shook his head in a puzzled fashion. "Who?"

"You know who. Kale."

"I was only thinking of how happy he's going to be. He knew you'd say yes; he told me I was a fool for being nervous." It wasn't exactly a lie.

"It's not right, the relationship the two of you have."

"What are you talking about?"

"You know what I'm talking about. Don't play dumb with me, Jason."

"I'm not, I really don't know. We have sex, but you know there's hardly a man in Perdana who doesn't sleep with his slaves."

"It's not that you sleep with him. That's fine. I'm not naïve, I know what men do. What's not natural, though, is that you're in love with him. A slave."

Jason stepped back from her. "Why does it matter to you how I feel about him? He's a loyal slave, and I'll take him to my bed as much as I please. I promise you, though, that I will never take a mistress. You'll never need to worry about that from me. And I think you're forgetting that I love you, Renee."

"More than you love him?"

"What kind of question is that?"

"A simple one. If I'm to marry you, I need to know that I'm the most important person in your life. I don't care what you do in your bed, that's your own affair. I'm not expecting things to be perfect, but I love you, Jason, and I need to know that you love me in the same way. I need to know that I'm above all others and not just a convenient bride. As long as Kale is with you, I'll never know that."

Jason's mouth twisted. "What are you saying, Renee?"

"I'm saying that I can only accept your proposal if you agree to sell Kale. You can replace him of course, but I won't be made a fool of in my own home. I won't marry a man who's in love with someone else. I don't expect fidelity, but I demand respect, and that means putting me first."

Jason's world tilted, and he put his hand on his head as if that could right it. Shaking his head, he turned back to her. "I've known him longer than I've known you. His loyalty alone demands mine in return. I won't sell him. There's no reason to, you're just being a selfish girl."

"I like Kale, Jason. I really do. I'd be fine if you wanted to keep him as long as he wasn't your personal slave anymore and you no longer bedded him."

"No." The answer was a reflex. That was not an option.

"Exactly. That wouldn't work because you're in love with him. I know he's been a good slave to you, but I can't live in a house with you and him knowing that you're in love with him. It's not fair to me."

"Fair? To you?" Jason's face began to get flushed, and his voice grew louder and faster. "But it's fair to sell a slave simply for being too good at his work? Because I have feelings for him? How is that fair? What did Kale do to deserve that?"

"Nothing, I know it. I hate myself for demanding this of you, but I deserve to know that my husband loves me above all others. You made me realize that I deserve that, Jason. You spoiled me. Before you, I didn't know that I could have it all. Now that I do know it's possible, I'm not willing to settle. If we married and Kale stayed, it wouldn't be fair to me, and I'd come to resent you, and that wouldn't be fair to you. Kale would know he was the cause of it, he's not an idiot, and that would not be fair to him. If you sell him, though, it's also not fair to him. Clearly you would be unhappy without him and resent me. Unfair for both of us again." Renee stepped up to Jason and touched his face, trying to turn his eyes to her, but he refused to look at her. He jerked away from her touch, and his entire body shook. "Perhaps getting married isn't the best idea. I don't see how it could make any of us happy. I wish it could be different, Jason."

For a moment Renee just stared at him as if willing him to look at her, but Jason stubbornly refused to meet her gaze. Finally, she stepped back, turned, and walked away. Jason watched her leave. Once she was out of sight, he strode to a nearby bench and sat down on it, slamming his fist onto the wood. All he could see was red. How dare she behave that way? She'd have been damn lucky to marry him. We'll see how she likes it when she marries a man who parades his mistresses around town and leaves her at home with a gaggle of children.

Jason kept slamming his fist onto the seat, letting the pain leech away his anger. When it became too much, he stood up and paced, trying to let off steam. It wasn't long before the anger was gone, and in its wake came a wave of grief. Jason doubled over and landed on his knees in front of the bench. He rested his head on his arms and began to sob. He had failed. This was his one chance to make a better life for himself and Kale, and he had screwed it up by loving Kale too much. What would happen to them now? How could he keep Kale with him once his inheritance dried up? His father would withdraw his offer of reconciliation. Why could no one just accept him as he was? Was it so hard to see why he was loyal to Kale?

After an hour of wallowing in his own grief, he realized he had to go home. It wasn't fair to Kale to put off the inevitable any longer. How would he break the news to him? Kale had been so sure that his master would succeed. How could Jason go home and tell him that he had botched it? It had been nice to have this time to wallow in his own self-pity. Once he got home, he knew Kale would try to make him feel better, and that just made him feel even more wretched. He knew he didn't deserve Kale's comfort when he couldn't manage to do anything right by him.

CHAPTER THIRTY-NINE

Kale wished he could say that he was completely calm about this whole thing. He wished he could just sit and read or draw and wait for Jason to come home, but he wasn't that calm. He cared too damn much, and it bothered him. It rubbed him the wrong way, just like it always did when he realized he was coming to care for someone else more than he cared for himself. He had spent the first hour or so after Jason left nervously cleaning their room. After a while though, he saw that he was just going to drive himself crazy, so he went downstairs to see if any of the slaves were free for a card game.

Down in the basement, Charlie was the only one around.

"You up for a game?"

Charlie looked up from where he was playing solitaire, and Kale could tell from his expression that he must look desperate.

"Sure."

Kale's mind wasn't on the cards, and he played badly. Charlie had to notice the nervous tapping of Kale's foot, but he didn't comment. Instead he filled the silence with mindless prattle. Charlie was good like that, always available to talk, but never pushing for information. Kale didn't know what he would say to him anyway, if he asked. There was no reason to feel this unsettled about his master proposing. The only reason a slave would have reason to feel nervous was if their place wasn't secure, and if there was anything Kale was sure of, it was his place in his master's life. After losing for an hour, he put down his cards.

"I think I'm done for the night, Charlie."

"Yeah. You want to go outside?"

"No, thanks."

"Want to fuck?"

Yeah, he wanted to fuck all right, only the man he wanted to fuck was off proposing. More than anything right now, he wanted to throw Jason down and claim him, as if he had any right to do so. Kale smirked. Jealousy was not an attractive quality. But dammit, he had worked hard to get his life to be as easy as possible, and now things were venturing into the unknown. Life was good, and he didn't want it disrupted.

"Not right now. I think I'll just go upstairs and wait." Charlie nodded at him, and Kale went to the door. Just as he was about to walk through it, Charlie spoke up.

"Hey, whatever it is you're nervous about, don't be. He's crazy about you, he'd never hurt you."

Looking back at him, Kale smiled. "Thanks, Charlie." Charlie looked satisfied, and Kale left.

Back in Jason's room, Kale didn't know what to do with himself. There was no way to tell how long Jason would be out. For all Kale knew, he wouldn't even come back tonight. After doing some unnecessary cleaning and tidying, he grabbed his sketchpad and a charcoal pencil and lay down on the bed. As he started to draw, he considered how comfortable his life had become that he could even do this. Tonight, things were going to change, but they were only going to get better. Instead of being nervous, he should be excited. Maybe he was, maybe that was what the swarm of butterflies in his stomach meant. He lived in a nice house, slept on a nice bed, and got to indulge in his own pastimes. Looking at his life from a distance, he might not have even been able to tell that he was a slave. It felt good—and a little dangerous. For the first time in his life, he really had something to lose, and it scared him.

It wasn't much later when Kale heard footsteps climbing the stairs. The butterflies, which had managed to settle while he drew, were kicked into action again. His hand began to shake as he continued to draw, not really looking at the page, but willing his eyes not to watch the door.

The door opened, and Kale looked up; the butterflies instantly flew from his stomach to his heart and landed. Jason's slumped shoulders and wrinkled clothes did not match the image of a newly engaged man. When he looked up to his master's face, puffy red eyes looked back at him begging for reassurance. Kale quickly threw his sketchpad down and went to Jason. "What?"

The word seemed to break through Jason's fragile façade, and his face shattered like glass. Tears fell from eyes that had already cried too much and Jason collapsed onto Kale. "I failed." His voice broke and sobs began to rack his shoulders.

"Shh. Come on." Kale led him to the bed and helped him gently onto it. When he pulled away and looked at Jason, a pain flared in his chest. "What happened?"

"She said no."

"What?" Even though he knew that's what it had to be, he still couldn't control the level of his voice.

Jason winced. "Well, she actually said yes at first."

Kale got on the bed next to Jason and pulled him into his arms. "All right, so then what happened?"

"I honestly don't know. One minute she looks like the happiest woman in the world, and the next she's telling me that she can't marry me unless I sell you." Kale went as still and cold as stone. "Of course, I told her that was out of the question. I tried to reason with her, but there was no changing her mind. She said she had to know that she was the most important person in my life, and I couldn't give her that, so she left. It didn't take very long; I've spent most of the evening at the park wondering how this all happened."

"You turned her down for me?" Kale asked with a note of awe in his voice.

The question seemed to pull Jason out of his dreary thoughts, and he lifted his head from Kale's chest and looked him in the face. "Of course, what else could I do?"

The genuine look of puzzlement on his face warmed Kale even more than the words did. To Jason, things really were that simple. A hopeless romantic through and through, his logic seemed to step back wherever his feelings were concerned. A part of Kale wanted to explain to him how stupid he was being. Here was a woman who could offer him everything, and he was giving her up for a slave. Somehow, though, he knew that's not what Jason needed right now; right now he needed comfort.

"You really are amazing, and she's a damned idiot for turning you away." Jason laid his head back down on Kale's chest, and Kale stroked his hair.

"I really thought she was the one for me to marry. I let myself start to picture it. I was such a fool. First Eric and now her. When will I learn?"

"First of all, you're not a fool. You love freely, and there's nothing wrong with that. Second of all, it's not really fair to compare Renee to Eric. Renee was wonderful and easy to like. You couldn't have known it'd end like this. She never seemed to have a problem with me before."

"And what about Eric?" Jason's voice was muffled against Kale's chest.

"Well, Eric wasn't one of your better moments." Jason chuckled and ended up choking back a sob as he hiccuped. "Still, Eric was a master manipulator. He would have trapped anyone."

"But he didn't. He trapped me. Why is it that everyone I love ends up hurting me? Everyone except you, of course."

"I don't know." Kale smiled at Jason's faith in him.

"I would have given anything for her, done anything."

"I know." Kale kept stroking his hair. It was true; when

Jason got it in his head to love someone, he gave himself over wholeheartedly. It's why he kept getting hurt. He didn't understand the concept of holding himself back, building a wall to guard against pain. Not the way Kale did.

"Why did she ask me to do the one thing I couldn't? How would she even be able to love me if I turned my back on you? I could never love someone who would do that."

"I guess she just expected you'd do it. To her it's probably not turning your back on me, it's turning toward her."

"I would have loved her, you know. Just because I loved you first doesn't mean I wouldn't have loved her."

Kale lifted Jason's chin so he was staring down into his face. "You are so incredible, you know that? Frankly, you're too much. No one could ever live up to this idealized vision you have. You don't even understand how amazing you are. I know you would have loved her; I know you did. Don't you understand that people can't comprehend someone being able to love that much?" Jason's eyes looked up at him, so full of hurt and hope that it pricked at something in his heart. Not able to look at him anymore, Kale simply leaned down and kissed him.

Jason clung to Kale as if he could make everything better. Kale didn't know what they were going to do, but he knew what he could do now. Wrapping his arms around Jason, he maneuvered him so that Jason was under him. Once he was situated, he broke the kiss and looked down into Jason's eyes. Kale shook his head. Everything about Jason amazed him, and it was painful to see him swimming in self-doubt. "No one is worthy of you, least of all me. But you have me; I'm yours. I may not be rich or an intellectual, but I see you for who you are." Not waiting for a response, Kale descended on him, kissing up the last of the tears on Jason's cheeks.

Moving down to kiss his neck, Kale began to unbutton Jason's waistcoat. Once that was done, he began to undo the buttons on Jason's shirt, slipping his hands underneath. The first touch of his hands sent tremors through Jason's flesh and caused Kale to smile. Getting up on his knees, Kale tugged at Jason's shirt until he rose up just enough for Kale to dispose of the clothing. Kale followed Jason as he lay back down and began kissing his chest. This wasn't about passion. It was about showing Jason what he thought of him. He covered Jason's body with slow kisses that could only be described as worshipful. When he reached Jason's bottom rib, Kale felt a shudder as he suckled it, followed by a sniffle. Looking up, he saw tears coming from Jason's eyes.

"What's wrong?" Kale went back up to his face and stroked Jason's brow.

"Nothing, they're happy tears. I was just wondering how she could ever expect me to give this up."

"Well, don't think about her anymore. I'm here."

"Yes, you are." Jason smiled and lifted his head up for a kiss. Kale was happy to oblige. Moving his hand to the crook of Jason's neck, Kale deepened the kiss. When he began to feel Jason's erection against his leg, he broke away. Tonight he wanted to prolong things. He finished undressing Jason and then removed his own clothes. Going back to Jason's ribs, he picked up where he'd left off. Slowly his lips and hands explored every inch of Jason's body, paying homage to the man who had given up everything for him. The only place that was left untouched was his cock. That would wait.

Kale sat up on his knees and gazed down at Jason, marveling at how perfect he looked, pale skin against the dark green of the comforter. If things were different, Kale would have taken him, rough and passionate, but as much as Kale wanted to, he couldn't. He was the slave and Jason was the master, but more importantly, Jason needed to feel in control right now, empowered. More than anything, Jason needed to know that he had Kale and wasn't going to lose him.

Kale reached across the bed and got the oil from the bedside table. Slowly, he prepared himself, locking eyes with Jason and seeing the lust building in them, a lust he knew was mirrored in his own eyes. When he was done, he moved on all fours to Jason's side and leaned down to whisper in his ear. "I'm ready for you, master. I'm yours, and I'll never turn you away." When he pulled back, he saw a flash of possessiveness in Jason's eyes before he got up and ran a hand down Kale's side as he positioned himself behind him.

"Yes, you're mine, and I'm never giving you up." Jason entered him in one long thrust, groaning as Kale gasped. It wasn't harsh, but it was firm and exactly what both of them needed. For a moment, Jason was still inside Kale, letting him adjust while he rubbed his hands up and down his back murmuring, "Mine." Then he started thrusting, quickly finding a rhythm. Kale bucked his hips back, meeting each stroke and groaning at the pleasure he felt. Gods, he hoped Jason wouldn't take long. His body was already thrumming with the effort to hold back. There was no way he was going to allow himself to come first.

Kale began to grip Jason each time he entered, showing his eagerness and urging him to lose control. Just when Kale thought Jason was close, Jason leaned over him to speak in his ear. "Eager, are we? I don't know why. You won't be coming tonight until I say."

Kale groaned and buried his head in the bed. At least Jason was back in control where, whether Kale liked it or not, he needed him to be. How had he gotten to the point where this man commanded him so completely? The thought was fleeting; at the moment he didn't care. All he cared about was completing Jason and then hoping his master would let him come.

Thankfully, Jason began to pick up the pace. Only trouble now was that the faster pace meant it took all of Kale's concentration to not come. "You're mine, Kale; I chose you. Whether you like it or not, you're the one I'm going to be with." He liked it all right, he liked it too much. Jason's hands moved from Kale's back to grasp his hips painfully. The pain cut through Kale's need and centered him, giving him something to focus on to keep his orgasm at bay. A few more harsh thrusts and Jason stilled, crying out as he came.

Spent, Jason fell on Kale and rolled over, bringing him with him so they were spooning. Jason's hand crept over Kale's hip and lightly stroked his erection, eliciting a whimper from Kale. "You're going to have to hold this for me for a while if you want release tonight." Kale's only answer was to desperately thrust forward into Jason's hand. "Are you disobeying me, Kale?"

Immediately, Kale stilled. "No. Yes. No, master."

"Hmm. Now roll over and take care of me. The sooner you get me ready to go again, the sooner you can come."

Kale rolled over and glared at Jason, relaxing boneless and sated with that pleasant post coital glow. Jason laughed. "You really need to learn to control that temper of yours. Patience is a virtue."

"One you don't seem to have." Kale plopped next to Jason and began to rub his chest.

Jason laughed and covered Kale's hand with his own. "True, but I never did claim to be virtuous. You're the only one who seems to think I'm perfect."

"And you're the only person who seems to think I'm worth anything. I guess we're cut out for each other."

Jason sobered immediately and grabbed Kale by the hair, forcing him to meet his eyes. "Don't speak like that. You really think I'd own a worthless slave? That I'd take a worthless man to my bed? Just because you had to settle for me because I was lucky enough to get you doesn't mean anyone thinks you're worthless. And anyone who says otherwise can come tell me to my face."

Kale marveled at the sincerity in Jason's voice. He really believed Kale was worthwhile, and he would fight any man who challenged that. He'd lose, but he'd fight them just the same. Jason held Kale's head firmly in his grip until Kale nodded his understanding. After he was released, Kale got up and fetched a washcloth to clean Jason. By the time he was done, Jason was already beginning to harden again. Wanting his own release, Kale reached down and began to stroke Jason's shaft back to a full erection. Jason relaxed into the bed and closed his eyes, enjoying the sensation. Looking down on Jason, Kale was so absorbed in studying his face that he was surprised when he felt Jason's warm hand curl around his own, halting his movement.

"That's enough. I have other plans."

Kale grabbed the oil, readying to be taken again. Jason reached out and took hold of his wrist. "Give it to me." Puzzled, Kale handed over the container and watched wide-eyed as Jason poured some out and began to finger himself. Kale froze, not wanting to believe his luck.

Jason chuckled. "Kale, I know what you need tonight, what you've wanted since I came home. I might not have succeeded tonight, but I'm still going to take care of you."

Kale's mouth had gone dry. "I don't need to; you can take me again."

Jason got up on his knees and came flush against Kale. "Yes, you do need it. And even if you didn't, I do. I need to know you love me, that you want me as much as I want you. Tonight, I need to feel that I'm yours."

Kale closed his eyes and shuddered. How well Jason knew him. When he opened his eyes, he saw Jason looking so vulnerable that it was hard to believe he was the same man that had just taken him so forcefully. Leaning forward, he kissed him and felt Jason's body melt against his. Snaking his hands up his back, he gently lowered him to the bed. Once they were situated, Kale looked down at Jason. "Are you sure?"

"More sure than I've ever been of anything."

Kale simply nodded and inserted a finger. He wasn't going to risk hurting him or worse. After he had carefully stretched Jason out and slathered himself with oil, he lined up his cock and slowly slipped in, groaning as the heat of Jason's body enveloped his own. Once inside, he settled, letting Jason become accustomed to him. This felt so good, so good to be surrounded by Jason, to feel his heat on his cock, so good to be allowed to do this because Jason sensed it was important and cared enough to let him. He opened his eyes and looked down on Jason who had a look of sheer contentment on his face that made Kale wonder how he'd gotten this lucky.

"You may come whenever you're ready, Kale." Jason clamped down on him to emphasize his point.

Kale leaned down and kissed Jason on the lips, grasping his head between his hands, as he slowly began to thrust, savoring the moment. When he pulled away, he kept his eyes on Jason's face, wanting to see all of his reactions. The looks of pure bliss that erupted on Jason's face gave Kale a feeling of pride at being the one to deliver such pleasure. Kale felt more than ever that he belonged to this man, but he also acknowledged for the first time that Jason belonged to him as well.

The sheer emotion of the moment was overwhelming. He couldn't control himself anymore. Quickening the pace, he dropped his head to Jason's chest and wrapped one arm around him. With his other hand, he reached between their bodies and grabbed Jason's cock. Even though his head had succumbed to a haze of feeling, he knew that he wanted Jason to come with him. There was no way that he would answer Jason's generosity with selfishness. It was sloppy work as his pleasure mounted, but he managed to stroke Jason in time with his thrusts.

Jason's hands came to Kale's head, holding him tight and running his fingers through his hair as he moaned in pleasure. Pressed up against Jason's body, Kale became intoxicated by the heady scent of sweat. Darting his tongue out, he tasted the salt on Jason's skin, and it made him hungry for more. Groping with lips and tongue, he found Jason's nipple and began to play with it. The sounds coming from Jason were now more urgent, and Kale felt his hands tighten in his hair. Kale increased the rhythm of his thrusts and stroking until Jason's grip turned to a vice and he came with a loud growl.

Kale released the nipple and shouted out his relief as he came too.

Once the last wave of pleasure had receded, he rolled off Jason, only to be pulled into a deep kiss. When Jason broke away, he rested on Kale's chest. The weight felt comfortable and right, and when Kale began to stroke Jason's back, he felt the most possessive urge he'd ever experienced.

Jason nuzzled against Kale, and goose bumps began to break out on their skin as the cooling air hit the sheen of sweat that covered them both. "I'm so lucky to have you."

"What, you don't think Demetri would have been as good in the sack? No, I'm the lucky one. I never thought I'd have a master like you."

Jason's voice was heavy with sleep. After two orgasms, he was struggling to stay awake. "Demetri's an ass, and I was stupid for wanting him. Wouldn't trade you for the world."

"Or a woman."

Jason laughed, and Kale thought it was the sweetest sound he had ever heard. "Or a woman."

A few minutes later, Jason went limp and heavy on Kale's chest. The look on his face was so pure and unguarded that it took Kale's breath away. Yes, Jason was his, he knew that now. Tightening his grip around the other man, Kale also knew that he would do whatever he had to in order to take care of what was his.

CHAPTER FORTY

Twenty-three. That's how many pages Kale had turned in his novel, and Jason still hadn't turned one in his philosophy text. From his position on the sofa, Kale had a clear view of his master sitting at his desk, pretending to study. Not only was Jason not turning the pages in his book, he also wasn't taking any notes. After an hour of this, Kale set his novel down.

"Let's go out."

"Hmm?" Jason looked back at Kale as if he had been unaware of his presence. "Oh, no thanks."

Five minutes later, Kale got up and put his hands on Jason's shoulders. "Come on. Your philosophy homework can wait."

"No, Kale, it can't." This time he didn't even honor Kale with a glance.

Kale sighed and tightened his grip on Jason's shoulders. "Master, this isn't healthy. You're not getting any studying done, we both know that. Let's take a break, and when you come back, you'll be fresh."

This time Jason did look up at him, and Kale immediately wished he hadn't. The face he saw was of a man desperately trying to keep himself together. "Please, Kale, just give me this. Let me be."

How could he not? Setting his lips in a grim line, he nodded, and Jason turned back to his book. Just as Kale was about to pull away, Jason's hand darted up and patted Kale's where it rested on his shoulder. Kale felt comfort in the gesture, but not enough to put him at ease. He gave one last squeeze and went back to the sofa, not even bothering to use his novel as cover for his worried glances at Jason. Last night, it appeared, had only been a temporary fix. It had been foolish to think that Kale could make everything better, but he had thought they would weather this together. How could he help if Jason wouldn't let him?

The melancholy was palpable, and Kale itched to get away, but he didn't dare leave Jason when he was like this. The last thing Jason needed was to be alone. The look on his face disturbed Kale. The whole situation was disturbing. Jason was clearly unhappy, and like it or not, Kale was the cause. If he wasn't in the picture, then none of this would be an issue. Jason had found the perfect woman for him in every way, and he had cavalierly thrown her to the wind in favor of Kale, a slave. How did those words even belong together? A master giving up his own happiness for a slave; it was unsettling.

Why would Jason do this for him? Kale knew that his relationship with his master was special, but he was under no illusions about his status. He wasn't a lover, he was a slave. A beloved slave, most definitely, but still a slave. Jason made his life comfortable because he was a caring and giving man, far too indulgent, but he was still the master, and it was Kale's job to make his life easier, not harder.

What made him worth this kind of sacrifice? What was so special about Kale that he was worthy of this kind of devotion? All he had done was try his best to make Jason happy; any other slave would have done the same. Now Kale's very presence had taken away any chance of Jason's happiness. That cut him deep, and he didn't want to stop and examine why; it was too uncomfortable. All he knew was that it was wrong and every fiber of his being rebelled against letting Jason make himself this miserable. Of course, that was silly and futile. Kâle didn't let Jason do anything. Whatever

Jason wanted to do was his prerogative. All Kale could do was sit by and watch.

Right at the stroke of one o'clock, Kale made his second attempt at getting through to Jason.

"It's time for lunch, master. I'll go get something from the kitchen and bring it up." For a moment, Kale thought Jason hadn't heard him, but when he opened the door to leave, Jason spoke.

"You've wanted to get out of here all day, and it's not fair to keep you cooped up. Just bring up enough for me. You may take your lunch downstairs."

Kale opened his mouth to protest, but thought better of it. Maybe it would be best to have a little break. It was clear that Jason didn't want him around. A few minutes later, he didn't even look up when Kale brought him his lunch.

◆ ◆ ◆

"Where is everyone, Marge?" Kale ladled out some stew for himself.

"Oh," Marge looked up from kneading bread dough, "Simon and Jacob are out with their masters, no doubt getting into trouble, and Charlie is off running some errands."

He had been hoping that Simon or Jacob would be around to distract him. Sitting down at the large wooden table, he only lasted one bite before Marge caught on to his mood.

"What's wrong?"

Kale looked up from his bowl and considered answering her. A part of him needed to talk about this, but he knew no one would understand. Putting on his most innocent face, he shook his head. "Nothing." He went back to eating his stew.

He shouldn't have been surprised when Marge sat down opposite him, but the feel of her rough hand closing around his was unexpected. "That bad, huh?"

When he looked into her face, he was floored by the concern he saw there. It was easy to forget, cocooned away in his little world with Jason, that there were other people who cared about him. "It's my master," he said. "He proposed to Renee, and she turned him down."

Marge removed her hand so he could continue eating. "And why does that have you so upset?"

"He's miserable, and it's all my fault."

"How," she said, her face screwing up in confusion, "did you get there?"

"She told him she'd only marry him if he gave me up, and he refused."

"I'd trust your master if I were you. He's a big boy. He can make his own decisions."

"But he can't, Marge, not when it comes to this. There's no way he understands the implications of what he's done. You know how he gets; he's too caught up in what he thinks he feels for me to be thinking rationally."

"What he thinks he feels?"

Kale gave her a pointed look and decided to move on, ignoring the comment. "I don't think Renee's the type to gossip, but it's eventually going to get out that he turned her down in favor of a slave. What are people going to think of him?"

"It doesn't matter what people think, as long as he's happy."

"Of course it matters, especially to him. He'll become an outcast. I can't stand to see him on the outside looking in at what he's always wanted. And all for what? To prove some stupid point to me?"

"Have you stopped to think that maybe it has nothing to do with you? Maybe he truly wants you more than Renee."

"That's the most absurd thing I've ever heard. And out of you of all people." Kale shot her a look of disapproval. Were there no sane people left in the world? "I'd expect you to be more sensible. How is he going to support himself? The money his mother left him is going to run out someday, and then what? No one in respectable society is going to associate with him even to employ him. No self-respecting man will let him marry their daughter. There's not even a chance of him getting a male lover as a benefactor. What man is going to be cuckolded by a slave? He's going to end up having to sell me anyway just to pay the bills."

"Is that what you're worried about?" Marge smiled and cupped Kale's cheek with her hand. "That boy will never sell you, dear, there's no need to worry about that. It will all work out, you'll see."

"Thanks, Marge." The words came automatically, but he knew she was wrong. The only way this was going to work was if he fixed it. "I've kept you long enough. I'll get out of your hair now."

"You're never a bother, boy, you know that. You should go talk to your master, share your fears with him, Kale. I think he's the one you need reassurances from."

No, what he needed was some time alone to figure out how to fix this. Lying down in the garden with the cool earth beneath his back and the endless blue sky above him, he was finally able to think. He hadn't anticipated having this problem. It was odd that Renee was willing to marginalize a slave in order to bolster her own entitlement when she claimed to wave the progressive banner. It appeared her liberal ideals only held where she was concerned. It didn't matter, though. Renee could still offer Jason more than Kale ever could.

The chill air in his lungs cleared his mind, and it was ridiculous how quickly he came to a decision. It was inevitable; Kale needed to be sold. It would happen eventually, but if he removed himself from the picture now, there was a real chance that Jason could reconcile with his father and even Renee. Sitting idly by was not an option. Even though there was nothing Kale could do directly, he could force Jason's hand. It was startlingly simple, and Kale didn't know why he hadn't thought of it before. It would be easy enough to convince Jason that he should be rid of him. Kale just had to be prepared to stick it out no matter how ugly it got.

Entering Jason's room, Kale was surprised to find that the atmosphere had lifted. Probably a sign that he had made the right choice.

"Good," Jason looked up from his desk, "you're back."

"Was I needed?"

"Needed, no, but wanted. I was just about to come find you, but I didn't want to disturb you." Jason put down his pen and pulled Kale over to the sofa. "I'm sorry I was so distant earlier. I was just doing some thinking. The awkwardness of eating alone snapped me out of it. Do you know, I don't think I've eaten alone in months? Was it awkward for you?"

"Well, I wasn't alone. I ate with Marge." Jason's smile faltered a little. Normally Kale would say something to assure Jason that he missed eating with him, but he thought better of it. There was no need in light of his recent decision.

"Oh, well, that's good." As quickly as the smile faltered, it returned to full strength. "I want to make up for my behavior earlier, especially after we had such a wonderful night last night."

Gods, there was Jason's trademark blush. Whatever it was Jason wanted now, Kale knew he would give it to him.

"So," Jason bounced to his feet, "grab your sketchpad. We're going to the park."

For the second time that day, Kale found himself lying in cool grass watching the clouds go by. This time, though, he had his sketchpad propped up on his knees. Usually he drew only what he saw or read about, but today he was inspired to draw the gods. The image of the heavenly court was one he had long imagined. As a young boy, it had been comforting to believe the deities of his mother's faith looked down on him. If only his mother could see him now, she would be so happy. All of his life she had worked to educate him as best she could so he might have a chance at a good life.

And he was about to give it all up.

"You know," Jason said, "I think this may be my favorite. I know I say that every time, but this time I mean it." On the page, the court feasted as some of the more serious gods cast a mournful eye on the world they had created.

Kale smiled. He never forgot that Jason was watching him, it was impossible to forget that presence so near, but he had gotten used to it. There was a time when Kale thought Jason would grow tired of watching him, but it never came. They had long ago passed the point where words were necessary, so Kale just smiled at him and kept drawing, knowing without looking that Jason's eyes never left him and the picture.

Walking home hours later, Kale was hit with how good this day had turned out to be. Why was he willing to give this up? Why should he be the one to sacrifice when there was so much uncertainty ahead of him? There had to be a reason, and it couldn't be that he cared for Jason. That was insanity as surely as Jason turning away Renee for him was. Of course Jason would grow to resent Kale over time. It wouldn't take long for him to realize what a mistake he had made, only then it would be too late, and Kale would bear the brunt of Jason's anger. Life might be comfortable now, but soon it wouldn't be. Kale had lost all hope of keeping the life he had the minute Jason went to propose. It would be much better to take his chances with an indifferent master than a master who rightly blamed him for all of his disappointments.

"Tonight was perfect," Jason said while he undressed after dinner. "I can't remember what life was like before I had you."

"It was simpler, trust me."

Jason rolled his eyes and reached for Kale's hand as he crawled into bed, pulling Kale down next to him. "No, it was boring. And virtually sexless." Jason was already stripping

Kale of his clothes. The sensible part of Kale's brain was telling him to feign a headache or tiredness. Sex was not a good idea after his earlier resolve, and Jason never pushed him when he didn't want to. But the feel of Jason's hands, smooth and soft as they removed his clothes, was too enticing.

Afterward, Jason fell right asleep. Kale wanted to as well, he was certainly tired enough, but his mind wouldn't let him. It had been stupid and weak to give in and have sex tonight. Then again, who knew how much sex he'd be having in the future? His whole plan was stupid. Who in their right mind traded this in? Even if he was going to be sold down the line when it was necessary, why not get everything he could out of the time remaining? Kale was fooling himself if he thought Jason would ever come to resent him. The same naïveté that kept Jason from seeing the mistake he had made would also prevent him from ever blaming Kale for whatever followed.

A particularly loud snore broke through Kale's haze of thoughts, and he looked down at Jason sleeping, nestled against him. Kale ran his hands through Jason's hair, and Jason just nestled in closer. Lifting his lips in a sad grin, Kale knew why he had to do this, why he had to give up everything in his life. It was for this man sleeping against him. Jason deserved to have the perfect life he had dreamed of, and Kale was determined to give it to him, or at least give him a chance at it. Having his plan firmly in mind, Kale relaxed into sleep. He would need the strength for what was to come.

Chapter Forty-One

The next morning, Kale was the first one awake. Try as he might, he couldn't fall back asleep. He was too tense with the knowledge of what he would have to do today. The best course of action would be to withdraw from Jason completely. It would do no one any good to pretend he could stay.

Kale steeled himself mentally against the resistance he knew he would face. Jason would be devastated at first, but it would pass, and after it was done, he would never have that haunted look again. As much as Kale wanted to stay in bed and savor this time with Jason, he knew it would serve neither of them in the long run. So for the first time in weeks, he got out of bed before Jason and started going about his day.

A couple hours later, Kale stood beside the bed as Jason woke and felt around the sheets looking for him. When he didn't find Kale, he shot up and scanned the room, squinting against the morning light. When his eyes focused on Kale, he smiled. "What are you doing up so early?"

"I needed to get some work done."

"Well, come here. After last night, I'm not ready to be up yet. Thought maybe we'd get another fuck in."

"Yes, master." Kale climbed into bed, but was stone cold despite Jason's efforts to cuddle.

"What's wrong with you?" Jason hovered over Kale, his

eyebrows furrowed in a mixture of puzzlement and concern.

"Nothing, master." Kale's voice was neutral. The sooner Jason realized that they were not lovers, the better.

"Yes, something is wrong. Tell me what it is."

Kale turned his head to meet Jason's gaze. "I'm just being your slave. That's what you turned down Renee for: a slave."

"No, I turned Renee down for you. You're more than a slave to me, and you know it."

"No, I'm not more than that. Renee could have given you everything you wanted. You were a fool to turn her down."

"She was the one who turned me down." Jason quirked a half smile in an attempt to relieve some tension, but Kale wasn't relenting.

"You didn't give her what she wanted."

Jason sobered. "She wanted me to give you up. It was out of the question, Kale."

"Why?" Kale let the stone façade slip a little as he raised his voice. "Why do you insist on holding on to something that isn't even what you really want? She's perfect for you."

"You are what I really want, and she wasn't perfect for me, obviously, or she wouldn't have asked what she did." Jason's voice was firm. "She'll never be as perfect for me as you are. If you don't want to fuck, that's fine. You know I'd never force you, but stop talking about this nonsense."

"Is that an order?"

Jason just looked at him with his lips drawn in a tight line.

"Come on, master, I'm your slave. Is that an order?"

"Yes, it's an order." The words came out short and low, and Kale took a perverse sense of satisfaction from knowing he had gotten to Jason.

"Very well, would you like me to prepare myself for you, master?" Kale imbued his voice with as much innocence as he could.

Kale got his intended response. Jason narrowed his eyes as he ground out, "No, just get back to doing whatever it is you were doing."

"As you wish." Kale got up from the bed and threw in a small bow when he was standing just for good measure. Jason turned away as Kale left the room, headed to the kitchen to bring up breakfast.

There was a tense silence as Kale prepared Jason for the day. Like the previous day, Jason immersed himself in his studies, only this time it was Kale who had pushed him there. Instead of being bothered by the distance, Kale saw it as a small victory. After tidying up around the room a little, Kale was at an impasse as to what to do. He really didn't want to draw, it just felt wrong right now, and reading was out of the question. Then he realized what he had to do, what would grate on Jason's nerves and make him see how annoying it was to have Kale around.

He walked to a corner of the room within Jason's field of vision, slowly turned, and knelt. Kale could almost hear the grinding of Jason's teeth when he sank to his knees. It was hard to keep back a smile. How predictable Jason was. As time went on, Kale's knees began to get sore; he wasn't used to spending this much time kneeling. In fact, he wasn't used to spending any time kneeling lately. Life from now on was going to be sore, he was just going to have to get used to that. Eating breakfast together had been a mistake. It was one of the nice comforts that Kale was reluctant to give up, but he had to. If Jason was giving up a lifetime of happiness for the perfect slave, then the perfect slave was what he was going to get.

Once the pain in his knees set in, Kale found himself staring at the clock, willing the steady rhythm of the second hand to lull him away from his discomfort. At half past one, Jason threw down his pen, and Kale released a breath he hadn't realized he'd been holding. The sound of Jason's chair scratching against the wooden floor as he pushed it back was unnaturally loud in the quiet room. "Go get us some lunch and bring it here."

Standing up proved painful in a different way as Kale

257

stretched his stiff muscles. As soon as Jason had finished speaking, the heavy silence settled back over the room, and Kale didn't dare break it. He simply left as Jason flung himself onto the bed.

Lunch would not be a repeat of the breakfast mistake. Jason wouldn't be happy, but that was his problem. That was the whole point, wasn't it? To show Jason that he was not happy with Kale? Jason was sitting at the table when Kale returned, and Kale walked straight to him and began to arrange the flatware as if nothing was wrong. It didn't take long for Jason to spot the change, and he eyed the single entree plate and pursed his lips, looking up at Kale. "What is this, Kale?"

"It's your lunch, master." Kale backed away and stood off to the side as he had been trained to do so many months ago.

"Sit down." Jason pointed at the chair opposite him.

"It wouldn't be appropriate, sir." Kale tried to imitate the voice of the more uppity slaves he had encountered since coming to Perdana.

Jason banged his fist on the table, rattling the flatware. "Dammit, Kale, sit your ass down."

Kale wasn't a fool. He knew when to give in. Stiffly, he walked to the chair and sat down, clenching his jaw.

"Now what the hell is going on?"

"Nothing, sir."

"If you say 'nothing' one more time, Kale, so help me gods, I'll tan your hide so bad you won't be sitting for a week. You've been distant and cold all day. And now you won't even eat with me. What is this about?"

"This is about you turning down Renee."

"This again? I thought I told you to stop talking about it."

"Well, you asked."

"What exactly is your problem, Kale?"

"I don't have a problem. I'm just a slave."

"You know you're more than that to me."

"No, I'm not. That's all I am, master, a slave. We're not

lovers; we're not destined to be together. You're a master and I'm a slave, that's it." Kale could feel the blood rushing to his face as he picked up steam. "I do what you want to make you happy because then I stand a better chance of getting what I want. And you know what? It worked. I haven't had to sleep in those damn slave quarters. I've gotten away with doing next to no work. I've gotten to eat good food. I spend hours on my own hobbies. All because I fuck prettily. A stranger on the street wouldn't be able to tell I'm a slave. Which was exactly Renee's problem, by the way. You need to get it through your head that we're not lovers. I did what I had to in order to be as comfortable as possible. Now, I may be a bastard, but I'm not going to sit here and let you throw away your happiness for me."

As Kale came down from the passion of his speech, he focused his eyes on Jason. Jason's face had gone pale during the diatribe, and now that it was done, he sat with his mouth loosely open. Shaking his head, the color began to return to it, and he picked up his knife and fork again. "Do you really think me so obtuse that I wouldn't know you after all this time? It's clear what you're doing, Kale, and it won't work. I'm not getting rid of you. Stop trying to annoy me in hopes that I'll sell you." Jason smirked. "Gods, Kale, you can be so dense sometimes. The fact that you would do this, would try to get yourself sold in some twisted attempt to ensure my future happiness, just proves how right you are for me. Would Renee do this for me? No. She wouldn't even live under the same roof with you for me. Yet here you are ready to face an uncertain future in a misguided attempt to make me happy. Your actions just solidify my decision. Now, eat the rest of this." Jason shoved his plate of food across the table to Kale. "I'm not hungry anymore."

Kale hesitated with his hand over the fork and then picked it up and began to eat. This was entirely unexpected. Kale had never stopped to consider what he would do if Jason saw through him. In truth, he hadn't thought that was

259

even a possibility. As he ate, he considered how much more difficult this had just become. Why did Jason have to have such faith in him? Why did he have to make this harder than it already was?

Once he was done eating, he had decided to abandon his plan for the day. There was no more worthwhile work he could get done, and he needed some time to think. More than anything, he needed a little time to build up his defenses. This was going to be harder than he thought, and he simply didn't have the energy to continue tonight. The fact that Jason could so easily see through him made him feel vulnerable, and the truth left him with an odd feeling that this was all wrong.

Chapter Forty-Two

Dreams of his life before Renee Arlington entered it woke Kale early. It had been an uneasy night. It was one thing to hold onto his resolve during the day; it was quite another to not give into the temptation to cuddle with Jason in bed.

Things had to go differently today, he couldn't let this continue, and he certainly couldn't spend another night in this bed. It wasn't fair to him, and it wasn't fair to Jason. Since Jason was proving harder to convince than he had anticipated, he was going to have to resort to more drastic measures. Watching Jason sleep, Kale frowned. He was going to hurt him today. It was unavoidable. But the pain would pass, and soon he would have Renee to comfort him and make him forget. There was not time to do this slowly. Every day was one day more that Renee could decide to tell someone what had happened, and then it would be hard for her pride to take Jason back, even without Kale.

Unlike yesterday, Kale decided to stay in bed. Perhaps Jason waking up with him still there would get things off to a better start. Although it didn't really matter; it wouldn't lessen the pain any. Kale didn't have to wait long. Soon, Jason was stirring and reaching for him. Kale simply remained on his back staring at the ceiling. He couldn't afford to offer Jason any comfort.

When Jason finally propped himself up on an elbow, Kale

spoke. "You've ruined everything. You realize that, right? This was our one chance at a good life, and you destroyed it with your insistence that you're in love with me. My gods, how stupid can you be?" Kale kept his face resolutely turned toward the ceiling. He couldn't bear to see the shock and pain that was surely on Jason's face.

"Look, I'll find someone to marry." Jason's voice was raspy, as if his mouth and throat had dried out. "I'll find someone who is all right with the fact that you're in my life. I'll find someone who understands that you are non-negotiable."

Kale closed his eyes. Why did Jason have to keep saying these things to him? Couldn't his master just let Kale get on with stabbing him in the back? "And who are you going to find, master? What woman in their right mind would take you after they hear that you gave up Renee Arlington in favor of a whoring slave? Even if you could find a woman, there's not a father in this town who is going to let you marry into their family. Face it, it's over."

"What?"

"You'd be better off just selling me and running back to her and hoping she'll take you."

"No, I won't even consider it."

"Why?"

"Because I love you and you love me."

Kale turned and looked at him. If he had to do this, he was going to make sure he only had to do it once. "Do I?"

Jason's face wrinkled in puzzlement, and his eyes flashed worry. "Of course you do."

"Really? When have I ever said those words to you? Think back through all our time together and tell me when I ever told you that." Kale couldn't even bring himself to say the words "I love you."

Jason stared off to the side, and his eyes began to dart back and forth as if searching for something.

"You won't find it because it isn't there. I've never said it.

I tried to tell you this yesterday; I'm just a slave. Anything beyond that is in your head."

"What are you saying, Kale?"

"I'm saying that whatever reasons you had for keeping me, I assure you they're not good enough."

"No, I refuse to believe that. We're in love."

Gods, why couldn't he just accept it? Why was he forcing Kale's hand? Taking a breath that didn't give him the strength he was hoping for, he plunged ahead. "How could I ever love a man who brutalized and humiliated me the way you did when you were with Eric? What did you expect me to do, rebuff the advances of the man who held my life in his hands? You are nothing more to me than Carter Cartwright was: a master to be pleased."

The color left Jason's face, and his eyes snapped closed. Kale looked away. Every second he was closer to telling Jason that this had all been a joke, that they'd figure something out. Kale was giving up a lot here, but he knew that if he stayed, it would only be on borrowed time until he would have to be sold to pay the bills. So he really had nothing to gain by staying. But Jason did have something to lose if Kale stayed. The time had to be now; Kale needed to make an exit.

Jason opened his eyes. "I'm sorry. I didn't know you felt that way." His voice was soft and hollow. "I should have known. No wonder you want to get away. All this time I thought I was trying to hold on to a lover, and you were trying to be rid of a rapist."

Kale clenched his fists to keep himself from grabbing Jason to him. The pain in Jason's voice was tearing him to shreds. He couldn't think up a response, so he just shut his eyes and nodded.

"You don't have to stay here, you're dismissed."

Kale rose from the bed and walked to the door. This was it. He was really walking away from this life for good. No more lazy days spent reading and drawing, no more having a master who actually cared for him, no more good food, and no more nights on a comfortable bed with a solid body in his arms. He never thought he'd leave that bed for the last time this way.

CHAPTER FORTY-THREE

Numb. The absence of feeling. Lying on the bed, Jason felt like he was floating, like what had just transpired was all part of a dream, a twisted, horrific dream. But if it was, why wasn't he waking? It had to be a dream. If it was real, he would feel something right now, wouldn't he? Watching the person you love with every fiber of your being walk out of your life forever should elicit some response. Kale had tried telling him, but in his stupid, childish, romantic notions, he had convinced himself of a lie. As he looked at the door that had closed behind Kale only moments before, his eye caught on something else. Sitting on his desk was the drawing Kale had done of a weed in the park.

And the tears began to fall.

Suddenly he was holding that picture, tracing it with his finger. It was a weed, but Kale had seen something beautiful in it, and it was. That's how Kale lived his life, standing strong amongst whatever chaos or burden was thrown his way. Jason had taken that stunning soul and brought it to this cold and dirty city. What was worse, he had become all the ugliness that was in this picture. He had raped Kale and spoiled the most beautiful thing that had ever entered his life.

Dear gods, what had he done? Thinking over all the times he had beat Kale, all the times he had taken him to bed, his knees went weak and he collapsed to the ground, clutching the picture to his chest. The guilt was suffocating and Jason sucked in gulps of air as he sobbed. All these months he had hoped to make it up to Kale and show him the true extent of his feelings. Ever since he realized how wrong he had been about Kale, his greatest fear was that Kale would not be able to love him because of his foolish actions. For a while he had been able to let himself believe that Kale understood, that he forgave him, and that he loved him.

That was foolishness.

Jason pulled the sketch away from his chest and smoothed it out. How could the man who created this ever love a man like him? Jason was a monster. Given the way he had treated Kale, it was no wonder that he went along with his advances. The man he was before, it wouldn't have been hard to imagine Jason beating Kale and then raping him anyway if he had refused. How much easier had it been for Kale to just go along? If he was anything, he was a survivor.

Down the hall, a door shut. The noise sent a jolt of fear through Jason, reminding him of the outside world. Would Kale be back to bring breakfast? Staying here was too risky; seeing Kale right now would be agonizing. Smoothing it out one more time, Jason put the sketch back in its place and turned to the bathroom. He would have to hurry if he was going to get out of the house before Kale appeared with breakfast.

For once, he didn't care how he looked. Given his emotional state, there was nothing that could make him look nice anyway. Five minutes after he had decided to leave, he stepped out onto the sidewalk, still fastening cuff links. Instinctively, he turned right, the shortcut to the park, but then thought better of it. Too many memories, too many lost opportunities. To the left was the university, the only other place in the city he felt he could go.

Even there, he was assaulted with painful memories. This place had been the origin of all his hopes and dreams in the city. That first day here, he had seen the whole world laid out before him, ready to be conquered. A fine job he had done of it. Passing Rosemont Hall, he felt almost physically sick. The secret society housed within was what had driven him for so long toward his own destruction. Finally he stopped in front of the library and realized this had been his destination. Walking into that grand entryway, he paused. There was no doubt this was the most beautiful building in Perdana, but as Jason looked around at the massive domed ceiling and the intricate stained glass, all he could think of was Kale's drawing. He had been right. Jason had spent hours looking at that picture since that day, and here now he saw there were differences between it and the real thing. He couldn't help feeling a little disappointment. He would always prefer Kale's creation to the reality.

Stepping back outside, he had to blink against the sunlight. He saw people walking, going about their days, and it seemed utterly absurd that here his life was falling apart and the rest of the world went on without noticing. He began to walk, going nowhere, wanting to wander off to a part of the city where he wouldn't think of Kale, as if such a place existed.

All around him, he saw families and lovers. He had neither, perhaps he never would. Father had never understood him. He was the reason Jason wanted to get away to Perdana in the first place. Then there was Eric, his first real love affair, if it could be called such. When Eric had dumped him, it was the first time he realized people could be that deceitful. Then there was Kale, whose deceit wasn't nearly as cruel, but just as painful.

How could anyone love him when Kale didn't? What did it say about a man when the one person who knows him better than anyone turns away from him, views him as a monster? Kale knew him as no one else did. There were no secrets from him, no hiding, and it had seemed as if Kale loved him, as if he accepted him. There was no hope of anyone truly loving him.

Across the street, a young man whispered into a giggling girl's ear as she blushed. They looked lost in their own little bubble. The way the girl smiled reminded him of Renee. Were these two planning a future together as he had with Renee? He loved her, and she couldn't accept that he had enough room in his heart to love more than one person.

Did that matter now?

Now that Kale was going to be out of the picture, there was nothing keeping them apart, if that was truly the only thing keeping her from accepting his proposal. Perhaps Kale was right, and he should propose to her again. If she accepted, he could be happy. The question was, was he ready to put his heart on the line again so soon? Of course, if he was to have any chance with Renee, he needed to act quickly. If she moved on, she wouldn't be likely to want to come back to him.

But what if she said no? What would he do? Live his life alone? A cold shiver passed through his body. He wouldn't be alone. He knew in that moment that if Renee turned him down, he would simply keep Kale. It was weak and small, but the thought of being alone in the world, without anyone who cared or knew him, was just too much.

The pungent smell of cigarette smoke wafted down the street to him. Looking up, Jason spotted a familiar place: Flannigan's, the bar he had visited with Kale. It was tempting to go inside and drink himself into oblivion. But he couldn't, not here, not where they had sat talking about the future. How was he ever going to give up Kale? All of his plans had Kale in them. In every scenario, Kale was by his side. He wasn't just giving up a months-long relationship; he was giving up an entire lifetime. Could Renee step in and fill the void that Kale would leave? No, there was no way he could ever love her the same way he did Kale. Plus, it wouldn't be fair to expect her to fill another person's shoes. She was her own person, he loved her for it, and he would never want to change her. Still, the question remained: could he envision a life with Renee that didn't include Kale? He closed his eyes and tried to picture it. Several minutes later, he sighed and opened his eyes. Yes, he could, but it wasn't a very happy life.

Would this pain leave, though? Would it fade into eventual nothingness as the pain from Eric's breakup had done? Rationally, Jason had to suppose so. Over time, he would get over Kale. He would make new plans with Renee. Together they would make new memories that would supplant the ones he had made with Kale. He knew he would never forget him, but with some time and work, he felt certain that he could at least move him to the back of his mind.

That was it. He would propose to Renee, and if he had any luck, she would accept. He would find a good buyer for Kale, and he and Renee would marry. Would Renee be willing to accept his proposal before Kale was sold? He hoped so. If she wanted to be with him, that was the only way. After all he had put Kale through, after the loyalty and devotion he had shown, he would not just sell him to the first person with the money to buy him. Kale deserved to live as happy a life as he could, and if it was the last thing Jason could do for him, he would do his best to make sure that he was contented.

His steps faltered. Kale had been devoted. Their life together had been effortless. Why did the one person he wanted most of all not return his love? He shook his head. There was no use going down that road. Jason had no one to blame but himself. He had sabotaged that relationship long ago, and all for the sake of his pride. That's all it had been. Jason wanted to show that he was a man, and he had hurt Kale, as if that was the type of man he wanted to be. Jason would pay the price for his foolish pride for the rest of his life.

There was only one thing left to do: go and beg Renee to take him back. Jason lengthened his stride. Renee's townhouse was on the other side of town, and he needed to get there quickly. There was no use being miserable about what might have been. The best he could do was work to make his future as happy as he could. He owed himself, and he owed Kale, that much.

CHAPTER FORTY-FOUR

Three days. Was that really how long it had been? Three days alternating between bouts of righteous indignation at Jason for turning her down and feelings of utter stupidity for making such a demand of him. It was time for all of that to end. Today Renee would resolve her feelings about the matter one way or the other and be done with it. After all, she was a pragmatist at her core, and it was absurd to let something as fickle as feelings get in the way of the most important decision of her life.

Staring at the blank page in front of her, she took a deep breath and reached for a pen. Getting her thoughts on paper would help her work through them and come to some sort of decision.

Two minutes later, the page was still blank. Three more minutes and the sound of her tapping pen was irritating her.

"This is stupid." What kind of woman decided who to marry this way? Throwing the pen down, she stood and began to walk in time with her thoughts. Turning Jason down had been one of the hardest things she'd ever done, but it was a matter of self-respect. "Really, Renee?" More like it was pride. Jason loved her. She couldn't deny that, it wouldn't be fair to him. He had only ever treated her with the utmost respect and affection. She also didn't have a problem with Kale personally. He had always been respectful and kind to

271

her. Of course, there was the unpleasant feeling she had when around him, knowing that he knew Jason better than she could ever hope to.

"Admit it, Renee, you're jealous. Of course you are. Kale has a part of him that I'll never have." It drove her crazy. But that wasn't really Jason's fault. So what was the problem?

"Yes, what is the problem?" Renee spread her arms in desperation and flopped into a chair. The problem was he chose Kale. No matter how nice Kale was, the fact was Jason chose someone else over her. Whenever given a choice, he would always choose him. "But when is that ever actually going to happen, Renee? I'm the only person who's making him choose. So why am I?" It was clear that the choice hurt him. It was not as if he casually threw her to the side when things didn't work out. The agony on his face had been clear, she could still see it when she closed her eyes, and it pained her. So why was she putting them both through this?

She stood up again and resumed her pacing, gesturing with her hands as if that would help her understand herself better. Since she was a little girl, she'd always had high hopes for herself. She was going to buck convention and get a higher education. Unlike the other women of Perdana, she would be respected on her own terms. "And he's the only one who's ever really understood that." From as early as she could remember, she knew that she didn't want to be considered second rate to anyone simply because she was a woman. "He's always seen me as an equal. All the parts of myself I've loved have been things he's loved too." As she had grown out of childhood dreams and into the world of reality, she had come to realize how unlikely it was that she would ever find a man like Jason. When she talked, he really listened. When she challenged him, he rose to the occasion instead of detesting her for it. Life with Jason would be almost ideal.

"Almost."

But did she really deserve to be so picky? She began to chew her thumbnail as she thought it over. It felt like she was looking a gift horse in the mouth. After all, if she didn't marry Jason, she'd have to marry someone. Papa's health was failing, and he insisted that she settle down soon so that he would have some peace before his time came. The mere fact that Papa had been willing to let her choose her husband for herself had been such a privilege. This choice could just have easily not been hers to make. After this, though, she knew her father would have to make it. There was no way she could fall in love again. She would have to resign herself to life as a trophy wife, to be seen and not heard. Her purpose would extend no further than having children, entertaining guests, and being a dutiful wife who would be an asset to an upwardly mobile man. There would be no intellectual conversation, no love, merely a mutual respect if she were lucky.

"And there will be mistresses. Jason was right about that." Jason would never take another lover. If anything, he was faithful, even if it was to two people. Would him having an affair with Kale really be worse than being married to a man who flaunted mistresses? "I don't see how. At least I know he loves me and he loves Kale." That had to be better than him cheating on her just for sex.

"Isn't he just asking for the same thing I am?" Renee stopped her pacing. She had never thought of that before. All he wanted was to be allowed to love and be loved. Was she being selfish in demanding all of his heart? Wasn't his devotion and warm heart what she loved about him? Why was she penalizing him for these things?

"It isn't fair. It isn't fair to me and Jason, and it isn't fair to Kale. Poor thing has to be upset over this." The pacing started again, only this time more urgent, more purposeful. "Do I love him? Yes. Do I want to be his wife?" The smile that broke out on her face answered her question before her mind could catch up. "Yes. And if that means letting him love Kale too, then so be it. There's enough love and happiness to go around."

It wasn't too late to fix this. Not wanting to waste a moment, she went to her wardrobe and grabbed her gloves and a hat. Stopping to look in the mirror, she arranged the hat and smoothed out her dress. The smile that shone back at her stole her breath. Why had she wasted even a moment being unhappy? Just as she reached for her parasol in the entryway closet, there was a knock at the door.

Chapter Forty-Five

Jason stood outside of Renee's building trying to push down the queasy feeling in his stomach. He needed to focus on getting this done. If he was lucky, he would leave here with a fiancée and could begin moving on and trying to find some happiness. He didn't even want to think about what would happen if she turned him down again. It was bad enough the first time, but at least then he'd had Kale, or at least thought he did. Jason didn't like to think that he'd keep Kale against his will to avoid being alone, but if Renee turned him down this time, he honestly didn't know what he'd do. At the mere thought, he saw nothing but darkness spread out before him, threatening to consume him.

Finally, he worked up the courage to knock. Renee answered almost immediately, and her eyes widened at the sight of him.

"May I come in?" Jason winced at the desperation in his voice.

Renee shook herself free from the shock of seeing him and opened the door wider, gesturing him inside. "Of course. What's wrong?"

Jason put on a wry smile. "I look that bad, huh?"

"No, no, you just look upset about something."

"Well, there's nothing wrong." Was it bad luck to lie while proposing? "I actually come bearing good news. I'm selling

Kale." Jason looked at Renee, hoping she would understand the implications.

Instead, she looked shocked. "What? Why?"

"I was being foolish earlier. I love you, Renee, and I want to be with you." Jason took a deep breath and took her hands in his. "You're more important to me than a slave. I was just being stubborn before. I realized that marrying you is the most important thing in the world to me." His grip unconsciously tightened on her hands. "Please tell me I haven't lost you. Please give me another chance." The first time he'd proposed, he had been standing, gazing down into her eyes. This time it seemed fitting to get down on one knee. "I would be honored if you would be my wife." Jason hated himself for how vulnerable he felt. One word from her and he might very well give up on life. It was a horrible feeling, and he couldn't help thinking that it showed.

A soft hand on his cheek tilted his face up. He hadn't even realized he'd been looking down. Renee looked happy, but he didn't dare believe it until she said the words.

"Yes, I would love to be your wife." She broke into a smile then and nudged him to his feet.

"Thank the gods." Jason pulled her to him, hugging her as if he couldn't bear to ever let her go.

CHAPTER FORTY-SIX

Kale heard Jason leave. He didn't know where his master was going, but if he had any sense, he'd be going to Renee to propose. Kale wished he knew, but he supposed he had given up his right to be privy to Jason's thoughts and would have to get used to it. If, indeed, that was where Jason was going, Kale would have to get used to the idea that he would be sold. Still, it wasn't his place to presume. As of right now, he was still Jason's slave, so he decided he should act like it. He went up to Jason's room, did what cleaning there was to do, and knelt to wait, trying not to let his thoughts torture him too badly.

It didn't feel like long before he heard the front door open and close. Straining to hear, he soon heard the familiar footsteps on the stairs; there was no mistaking that it was Jason. Try as he might, Kale couldn't tell much from Jason's footsteps. They seemed neither slow and sad, nor quick and happy. When Jason finally opened the door, Kale kept his head down, fighting the urge to look up.

"Kale, I came to a decision earlier." Jason paused and Kale looked up, figuring that's what he waited for. "I'm going to sell you. It isn't fair to you to have to remain in the service of someone who forced himself on you. I'm terribly sorry for what happened, and I deeply regret it. I recognize you've been a good and loyal slave to me, far better than I deserve.

I'm going to do my best to find a good master for you. I'm not going to sell you to just anyone." It took every ounce of self-control Kale possessed to keep his feelings from his face. This was what he wanted, after all.

"Furthermore, I have told Renee of my intention to sell you, and she has graciously agreed to accept my proposal of marriage."

This was exactly what Kale had wanted. Forcing a smile on his face he said, "Congratulations, master. I wish you many years of happiness."

"Thank you, Kale. It's kind of you to say so after what I've put you through. I'm just glad everything worked out for the best. I'm going to be having Renee over for dinner tonight. Can you make sure to let the rest of the house know they're invited?"

"Of course, sir. And is there anything I should request be made special?"

"Not that I can think of."

"If that's all then, sir, I'll go begin the preparations."

"Yes, Kale, that's all. You're dismissed."

Kale left and went down to the kitchen to tell Marge what was happening and to make a request for dinner. With that done, he headed out to the back garden. No one would be around right now for him to invite to dinner, so he figured he would spend some time in the fresh air.

Right now, he should feel victorious. He was getting everything he wanted. He had convinced Jason to sell him and marry Renee. Renee had taken Jason back. Why did his victory feel so empty? He realized that he didn't really want to know. He just sat and stared at the tiny garden.

How simple these flowers had it. No worries, no cares, their only job was to be pretty. All Kale had wanted was a simple life. He thought he knew his job: to follow orders and keep his master happy. Of course, the difficulty came when those two things conflicted with each other.

Kale must have been out longer than he thought, because

Charlie was suddenly standing nearby. "How long have you been there?" Kale asked.

"A little while. It looked like you were thinking, and I didn't want to disturb you. What's on your mind?"

"My master proposed to Renee again, and she accepted."

"Really? I thought she wasn't going to marry him as long as he kept you. What changed her mind?"

Kale met Charlie's eyes for the first time and Charlie gasped. "No, you don't mean he's...?"

"Yep. I got myself sold as soon as he can find a buyer."

Charlie walked over to Kale and sat down next to him, placing a hand on his shoulder. "I'm so sorry, Kale."

"Nah, don't be. It's what I wanted, right? He's having her over for dinner tonight. Everyone's invited. Think you can tell the others for me?"

"No problem. You sure you don't want to talk about this?"

"Yeah. What's there to talk about? If a slave is standing between a man and happiness, the man gets rid of the slave."

"But are you sure you were really in the way of his happiness?"

"Of course."

"How'd you get him to agree to sell you? I'd have never believed it. That boy gets puppy dog eyes every time you're around."

"He just likes that I take care of him. I told him I could never love someone who beat me the way he did when he was with Eric."

"I'm surprised he bought the lie."

Kale turned to Charlie. "What do you mean? It's not a lie. I don't love him."

"Ah, I see. A lot easier for him to buy it when you do, too."

"It's not a lie," Kale growled.

"Sure it's not. All I know is I don't think I've ever seen two people more smitten with each other than you two."

"Look, I don't love him. I don't know if he ever loved me; you'd have to ask him. All I did was what any other slave would do. I kept him happy, and it got me just what I wanted. I haven't been sleeping in the drafty basement now, have I?"

"No, you haven't."

"So just lay off."

"All right." Charlie stood and wiped the dirt from his pants. "I'll go let the others know about dinner. If you've got some time between now and then, do you want to fuck?"

"No, thanks." The words came automatically, but when Kale stopped to analyze them, he realized they were true, and he didn't want to think about why.

Charlie smiled a sad, knowing smile and walked away.

CHAPTER FORTY-SEVEN

It took a concerted effort for Renee to stop tapping her pocketbook. The restlessness was not brought on by excitement as it should be—this was an engagement celebration after all—but from nerves. Beyond this front door was Kale, the slave she had earlier resolved to tolerate for Jason's sake. That resolve had melted the instant Jason proposed again. If he had come to this decision on his own, why not let it stand? He was hurting now, that had been apparent from the way he looked when he showed up on her doorstep, but the pain would fade and eventually cease altogether. Once Kale was sold, they would move on, get married, and she would make him forget all about his former slave. They could be happy together. They would be happy together, she felt sure of it.

Renee couldn't help the anxious glances she tossed around as Jason greeted her and led her to the dining room. Her attention should be on her fiancé, she knew that, but something wouldn't let her stop looking for Kale.

There he was, standing against the wall of the dining room. When she entered, he stepped forward, and Renee's stomach clenched. He wasn't going to talk to her, was he? The thought of him serving at dinner was unsettling enough, but to actually have to face him?

"Excuse me, miss," Kale said. "I just wanted to offer my

281

congratulations on your engagement." There was no hint of bitterness or jealousy in his voice, just sincerity tinged with resignation. Should she say something in response? What could she say? It didn't matter. As quickly as he had appeared before her, he was gone again, back to blending in with the rest of the slaves.

The food was delicious and the company festive. All of Jason's housemates were there, and it was just the sort of small gathering she liked. In a few weeks, she would have to endure a formal engagement party, but tonight was about celebrating with friends. The boisterous conversation from Timothy and Phineas should have been enough to distract her from the sad undercurrent she felt, but it wasn't. Jason's smile every time she looked at him was too forced, and any time Jason saw Kale, he looked like he was in outright pain. Was it her imagination, or were the other slaves in the room eyeing her with contempt? It was likely they were the only ones here who knew why she had suddenly accepted Jason's proposal. As she chewed on roasted duck she couldn't even taste, Renee kept telling herself that things would get better. Once Kale was actually gone, Jason could start to move on. This pain was only temporary. They would have their whole lives together.

One course after another came and went in a blur until dessert. Looking down at the plate in front of her, Renee finally smiled. Chocolate covered cherries, a dessert so simple it was rarely served. "My favorite."

"What was that, darling?" Jason turned his attention to her.

"The chocolate covered cherries, they're my favorite. Thank you." There was a flicker of confusion on Jason's face before he smiled. Had she ever even told him about her love for the dessert? How did he know? Of course. Kale. He would have known from the party at the Woodhausen's. Jason had been off with the men while the women had dessert, but Kale had remained with some of the other slaves to serve.

Jason turned back to his conversation with Carl, and Renee looked over his shoulder to where Kale stood against the wall. He smiled and nodded at her. Renee did her best to smile back before she returned to her plate. That Kale would go to these lengths to make the night special for her was knowledge she'd rather not have.

It was unfair, the way she was treating him. Ever since she had figured out that Jason loved him, she'd viewed him as a rival. Meanwhile, he had done nothing other than welcome her into their lives and try to make her as comfortable as possible. It was as if he sensed how hard this must be for her and was trying to make it as easy as he could. And what thanks did he get for it? She was having him sold. Jason had come to the decision himself, but she knew he wouldn't go through with it if he didn't think it was the only way she'd marry him. In fact, she was surprised he had decided to go through with it at all. Before today, she had been certain that nothing would ever tear those two apart.

She choked down the last few bites of her dessert. The sudden knotting in her stomach made her want to leave the last cherry on her plate, but her upbringing wouldn't let her return this kindness with the ungratefulness of not finishing. She could ruin lives with no thought other than her own selfish desires, but leaving food on her plate was a breach in decorum. She hated herself for what she was doing, but she couldn't bring herself to put a stop to it. Everything she ever wanted was hers for the taking now, she just needed to see it through. Kale would manage. He was a good slave and would no doubt charm any master who owned him. Really, any pain or discomfort was only in the short term. Long term, everyone would be happy.

Keeping that thought in mind, she drank her wine and joined in the happy conversation around her, soaking up her night and pretending that she didn't see the pain Jason tried so hard to hide.

CHAPTER FORTY-EIGHT

"Damn." Jason threw his gloves on his desk and reached for his glass. The stress of finding a buyer for Kale was beginning to get to him, and he had taken to keeping a bottle of brandy in his room. Whether the smooth fire of the liquid going down his throat actually relaxed him or whether he just thought it did, he didn't care. Sitting alone in his room with a tumbler in his hand had become a familiar routine over the last few days.

Looking around, he was assaulted with Kale on every side. The sketchpad sat where Kale had last left it, only now it was nearly empty. Jason had taken the pictures and hung them around his room. Was it a punishment? Seeing them all —each one speaking of a man Jason would never have—was a sweet torture. Downing the last of his drink, Jason returned the glass to its place and reached for the decanter. His hand froze midair; one drink had been his limit when drinking alone.

"But I need you." The amber liquid? Or the man who drove him to want to numb his mind? Kale would have been able to draw him out of his dark mood, but Jason kept him at a distance. It was too hard to look at him, still loving him and knowing that Kale would never return those feelings. If he was around Kale too long, he began to think of the enormity of what he had done, and it drove him to drink more than he should, which is where his one drink rule came from. Things were easier if Kale stayed out of sight; no doubt he enjoyed the respite from having to tend to Jason.

His stomach clenched, and he backed away from the brandy, ending up on the sofa. No, he wouldn't add drunkard to the long list of his shortcomings. How could anyone love a monster like him? It was lucky he still had Renee in his life.

A persistent knock on the door jostled him from his thoughts. How long had the visitor been knocking? What had he been thinking of? Renee, Kale, life, sin, redemption—he didn't know.

"Yes?"

"Excuse me, sir." It was Charlie who poked his head around the door. "Miss Arlington is here to see you. She's waiting in the parlor."

"Thank you." A part of his mind knew he should be happy to see Renee, but it was so much easier to wallow in self-pity alone.

Renee jumped up to meet him when he entered. The happiness on her face didn't mask the shock in her eyes at seeing his condition. He had tried to straighten himself up, but some things couldn't be hidden.

"How are you?" she asked. The kiss she gave him on the cheek felt soft and delicate, so unlike the firm kisses he had shared with Kale.

"Not well." They moved to sit down. "I just returned from meeting with a potential buyer."

"How did it go?" Renee slid forward in her seat.

"He showed interest in using Kale as a valet." Jason was adamant that Kale not go to a master who would use him for hard labor. "He's wealthy, an upstanding citizen. I don't know him well, but by all accounts he's a nice and fair man."

"But?"

"His slaves. They were taken care of, but they didn't exactly look happy."

Renee gave an exasperated sigh and sat back in her chair.

"They're slaves, Jason."

"I know that, Renee. But I need him to be happy. I'm selling him and moving on to get married." She was losing patience with him, he could tell. "I'm entering the happiest time in my life, and I'm not just going to dump him at the first convenient place. Besides, that's not the only reason it wasn't a good fit."

"Well?"

"This man is in the same social circles we are." Renee clearly didn't see the problem with that. Jason shifted in his chair, and he nearly whispered what came next. "It means there's a chance I'll see him, Renee. I can't do that; I can't risk it. I'll just have to look harder for someone acceptable with whom we're not likely to cross paths in the future." Would Renee accept that and let it go?

The truth was Jason couldn't picture a future with Kale belonging to any of the people he had gone to see. If he were honest with himself, he couldn't picture a future with Kale belonging to anyone but him. For so long, the future had seemed certain. Details were up for grabs, but one thing had never been in question: Kale would be with him wherever he was. Even though he thought he had come to terms with a future without Kale, he knew he hadn't come to terms with a future where Kale belonged to someone else.

◆◆◆

Renee grimaced. It would be uncomfortable if they should chance to see Kale again, but it was highly unlikely, and it had to be better than the current situation. The atmosphere in the house was unbearable. Jason was worn from the stress, and the few times Renee had seen Kale, he looked like a man condemned and waiting for sentence to be passed.

"Dear, Kale is used to being sold. It won't be awkward for him, and it won't be for you once we're settled."

"Yes, but that's not the point." Jason's leg began to shake with tension.

"Then what is?" Renee leaned forward again. He seemed itching to tell her something. "Tell me what's going on."

"Renee, all this time I thought he loved me, and he was merely cowing to me." He broke. "I beat him viciously when I was with Eric. When I started to make advances toward him, he did the only thing he thought he could and accepted, but it wasn't out of affection for me. It was out of fear. I no better than raped him. When I told him what you said after I proposed, he told me the truth. He was looking to get away from me. I imagine that's why he arranged for us to meet. He knew we'd hit it off, and you were his best chance at diverting my attentions away from him."

"He's the one who first told you about me?" That was news to her.

"Yes. He'd been trying to help me meet a woman for ages. I always blew them off. They were all so boring. When he heard about you, he knew you would be a perfect match for me, so he arranged for us to be at the same party."

"He was helping you find a wife?" Why?

"Yes. I thought we were looking for a wife for me to secure our future. Turns out, he just wanted me to focus my attentions toward someone else. I can't say I blame him. Still, it hurt to find out that the future we had planned together was just a farce. When he had me meet you, I fell for you in a way I didn't think I'd fall for any woman."

Renee looked at Jason and was amazed at how blind he was. Kale was feeding him a line, she felt sure of it. There was no way he hadn't reciprocated Jason's feelings. Everything Kale had done had been because he loved Jason the same way Jason loved him. Here Kale was giving up everything for Jason's happiness, and all Jason saw was the lie Kale had told. It would be funny if it weren't so tragic. If there was ever a time to speak up, it was now. A word from her would end this. But she was so close. How could she compete with

Kale? What about her happy ending?

"Jason, you've got to snap out of this." It came out sterner than she intended. Not anger at Jason, but at what she was about to do. "Perhaps it's best if you just send him to a dealer to be sold. Don't handle it yourself; it will never get done. Just sell him to a dealer who will take care of it from there. It's not like you need top dollar for him, anyway. This is tearing you apart, and I won't stand for it anymore. You've got to get this done. Take him to the dealer tomorrow."

"I can't do that." Jason's eyes widened and the color faded from his face. "I won't do that to him. He deserves more."

"Have you looked around you? Is this what he deserves? Walking around with that haunted look on his face like he doesn't know what's coming? The best thing you can do for him is get this over with. End the uncertainty. Let us all move on with our lives."

"You really think he's unhappy here?"

"Wouldn't you be?" Renee reached forward and grabbed his hand where it rested on his chair. His skin was cool and clammy against hers. She willed the certainty and strength in her eyes to push the doubt and sadness from his.

"You're right." Victory. Jason took in a deep breath and leaned back in his chair. "As usual, you're right. I'll take him to the dealer tomorrow and be done with it. Just let me tell him."

Chapter Forty-Nine

Standing in front of Jason and Renee, Kale was nervous, and he wasn't sure why. On one hand, he didn't really want it to be over. Somehow in the last few days he had permitted a hope to be born in him that he wouldn't leave Jason after all, that somehow this could all work out for the three of them. On the other hand, he prayed every second that Jason would just find a buyer. Deciding to get himself sold was easy; this waiting around and having to stand by that decision wasn't.

Looking at Jason, Kale awaited what he had to say, wondering if it would be the life changing words he waited for or a mundane request for wine. Jason looked slightly calmer than he had the last few days. The tension was fading. Renee, on the other hand, looked uncomfortable, though she hid it well.

"Kale, I've decided I've been unfair to you."

Jason's voice washed over Kale, and he realized how much he had missed it. Hope blazed to life inside his chest. Was he to stay after all?

"All this waiting around to be sold isn't fair to you. I was trying to do the right thing by you, but Renee has shown me that it really isn't a kindness after all. I'll be taking you to the dealer tomorrow, and I'll let him handle your sale. You have the night off to enjoy as you see fit. Be ready at eight o'clock in the morning." Jason kept his head turned to the side, avoiding him.

Kale closed his eyes. This was it then. The relief pouring through him drowned out the heartache. Opening his eyes he said, "Thank you, sir. Is that all?"

"Yes, that's all." For a brief moment, Jason looked at him and then turned away again.

Was that sadness Kale saw in his eyes? It didn't matter. He bowed and left.

◆ ◆ ◆

Kale waited until the house had been quiet for a few hours. The last thing he wanted was to get caught in his enterprise and have a scene caused. He knew what was going to happen. He had chosen it, and wanted it to happen as quietly and smoothly as possible. He just needed one last look. Satisfied that his fellow slaves were deep in sleep and that no one else stirred, he carefully got out of bed and crept up the stairs to Jason's room.

Kale stood just inside Jason's doorway, the full moon his only source of light. Funny that he felt like a stranger in these rooms he had shared for so many months. Strange, how things could change so fast.

From Jason's bed emerged a familiar sound. Apparently not everything changed. Kale had to suppress a laugh. That first night he had hoped Jason's snoring had been the result of too much alcohol. Later, he learned that the boy never slept without snoring. During the months they shared a bed, Kale had become used to the sound. The nights now seemed eerily quiet without that snore lulling him to sleep, safe in the knowledge that he was loved. But Jason was no longer a boy. Looking at him sprawled out on the bed, Kale marveled at how much he had changed since the night they met. Odd that he hadn't noticed it before now. Jason had filled out, and his features had become more angular. He was a man now, no

292

longer the lost boy playing at adulthood.

Kale took a seat on the floor and just watched Jason sleep. It was nice to have this last bit of stolen time to see him. The past few days had been hard on Jason, and Kale was almost grateful that he had been kept out of Jason's presence. He didn't think he could have held on to his resolve in the face of Jason's pain. It would pass though; in a few days, this would be just a painful memory for Jason. In a few months, he would be married, and Renee would make him forget all his worries. She was a good woman, a good match for Jason, and she could give him everything Kale couldn't.

In sleep, Jason looked more at peace. It was easier for Kale to think of him as he had been: happy and full of life. It was easy to look at him as he slumbered and recall all the glorious dreams Jason had held for the two of them. Those dreams would come true, except instead of Kale at his side, it would be Renee. Not such a hard adjustment, Jason would make it in time.

After sitting in silence for an hour, memorizing every line of Jason's body as if he could ever forget, Kale realized it was time for him to go. How he longed to curl up beside his master and sleep the night away and then wake up and laugh away all of this misery. He would even gladly take a spot on the floor by Jason's bed if it was offered to him now. But no, he had made his decision, and now he must follow it through. Rising from his seat, Kale prepared himself to turn away from Jason forever. As much as he wanted to stay, he couldn't. It simply hurt too much. He'd be damned if he was going to cry and run the risk of waking Jason.

Getting ready to leave before he lost his composure, Kale remembered the other reason he'd snuck up here tonight. He wanted a memento to take with him, something to remember Jason by. Kale wasn't a fool. He knew what awaited him on the other side of this night. Already, he had used up all the luck he had ever hoped to have in his lifetime. Fortune would not smile on him twice. Up until now, his life had been fairly easy for a slave. That would all end tomorrow. At best, he would end up with a master who was indifferent to him. At worst, he would end up in hard labor and wouldn't live out another decade. Either way, he knew he needed something to get him through, something to remind him that he was once loved and freely gave it up, that he had a choice and chose the harder path. Jason was going to keep Kale's heart for the rest of his life. It only seemed fair that Kale got to keep something of his.

He picked out the memento he wanted and took it. He allowed himself to pause in the doorway and take one last look at Jason. His sob was muffled by a snore as Kale closed the door on the life that could have been and went downstairs to his place in the world of reality.

◆ ◆ ◆

When the other slaves began stirring in the morning, Kale was sitting on his made bed, ready to go. Sleep had eluded him. After his time in Jason's room, he found that he just wanted it to be over. If he had been able to take himself to the dealer, he would have, just to be gone from this place. Now, he waited.

The other slaves rose and readied for the day. Kale couldn't stand the look of pity in their eyes, as if they were looking at a prisoner awaiting the hangman. That was how he felt though, simply awaiting his fate, powerless to stop it. Except, of course, he wasn't powerless, not really. He had a choice and he knew it. Even now, he could go to Jason, tell him it was all a lie, that Kale was just trying to do what was best for him. This very moment, they could be holding each other in bed. He would make Jason forget about Renee Arlington, and they would live their lives in happiness together. It would be so easy, but he knew he wouldn't do it. The time had come to put away childish things. He was a slave; he couldn't claim to love a free man and then drag him down. Perhaps at one time he could have. If he didn't love Jason, he knew he could. He would have been all too happy to lead Jason along and reap the rewards of his master's affection, if he just didn't love him back.

But he did love him, that much he had to admit to himself. After all the fighting he had done to try and deny it in the past, he was amazed at how natural it felt to finally admit it. He loved Jason, and so his sense of honor would not allow him to do anything that might harm Jason in the long run, including staying with him.

As the other slaves left to go about their work, they murmured a few words of farewell. There was not much to say, and Kale wasn't of a mind to hear them anyway. Once he was left alone, he began to panic. When he had been sold away from his family, he thought nothing could be so scary. How wrong he was. His thoughts did not linger long. For once, Jason had gotten up early, and he sent for him not long after the slaves had left.

Arriving in the entry hall, Kale was taken aback by Jason's appearance. His face was drawn and tight with deep lines etched into the skin, the face of a man resolved to do an unpleasant task. He looked older than he should, and Kale hoped this experience wouldn't prematurely age him. That would be a shame and a damn waste. Thank the gods Kale had snuck that last look of him in his sleep; he didn't want this to be the last picture of Jason he held in his mind. When Jason looked at him, Kale could see a little glimmer of something in his eye, but it passed quickly. Jason didn't say anything, simply put on his hat and walked out the door, expecting Kale to follow.

Kale did follow without as much as a backward glance at the house. This place was never home to him. The man standing in front of him had been his home. Getting into the carriage after Jason, Kale went smoothly to his knees. He knew his place. He would leave this house the way he came to it.

The ride to the dealer's was tense. Jason stared impassively out the window, and Kale tried, unsuccessfully, to keep his mind blank. It was easy to see that Jason was troubled. Kale fought every urge in his body to comfort him and wondered for the thousandth time if he was doing the right thing. A look up at his master said he was not. Kale had told himself he was doing this for Jason's own good, for Jason's happiness. Yet Jason looked worse than at any time Kale had known him. Perhaps he should speak? Even if only to let Jason know how much he loved him?

Kale's mind lurched as he realized that he never told Jason how he felt; he had only come to the awareness himself last night. Hadn't that been why Jason believed the well-crafted lie? Shouldn't he remedy that now? How could he let him go on not knowing just how he felt? Kale looked up at Jason, ready to speak.

As he opened his mouth, he was struck by his position. On his knees at his master's feet, he realized just how much of a master Jason was to him. He couldn't confess his love to him because they weren't lovers. Jason was his master, not just on paper, but in every way. For the first time in his life, Kale was putting the needs of another person before his own. Jason had truly mastered him. Telling Jason his feelings would not result in anything good, it would just make this harder on Jason. Kale couldn't do it. He knew his place, and it was at his master's feet. In this place and at this time, Kale truly submitted for the first time in his life. His mind cleared, and he was calm for the rest of the ride.

It wasn't long before they arrived at their destination. The carriage stopped, and both men got out. Not a word was spoken between them, and even in his transaction with the dealer, Jason kept it as short as possible. It was almost as if the words had a hard time coming from Jason's mouth. Was the difficulty due to anger or sadness? Kale would have liked to know.

A few quick signatures and it was done. Kale was no longer Jason's problem. The dealer took Kale's arm and led him to a holding room. Once inside the doorway, Kale turned around and was startled to see Jason staring at him from the other end of the hall. Kale met his eyes, knowing it was his last chance. In them he saw anger, hurt, and frustration all trying to hide the little glimmer of love that he could see buried beneath it all. Just before the door to the room was closed, Kale saw Jason turn and walk away.

When the door closed, Kale went limp, spent from the strength it had taken to stay silent. Leaning against the door for support, he reached into the pocket of his pants and pulled out a lock of brown hair. How carefully he had moved the night before when he clipped this memento from his master's head. Holding it up to his face, he was overwhelmed with the smell of the man who had held him transfixed, and his face twisted in agony.

Sliding down to the floor, he began to cry and then to sob, emanating a sound so torn with grief that surely the gods looked down on him in sorrow. Tomorrow he would face whatever came, but today—just for today—he would grieve. Tomorrow he would take joy in his victory, but today he would mourn his loss.

When the tears were done, he lay down and went about the impossible business of figuring out how to live the rest of his life with this unbearable pain. Right before sleep overtook him, he muttered a word into the night that he had never before spoken, a word that held all his hope for the future and justified the price he had paid.

"Jason."

Thank you for reading *Measure of Devotion*.

Want to read more about Jason and Kale?

Visit
CaethesFaron.com/Measure-of-Strength
to learn about the sequel, *Measure of Strength*.

If you liked *Measure of Devotion*, please consider telling your friends about it or leaving a review.

To learn more about the author and sign up to be notified of new releases, visit
CaethesFaron.com/Newsletter.

Printed in Great Britain
by Amazon.co.uk, Ltd.,
Marston Gate.